ALL THINGS WORK TOGETHER

A *novel*

BY

MAURICE M. GRAY, JR.

WRITE THE VISION

This novel is a work of fiction. Any resemblance to real people, living or dead, actual events, establishments, organizations and/or locales is intended to give the fiction a sense of reality and authenticity. Other names, characters, places and incidents are products of the author's imagination.

Published by Write The Vision
Box 13083 Wilmington, DE 19850
(302) 765-8709
E-mail: writevision2000@yahoo.com
Web site: www.writethevision.biz

Library Of Congress Control Number: 2002096539

Gray, Maurice M, Jr.
    All Things Work Together by Maurice M. Gray, Jr.- 1st ed

ISBN: 0-9700514-4-1

First Printing- April 2006
Second Printing- May 2015

Printed in the U.S.A.

PRAISE FOR
ALL THINGS WORK TOGETHER

"Maurice Gray has once again crafted a compelling story of real Christians struggling to balance their desires with God's plan for their lives."

Victoria Christopher Murray,
author of *Stand Your Ground*

ACKNOWLEDGEMENTS

We do nothing in this world by ourselves; everybody needs a helping hand at some point, and I am grateful for the many people who have extended theirs to me. Thank you all for everything you've done, are doing and continue to do that blesses my life so richly. If I missed anyone, charge it to my head and not my heart.

God- For EVERYTHING.

My father Maurice M. Gray, Sr., for understanding why I just gotta write.

My sister Regina Gray, for proofreading this book a few chapters at a time, and for threatening to lock me in my room until I finished ☺.

My Uncle Joe and Aunt Jackie and all my cousins for relentlessly promoting my books- thanks y'all!

My other proofreaders Linda Beed (also a threatener!), Natalie Mangham, Nichole Christopoulos (your time is coming!) and Terrance Johnson, thanks for your feedback and your honesty.

My pastor, Rev. Silvester Scott Beaman and the Bethel African Methodist Episcopal Church family, for supporting me unconditionally and for bragging about me to anyone who will listen.

Patricia Haley-Glass, for teaching me how to publish my own works and for introducing me to so many of the authors I know now (Jacquelin Thomas, Victoria Christopher Murray, Marni Williams and Terrance Johnson just to name a few).

My first "road dawgs," the Writers Group: Jamellah Ellis, Kevin Johnson and Gloria Thomas Anderson. The signings and workshops we did together were wonderful! Keep on writing for Him.

My brothers of Kappa Alpha Psi Fraternity, Inc., who always encourage me to achieve even greater things with each new accomplishment

Bernard and Linda Beed, thank you for your hospitality during my first visit to Seattle. Linda, thank you for ruthlessly editing any manuscript I push at you (wow, who taught you how to do that? ☺)

My fellow authors Sharon Ewell Foster, Kendra Norman-Bellamy and Pat G'orge-Walker for your godly support and good humor from the start. Jeanette Hill, you're more than just a playwright. Get to novelizing already! ☺

Elissa Gabrielle and my fellow contributors to The Soul Of A Man anthology. Soul Brothers, I've enjoyed getting to know you all. Let's continue to be about our Father's business as we do The Soul Of A Man II.

Wanda B. Campbell and my fellow contributors to the Home Again anthology. We have a winner! I'm glad Wanda talked me into it.

Isaiah David Paul and K.L. Belvin, thanks for putting in such hard work on Soldiers Of The Cross. Let's keep it moving.

DEDICATION

I dedicate this book to my parents. Without their love, support and guidance, I wouldn't have been able to accomplish such a massive undertaking. I love you both.

Maurice M. Gray, Sr.

You gave me life and your name. Thank you for teaching me the meaning of the words "work ethic," and for showing me how a Christian man is supposed to conduct himself.

Joan K. Gray (6/18/36-8/8/05)

Thank you for instilling within me a deep appreciation for the written word. You taught me from an early age to love reading, which led me to love writing as well. I'll miss you until we meet again.

"For we know that all things work together for good to them that love God, to them who are the called according to His purpose."

Romans 8:28

1

"**G**et out my face before I kick your - - -!"

Fred Bennett stopped before he completely lost it. The startled man in front of him fell backwards, windmilling his arms in a vain attempt to stay upright. Fred caught him before he could hit the pavement, and flinched at the aura of alcohol and body odor surrounding the shorter man. He immediately felt ashamed of himself.

"Look. I'm sorry I went off like that. I, well, I got a lot on my mind today."

Fred found a five-dollar bill in his suit pocket. The man's eyes lit up, and he thanked Fred for the unexpected blessing before shambling off down the street.

Fred watched him leave, and then remembered what he needed to do. He straightened his tie, glared down a few nosy neighbors and pulled out his car keys, filled with renewed dread at having to face the next few hours.

Wasn't that guy's fault, Fred thought as he pulled out of his building's parking lot. *All he did was ask for a dollar. He didn't kill Merry.*

Images filled his head as he drove. Fred remembered meeting Merry Lucas on Ladies Night at the Diamonds High and then spending the entire weekend with her as a one-night stand unexpectedly became a relationship. Neither of them knew how to be monogamous, but they found in their closeness the courage to try. Unfortunately, Merry's past found her, and a hail of bullets destroyed their dreams. Instead of planning a wedding, Fred found himself preparing for a funeral.

A tear rolled down Fred's cheek as he pulled into the church parking lot, where a handful of cars sat. He checked his watch: ten fifty AM. The viewing started at ten, and the service was set for eleven sharp.

Fred pounded the steering wheel. *Merry might have been shady, but nobody should die and not have a lot of people at the funeral. Come on Fred, get up. Man up and get in there.*

He covered his eyes with sunglasses in a vain attempt to conceal any tears and went inside. With its red cushioned pews, high arching ceiling and ornate stained glass windows, Mount Pisgah United Methodist Church reminded Fred of his own church.

Strange, Fred thought, *the things you notice when you're at a funeral trying not to cry.*

As he moved towards the front for the viewing, he noted the sparse crowd. A middle-aged brown skinned woman with graying hair that Fred took to be Merry's mother Lorraine sat in the left front pew. Next to her sat a hazel-eyed young man in a wheelchair, who bore a striking resemblance to actor Terrence Dashon Howard. Fred recognized him from newspaper pictures as Merry's brother Bryan.

Fred's best friend Max Carson and Max's fiancée Donna Randall sat off to the right, and Fred's heart warmed to see Donna's best friend Yolanda Mason sitting with them. He nodded in their direction and then forced himself towards the open casket.

Merry looked like she was taking a nap before getting up to vacuum or cook or do anything rather than actually be dead.

"Oh God, why?"

Overcome with sadness, Fred forced himself towards the refuge of a seat among his friends.

Pastor Robert Hanson began the service exactly on time by reading John 11:25-26. The thud of his Bible closing broke the eerie silence.

"As youth pastor at St. Luke United Methodist church, I had many memorable children cross my path, including Merry and her younger brother."

He nodded at Bryan, who kept his head bowed.

"Merry and Bryan were regular attendees in our Children's Church. She was a bright and intuitive child, asking question after question until I gave a satisfactory answer."

He paused, praying briefly for guidance as he ran his fingers through his thinning blond hair.

"Merry left an impression on each of you, or you would not be here. I did not have the opportunity to get to know Merry as an adult, and it would be dishonest of me to try to eulogize her in the manner that she deserves."

He scanned the attendees' faces. "I ask each of you to come forward as you feel led and give a brief word about Merry, how you knew her and how she affected your life.

Lorraine indicated that she was unable to comply, and Bryan also shook his head no, hugging his mother as fiercely as his still-healing gunshot wound allowed. Fred saw him wince, and remembered the news reports of Merry's shooting rampage shortly before her own death.

If this is hurting me, Fred thought, *how much worse must it be on her family? The only one she didn't try to kill was her mother, and that's only because she ran out of time.*

Fred looked around the room, noticing three more arrivals. There was a white couple and sitting behind them, a heavyset, cinnamon-skinned black woman. Each of them had the same regretful look in their eyes that Fred saw in the mirror earlier.

That's it, Fred thought. *We're all wondering why she had to die or what might have happened if we'd been there for her.*

Before he realized it, he stood at the podium, fiddling with his new black tie and utterly clueless about what to say.

"Uh, good morning."

The others mumbled a reply.

"I'm Fred Bennett. I suppose I knew Merry as well as anybody."

Fred fought back tears before continuing. "We- - - dated for a few months, and eventually she opened up to me. I got to know Merry beyond that front she always put up."

He wiped away a tear that escaped his sunglasses.

"Merry was high maintenance. She liked to do things her way, she didn't like to be rushed and Lord *knows* she had a temper!"

The small congregation chuckled in spite of themselves, and Fred joined them.

"Merry was tough enough to keep a gun in her nightstand for home defense, gentle enough to enjoy a day at the zoo and polite enough to eat my cooking without gagging."

The congregation laughed again, and Fred relaxed a bit more. "She cared enough about herself to watch her diet and exercise, and she loved to relax with a good book. Terry McMillan was her favorite author."

Fred felt cleansed. Talking through his pain was soothing, and as much as he wanted to continue, he knew it was time to stop.

"Merry made some bad choices, but who hasn't? I wish I'd spent time with her near the end. Maybe if she'd talked to me instead of keeping it all inside, maybe we wouldn't have to be here today. But maybes don't count. Merry touched all of our lives, and she deserves to be remembered, not just for her crimes and how she died, but for the good things too. Thanks."

He returned to his seat, feeling lighter. Yolanda gave him a hug as he sat down.

The white man rose, but found himself overcome with tears and returned to his seat without speaking. The woman with him helped him regain his seat, hugging him fiercely as they both wept unashamedly. Fred looked away from them in time to see the heavyset woman approaching the podium.

"Good morning. My name's Mechelle Thornton, and my church home is Christian Fellowship Church, where the Rev. Theodore James Williams is my pastor. I never knew Merry's name until I saw her in the newspaper, but I know one thing about her; she was searching for something."

Fred listened attentively as Mechelle told of Merry's visit to her church, described the longing in Merry's eyes when the pastor presented Jesus and the disappointment Mechelle felt when Merry ran out the door without accepting Him.

"After she left, I felt such a burden for that girl that I couldn't do nothing else but pray. If I'd known where to find her, I would've gone to see her. As it was, I prayed she'd come back, or go to another church or that somebody somewhere would witness to her. After awhile, I couldn't even pray no more. All I could do was lift up a word for her in song. I'd like to do that now if it's okay."

With murmurs of assent from those assembled, Mechelle lifted her powerful soprano voice in a stirring rendition of "Precious Lord, Take My Hand." When she finished, there wasn't a dry eye in the room.

"That song stayed with me from the moment Merry left our church. She was asking the Lord to take her hand and lead her, but she didn't know how to reach out to Him."

Mechelle returned to her seat. Before she realized what she was doing, Donna approached the podium, her Bible in her right hand. The sling on her left arm moved, causing her bullet wound to throb as she walked.

Donna was there when Merry died, Fred thought. *Wonder what she has to say?*

Donna placed her Bible on the podium. A scripture came into her spirit, and she turned to it, fumbling with her good hand to hold the page.

"I want to start by reading from Luke, the twenty-third chapter, first the thirty-second and thirty-third verses and then skipping down to the thirty-ninth to the forty-third verses. I'm reading from the King James version."

Too nervous to look up, she kept her head down as she read the chosen passages. She then closed her Bible, said a silent prayer and looked up again, suddenly filled with confidence.

"I didn't know Merry very well. In fact, I only encountered her twice, and the last time I saw her, she shot me. I'm wearing this sling because she tried to kill my fiancée and me. But, newspaper stories and TV news sound bites aside, I *know* Merry wasn't just a "misguided soul," or "cold-blooded killer.""

Fred felt a chill snake down his spine as Donna's voice resonated with the power of the Holy Spirit. She closed the Bible and spoke, looking directly at Merry's family.

"Lorraine, Bryan, be comforted, because Merry is not lost. Her soul was bought with a price on a cross over two thousand years ago. Merry was dying and bound for destruction. But, God is merciful, and makes provision for those of us too foolish to accept Him the first time we learn of Him. John 3:16 says it all: *"For God so loved the world that He gave His only begotten Son, that whosoever believeth in Him, should not perish, but have everlasting life."* The next verse says, *"God sent not His Son into the world to condemn the world, but that the world through Him might be saved."*

Fred stared at Donna dumbfounded. He felt the Holy Spirit wash over him as the Word came forth through his best friend's fiancée.

Donna summarized the circumstances that led to Merry's death, sharing how she'd learned that Merry believed the only way to get her father Karl's Powerball winnings was to kill him and anyone who might inherit them before her. Max and Donna saved Karl and his wife from Merry, and Merry was furious. As she stalked them to seek revenge, her scorned ex-lover Roscoe Hemingway stalked her.

Merry went on a shooting spree, including an old enemy, her brother, her father and her stepmother, and finally Max and Donna. In the midst of her rampage, Merry finally listened to the voice of Jesus. When she aborted her plan to murder Max and Donna, Hemingway killed her, and the police killed him.

"Oh, I wish you could have been there! Max and I saw that man shoot Merry and we watched her die, knowing that we couldn't save her. But thank God Jesus *does* have the power to save!"

Donna closed her Bible with her good hand. "You all need to know that with her dying breath, Merry confessed Jesus as her Savior."

Lorraine Lucas leaped from her seat, shouting and dancing for all she was worth; Mechelle joined her a split second later.

"Like that thief hanging next to Jesus, Merry called out, and the Master answered! Merry was redeemed from hell and given everlasting life with God Almighty!"

Try as he might, Fred couldn't stop tears from streaming down his face. Nobody noticed; they were engrossed in their own personal communion with the Holy Spirit. Everyone in the crowd either shouted, danced, wept, lifted up holy hands or all of the above as Donna continued, feeling no pain from her injury.

"We can all take comfort in the word read to us by Rev. Hanson earlier from John 11:25-26, where Jesus said *"I **am** the resurrection and the life. Those who believe in me, even though they die, will live, and everyone who lives and believes in me will **never** die."* It may have been late to us, but in God's eyes, Merry found Jesus *just in time!*"

All of Donna's doubts and fears vanished as she preached to a group desperately in need of the Word. She felt a confirmation in her spirit that this was the path God wanted her to walk for the rest of her life.

"His blood is sufficient to cleanse *all* our sins! Jesus didn't *have* to die, but He chose to. It wasn't the nails that held Him on that Cross, it was His love for us! He laid his life down just to save you and me! And He took it back up again so He could prove that death couldn't hold Him! Hallelujah!"

Without warning, Donna came to herself, still standing at the podium. She was sweating profusely, and she felt as if she'd run ten laps around the building. Totally drained, she moved towards her seat.

Fred wiped away the last of his tears in time to see Max jump up and run to Donna's side. Max put her right arm around his shoulders and supported her weight as he guided her back to her seat. Words of thanksgiving and praise flowed from Donna's mouth as she and Max sat.

Max took Donna's good hand and prayed with her. Rev. Hanson prayed with Lorraine and Bryan and then returned to the pulpit. His voice was thick with emotion as he groped for the right words.

"I normally don't do this at a home-going service, but under the circumstances, it is appropriate. The doors of the church stand open. As the *preacher* taught us today, it's never too late to accept Jesus Christ as Lord and Savior. If anyone here does not know Jesus personally, today is a good day to meet Him. You don't necessarily have to join this church; if you want to give your life to Christ today and prefer to join a different church, I will send you there with my recommendation. You'll take *my* hand, but you'll give God your *heart*."

Immediately, Bryan started to wheel himself towards the altar. The white woman came over and wheeled him the rest of the way, tears streaming down her cheeks.

Mechelle began to sing "The Old Rugged Cross," and as she sang, Bryan Hurzen and Theresa Errell gave their lives to the One who died on that Cross so that they could be set free.

"Donna, that- -that was- -I don't have the words to describe how- -how *blessed* that was!"

"Max, that was *not* me."

Donna leaned on Max's shoulder, totally spent.

"I was hoping that scripture would comfort Merry's mother and brother, but after I read it, nothing that came out of my mouth was what I meant to say."

"God used you today sister. You might want to speak to your pastor about this."

Donna turned at the sound of Mechelle's voice in her ear, smiled, and hugged the larger woman. "I guess so. I don't do this every day."

"You might after that!"

Donna laughed and hugged Max again.

Bryan Hurzen just gave his life to Christ, but his heart was heavy because his estranged older sister was the one who shot him into his wheelchair. At that moment, Bryan wasn't sure whether to love Merry, hate her for the pain she caused him or forget she ever existed.

Seeing the turmoil on his face, Mechelle knelt in front of his wheelchair, clasped his hands and prayed fervently for his physical healing and for emotional healing as well. Rev. Hansen prayed with them, silently beseeching the Lord to grant favor to this young man as he made a new start in Christ.

In the opposite corner, Fred and Lorraine drifted together.

"You knew my daughter well."

Fred wiped his eyes for what felt like the hundredth time.

"I loved her. If things had been different, I would've asked her to marry me."

Lorraine fished a tissue out of her purse and blew her nose.

"Excuse me for crying again, but I'm just so glad she had you in her life!

Fred blinked back tears of his own. "You are?"

"My daughter blamed me for allowing her father to beat her as a child, and she was right: I did. We didn't speak a civil word for the last ten years."

Lorraine took a deep breath. "Karl was unstable. Life didn't go his way, and he beat his frustration into me and Merry until I finally got the courage to leave him. Merry never forgave me for staying as long as I did, and she moved out the instant she turned eighteen. After college, she all but vanished from my life. Until recently, I didn't know where she lived, where she worked, who her friends were, nothing. All I knew was she was angry at me and her father in particular and the world in general. That hurt me badly; I wanted to see her happy."

Fred sighed. "Me too. She was so sad all the time- it made me want to cheer her up. You wouldn't have known that to look at her though- she put up a good front."

"She never let on that her father's abuse bothered her beyond the immediate pain. I think that's how she coped."

Her voice trailed off. Fred was about to leave Lorraine to her grief when she spoke again.

"I just wish we could've spoken once more. It hurt that Merry wouldn't accept my apologies. I just wanted her to forgive me."

Lorraine broke down. Wiping his eyes, Bryan approached her. When Lorraine composed herself, she wheeled him towards the exit.

I know how she feels, Fred thought. *I don't speak to my mom much either, and it's been almost twenty years since Dad divorced her.*

Fred involuntarily flashed back to the worst day of his life. He was eleven years old at the time and had no clue anything was wrong in his house. When he came home from school, the utter lack of emotion on Joe Bennett's face scared Fred silly. Before Fred's astonished eyes, Joe told his wife in a quiet voice that he knew what she'd done, to pack her things and get out. Lena gathered her things, made a tearful apology and walked out of their lives.

Fred asked his father what his mother had done, and the only words Joe Bennett could spit out were "She's been running around on me. With other men."

As he grew older, Fred learned the whole story, which his father couldn't bring himself to verbalize. Lena loved Joe, but she fell victim to a bad combination; a weakness for alcohol and an inability to cut ties with some of her single friends. Lena would get drunk with them, meet a man and go home with him. It happened twice before word got back to Joe.

Once Fred learned the full story, he chose not to speak to his mother unless he absolutely had to. He was furious at the pain she brought into his life and his father's, that she could be so careless as to throw them away for a drink and some anonymous pleasure.

I don't speak to her all that much, but maybe it doesn't have to stay that way.

2

Yolanda Mason blamed her foul mood on the cold she felt coming on, but in reality, she didn't know why she felt so cranky.

"Is this everything?"

Donna Randall Carson chuckled as Max went over her huge volume of packed items for about the seventy-fifth time. Yolanda rolled her eyes, knowing that her extremely thorough friend had triple-checked every item as she packed.

Max finished studying the assorted bags and boxes.

"Yup. We already checked to make sure that I didn't pack any of your things by mistake, Yolanda. Now we can haul this to the cars."

"Oh joy." Fred scowled. "And we get to do it again next week when Yolanda moves. I thought slavery was over."

Max smiled. "They found an out clause just for us. Get to lifting."

Max and Donna barely returned from their honeymoon trip to Sint Maarten before facing the daunting task of consolidating the contents of two apartments into one. Max, Fred and Max's father had moved all of Max's things the day before, and today it was time for Donna's.

And then it's just me here, Yolanda thought.

Max and Fred braced for the job of wrestling with Donna's mammoth couch when the door buzzer sounded. Yolanda squealed with joy when she saw her visitors.

"Mami! Dad! You came!"

The Randalls had promised to be there, but the Masons said they wouldn't come until Yolanda's move (upstairs into a one-bedroom apartment) the next weekend.

Yolanda's father pulled her into a hug. "How could we miss Donna and Yolanda breaking up the roommate team? This is bigger than Mary Wilson leaving the Supremes!"

"Dad!"

Fred and Max cheerfully shook hands with Donna's two teenaged brothers. "We're glad to see you fellas. It's gonna take more than just us to get this couch outta here!"

Richard rolled his eyes and Roland scowled.

"Dag, just got in the door and they making us work! No whassup, no "how you be," nothing. Didn't they free the slaves already?"

Donna laughed. "Must be a testosterone thing."

After a crushing group hug, Yolanda pulled her parents and little sister over to where the men were preparing to lift.

"Hold up a minute, guys. Everybody doesn't know everybody."

Glad for the stay of execution, Fred, Max and the Randall boys sat on the dreaded couch.

"Dad, Mami, this is Fred. Fred, these are my parents, John and Gloria Mason. And this is my little sister Carmen."

Fred hugged Carmen first, and then turned to greet Gloria. "Buenos tardes Senora Mason. Me allegro podemos encontrar finalmente." (*I'm glad to finally meet you*).

Mrs. Mason blinked in surprise; after thirty years of marriage, her own husband didn't speak Spanish that well. Composing herself, she chatted with Fred, telling him that Yolanda spoke of him often and well before excusing herself to chat with Mrs. Randall and Mrs. Carson in English.

Glad I remembered Yolanda telling me her mom prefers speaking Spanish. You only get one chance at a first impression.

He turned to greet her father. "Mr. Mason, glad to meet you too, sir."

John Henry Mason chuckled and accepted the hand Fred offered. "I know I'm getting old when my daughter's friends start calling me "Sir." Well, it beats "What up, Pops?" After the way you handled my wife, I thought you were gonna speak fluent Ebonics to me!"

They both laughed.

"Where'd you learn to speak Spanish like that?"

Fred smiled. "I took it in high school, and then I had a Mexican roommate my freshman year in college. I made him speak Spanish to me as much as possible so I could learn it better."

Mr. Mason looked around the room. The elder Max Carson renewed acquaintances with Mr. Randall, and the three mothers were firmly entrenched in their conversation. Across the room, Max, Donna, Yolanda and the three teenagers chatted, leaving him isolated with Fred. He lowered his voice.

"Yolanda speaks highly of you."

"Glad you weren't around when we first met." Fred chuckled. "She hated my guts!"

Mr. Mason laughed. "Her mother had the same initial reaction to me. It must be genetic."

He lowered his voice again. "Is something going on with you and my daughter, or are you just friends?"

Yolanda looked over at Fred talking with her father.

Figures. He never likes any of my boyfriends, but let him see a guy who's just a friend- - -.

The "deer-in-the-headlights" look in Fred's eyes spoke volumes. John Henry chuckled.

"I thought so. She thinks you're just friends, but you're hoping for more. Am I right?"

Fred smiled. "Can't put anything past you."

"Nope. Like they say nowadays, been there, done that. I've been married to her mother thirty years, and it felt like I had to beg for sixty just to get her phone number!"

Fred laughed. "That bad?"

"I was a player. I had to convince her that I meant it when I said I only wanted to be with her. I bet that's where you are right now too. Am I right, "player?""

Busted, Fred thought.

"Ex-player. I turned in my player's card last year, and I wouldn't take it back now if somebody paid me."

"I hear you. Now you hear me. Whether she knows it or not, Yolanda cares for you. You're her best friend now that Donna's married, and Yolanda takes her friendships seriously."

Fred remained silent, waiting for Yolanda's father to continue.

"If you're serious about her, let her know. The longer you let her keep you in that "just friends" mode, the harder it will be for her to see you in any other light."

He don't know how complex all this is, Fred thought.

"Now that Donna's married, Yolanda's thinking about her own future. Don't let her get away because she thinks you're just her friend."

Max's voice cut through their conversation.

"Hey Fred! Break's over!"

Fred smiled. "The overseer's calling. Thanks for the advice Mr. Mason; I'll keep it in mind."

The older man smiled.

"You've got a good head on your shoulders, and Lord knows any ex-player knows how to treat a woman right. She could do worse than to give you a chance."

He shook Fred's hand and walked over to chat with Mr. Carson and Mr. Randall, leaving Fred pleasantly surprised and alone with his thoughts. He absently joined Max and Donna's brothers at the massive couch.

Her pops saw right through me. Didn't think I was that obvious.

"Yo Mr. Fred, you gonna daydream or you gonna help us lift this thing?"

Fred smiled at Roland's teasing. "How about this? When you start shaving, you can start busting on me!"

The men laughed and started lifting.

Four hours later, the dreaded couch had made it to the new apartment and the last of Donna's things were loaded for the final trip. Max smiled and looked around the room at his extended family and friends.

"I know it's hard to believe folks, but we got it all. Everybody, we really appreciate this. Thanks for coming."

The families and friends exchanged hugs and goodbyes all around. The Mason crew prepared to return to Baltimore, while the Randalls and Carsons went to help Donna and Max get everything into the apartment before heading home themselves.

"You okay, Yolanda?"

Fred noticed that Yolanda was sitting down again, and that she looked pale.

"I'm fine. I might be catching a cold, but mainly I'm just tired."

"Go lie down then." Donna hugged her friend tightly. "You did more than your share helping us out. We can handle the rest."

Fred pulled Max aside. "You know I'm there for you bruh, but right now, Yolanda needs me more than you do."

Fred looked to where Donna and Yolanda were just releasing their hug. Yolanda looked wistful, as if she didn't want to let go.

"I think you're right, Fred. Make sure you feed her while you're here, because Donna told me Yolanda hasn't eaten all day."

Max pulled Donna aside and explained to her why Fred wasn't coming with them.

"Good idea. I think it's sinking in that I'm really moving out. I'm feeling it too- I'm going to miss living here. Of course I *am* trading up!"

Max and Donna laughed and closed the door behind them. Yolanda got up to lock the door, and was surprised to see Fred still there.

"I thought you were going over to help."

"Nah, they got this. Besides, I got stuff to do."

Yolanda's eyes narrowed. "Like what?"

Fred guided Yolanda over to the couch. "This. You've been ripping and running since I got here. And did you eat today?"

Yolanda blushed and shook her head no.

"That's what I thought. How you gonna handle your little rug-rats on Monday if you're skipping meals? Kids can smell blood; you go in there weak and they'll have you for breakfast."

Yolanda chuckled. "Okay, I get the point."

"Good. Now, do you have anything in here I can cook?"

Yolanda protested, but Fred made her sit back and relax while he looked in the refrigerator.

"Unless you want a cold air sandwich, you might want to tell me what you're hungry for so I can go get it!"

She laughed. "So I haven't shopped yet. Sue me!"

After a brief consultation, Fred returned twenty minutes later with Boston Market bags.

"Darn Fred, did you leave any for the other customers?"

He smiled as he laid the food out on her dining room table. "I was gonna get you a Happy Meal, but they were out of toys."

Yolanda was impressed. Fred bought a family meal for four, including slow roasted chicken, macaroni and cheese, mixed vegetables and mashed potatoes. While she got out plates and silverware, Fred poured glasses of the Hawaiian Punch he'd bought to top off the meal. They prayed over the meal quickly and dug in.

Throughout the meal, Fred sneaked looks at Yolanda. Over the past nine months, they'd gone from adversaries to reluctant allies to friends. During that time, Yolanda took the auburn coloring out and returned her hair to black, but she still wouldn't cut it. It now reached the middle of her spine, and showed no signs of stopping on its own. And her raggedy old sweats did little to conceal her formidable curves.

"Fred, thanks for bringing me the food. I didn't realize how hungry I was until you called me out about not eating."

"You're welcome. That's what friends are for. And you know the best part of all this?"

They chimed in together. "LEFTOVERS!"

Fred and Yolanda laughed.

"Yeah Yolanda, you're good for at least another meal or two."

Yolanda looked surprised. "You're not taking any with you?"

"Naah. I went shopping last night. I got food for days now."

Fred knew Yolanda wouldn't rest while he was still there and got up.

"Leaving so soon? Got a hot date, huh?"

Fred laughed. "Hardly. I figured you ain't trying to sit up here entertaining me when you could be sleeping."

"Yeah, I could use a nap, but don't let me run you off. I was about to watch TV first and then lie down. Anything you want to see?"

They settled in with fresh glasses of punch and Yolanda's tape of a Christian movie, *Something To Sing About.*

They both made it through the movie awake, but the credits were still rolling when they both dozed off.

Raoul Carizales stood outside Kahunaville, awaiting his prey.

He should be out any second now, Raoul thought. *His buddies just got up to leave, and drunk as he is, he'll need a ride home.*

A minute later, the door opened and four men emerged. Raoul smiled to see the one he was looking for within arm's reach.

Perfect, he thought. He took a step towards one of the three white men.

"Peter Tarkanian?"

The man peered at him through vodka-dimmed eyes. "Yeah?"

"I'm here on behalf of Tyros Vouras. You missed your court date yesterday, and Mr. Vouras isn't pleased that you skipped out on the bail he so generously provided."

Peter tried to focus his vision. "Court date? Oh yeah, forgot about that."

Raoul put a firm hand on Peter's right arm. "If you wouldn't mind coming with me, we can get you rescheduled right now."

Peter rose up to his full six-foot height, and looked slightly down on Raoul. "And whaddif I do mind?"

Raoul met Peter's eyes with a concrete gaze. "Then you're still coming with me. It just won't be as pleasant for you."

He started to guide Peter towards his waiting car, but Peter dug his heels in, proving himself to be deceptively strong.

"I'll reschedule when I feel like it!"

Peter cursed Raoul, ripped his arm from Raoul's grasp and turned to walk away. Raoul smiled, caught up to Peter with three long strides and renewed his grip on Peter's arm.

"Maybe you didn't hear me. You. Are. Coming. With. Me. *Now*."

Peter ripped his arm out of Raoul's grasp again, and this time he threw a left hook. Raoul sidestepped and pivoted to meet Peter's next attack. Predictably, Peter rushed Raoul and fired a stiff right jab. Raoul intercepted Peter's fist in mid-flight and squeezed. As the pressure mounted, Peter yelped in pain and tried a kick. Raoul released the hand, grabbed the extended foot and flipped Peter to the ground before Peter even realized his hand was free.

"You're coming with me regardless. Don't make me hurt you."

Peter lunged at Raoul again, who responded with a lightning-fast martial arts thrust. The heel of his right hand struck Peter's chin hard; Peter was unconscious before he hit the ground.

"Okay folks, show's over."

One of Peter's friends stepped forward. Raul looked at him like he was a roach to be stepped on.

"I should warn you. I'm licensed to bring this man in because he missed his court date. I am also licensed to take down anyone who helps him resist arrest. Besides having your butt kicked, you would also be subject to a charge of aiding and abetting a criminal, not to mention any crimes you might already be wanted for. Want to be his cellmate?"

The man stepped back. Raoul handcuffed Peter, shoved him into the back seat of his black Suzuki Grand Vitara and got behind the wheel for the drive to the police station.

That was easy, Raoul thought. *It's always nice to keep in practice.*

Peter was arrested for beating up his girlfriend, and then skipped out on a $10,000 bond. For this capture, Raoul earned ten percent of the bond.

$1000.00 for ten minutes of work, and I still have time to go out after I drop this loser off. Guess I can't come back here though.

Raoul laughed and put in his Best Of Public Enemy CD. He ignored Peter's groans from his seat right under the speakers as Rebel Without A Pause assaulted his ears at a merciless volume, and sped off towards the police station.

Fred and Yolanda woke up simultaneously, and laughed at the position they were in. Yolanda's head was on Fred's shoulder, and Fred had unconsciously put his arm around her.

"That's my cue to get up outta here! I bored you to sleep!"

Yolanda cracked up. "No you didn't, but I think I'll go to bed now."

They stood and stretched. Fred joked about Yolanda drooling on his shirt and then turned to leave. Yolanda stopped him with a hug and a peck on the cheek.

"Fred, thank you. I really appreciate your staying. You didn't have to, you know."

Fred blushed ever so slightly, praying that Yolanda wouldn't notice how glad he was that she'd released the hug quickly.

"Hey, I wanted to make sure you actually sat down! I bet if I'd left, you probably would've done lesson plans or something instead of eating and resting like you needed to!"

Yolanda playfully slapped his shoulder. "I'm not that bad, am I? Don't answer that!"

They laughed again, and Fred bid her goodnight. He whistled cheerfully as he walked downstairs to his car, surprised to note that it was ten P.M. already.

Good, Fred thought as he started the engine. *I can get home and go to bed. It's my turn to drive tomorrow.*

Even though he'd just left Yolanda, Fred found himself looking forward to picking her up for church in the morning.

"Randy, you coming to church with me tomorrow?"

Dr. Randy Errell locked his office.

"I don't know. Somebody might come in needing attention."

Theresa Errell fixed a cold stare on her cousin and employer.

"I let you use that excuse last week, buster. If someone comes in tomorrow, Betty can page one of the other doctors."

Randy sighed. *No getting out of this one.*

"Okay, my head nurse has spoken. I'll go. But what church are you going to? Any left in Virginia we haven't visited yet?"

Theresa smiled. After giving her life to Christ at Merry's home going service, she conducted a relentless search for a church home. She'd dragged Randy along a few times, but he'd begged off on many other occasions.

"I liked that United Methodist Church from two weeks ago. Let's go back there."

Randy thought back, remembering a pleasant enough service.

"Works for me. What time do they start?"

"Eleven. I'll pick you up, but you better be ready on time, Mr. Sleeping In!"

The two of them laughed and headed for home, Theresa to her apartment and Randy to his house. Randy waited until his cousin got safely in her car and pulled out of the parking lot before leaving himself.

Why am I so gun shy about going to church? After everything that's happened, only a fool wouldn't believe He's real.

Randy braked for a red light.

Maybe it's this whole Jesus thing that has me nervous. It all seems pretty intense. I mean, Jen- Merry- whoever she was- could've died and gone to hell, but Jesus saved her at the last minute. That blows my mind. The news stories all said she was a blackmailer and a murderer, yet Jesus still accepted her.

If she could make it, then why is it that folks like Theresa who live right and do good things still have to do something to "get saved?" Why wouldn't Jesus just automatically include her on the "good people" list? Or me for that matter? I always thought I was okay. I don't drink, don't smoke, don't run around with a lot of women and I help people with my clinic. What else do you have to do to get on the list?

Maybe it'll all make sense to me if I keep going to church.

Randy drove the rest of the way home, still pondering spiritual matters.

3

Fred and Yolanda entered Calvary United African Christian Church just before service started, and looked for Max and Donna.

"There they are, Fred. They beat us after all."

With one hand positioned behind his back, head usher Ted Stansbury directed them towards the third pew from the front on the left side of the sanctuary. Yolanda laughed as Max and Donna arrived from the right and joined them.

"Running late huh? Then how'd you beat us here?"

Max laughed. "We were when I called. If you'd waited for us, you definitely would've been late."

He glanced sideways at Donna, who ignored him. Yolanda laughed to herself.

Bet she was in the shower forever as usual, Yolanda thought. *Hope Max doesn't think that will ever change.*

As the service progressed, Fred sneaked looks at Max and Donna, and laughed at their "cutesy" ways. Max and Donna held hands, shared a hymnal and a Bible throughout the service.

Look at them, Fred thought. *If they were grinning any harder, they'd lock their jaws.*

From her seat beside Fred, Yolanda also saw the newlywed bliss occurring further down in the pew, and it brought a smile to her lips.

They couldn't be happier. Good- every couple I know doesn't look that content.

Yolanda and Fred simultaneously reached for their Bibles and bumped hands. Fred glanced at Max and caressed Yolanda's hand in exaggerated fashion. Max scowled at Fred while he and Yolanda did their best not to laugh. Donna pretended not to notice.

I know Fred was just joking, but I kinda liked that!

Raoul woke up at eleven A.M. feeling on top of the world. Energized by his success with Peter Tarkanian, he returned home, changed and then went to the Diamonds High. It wasn't as frenzied as the clubs he'd enjoyed in New York, but it fit his needs.

After a few hours, he chose one of the half-dozen women he'd danced with and decided to try to take her home. If he didn't get the first one, he wouldn't try again.

Raoul enjoyed setting such challenges for himself, and winning them. He randomly chose his second dance partner, a dark-skinned black woman with an exotic accent and eyes that reminded him of supermodel Naomi Campbell.

They had danced to a reggae number, and impressed each other with their fluid gyrations. When he approached her table again, she gave him a "Do you really think you're worthy?" look. Undaunted, he sat down anyhow.

She couldn't have left all that long ago. Her side of the bed is still warm.

He cleared the condom wrappers from his night table, and smiled to find a note hidden underneath.

"Call me when you want to dance again."
Coral

A phone number was neatly printed underneath her name. Smiling even wider, Raoul went to shower.

Fred and Yolanda waited for Max and Donna to finish chatting with Pastor and Mrs. Nathan and then headed out into the sunshine.

"So, what's up with America's favorite newlywed couple? Feel like hanging out with us lowly single folk today?"

Yolanda laughed. She had been about to ask the same thing, but Fred beat her to it.

"Actually we can't. Donna and I were going to have dinner with my parents today, but Donna's folks called last night complaining that we haven't been to visit since we got married."

Max rolled his eyes. "So, in the interest of family harmony, we're picking up my parents and going to Baltimore to have dinner with *Donna's* folks."

Fred chuckled. "You're not exactly turning cartwheels."

"I like my in-laws, but I'd like it better if somebody would take the wheel now and then when we go places."

"But wasn't that in the wedding vows?" Yolanda laughed. "Love, honor, obey and do all the driving on road trips."

Fred laughed. "And you know if Speed Racer there drove, you and your folks would spend the whole trip clutching the seats in fear. Of course you *would* get to Baltimore in about twenty minutes."

Donna glared at Fred. "Just because I happen to know what a gas pedal is for, unlike a couple of men I know- - -."

Fred and Max both laughed at how ironic it was that they drove calmly while Donna and Yolanda graduated from Lead Foot Driving Academy. The Carsons made their farewells and hurried off. Fred and

Yolanda watched them, missing the days when the four of them would have spent the rest of the day together.

"Hey 'Landa, how about we go get something to eat? I'm suffering from Extreme Triflingness, which in this case, means there's food in my apartment, but I'm too lazy to cook anything!"

Yolanda laughed. "You read my mind! After sitting through service with the Huxtables, going home to the set of Living Single just ain't making it!"

They laughed, got into Fred's car and headed for Old Country Buffet. Ted looked up from his post-service ushering duties and stared after them wistfully. A sigh heaved his plus-sized form.

Why do guys like that always get over? I know he's a man of God now, but he lived crazy before. I've always lived right, and women like Yolanda Mason won't give me the time of day even if they have a watch on.

He sighed again, reentered the sanctuary and started to clear away discarded worship bulletins.

"Okay gentlemen and lady, we've put this off long enough."

Max tried his best to feel like he belonged, even though his promotion to editor was recent. He'd sat in on City Voice Monday morning editorial meetings before, but only those related to story content. This was his first personnel meeting, and he was proud to be there. In his excitement, he was hard pressed to pay full attention to the managing editor.

"Thanks to Max being too talented to remain an assistant editor, we have an opening to fill."

Polite laughter rippled through the room.

"We've been getting by with three assistants, but you all know we work best with four, and with us going to daily in a few months, we need to be at full strength."

Max slipped in a quick, silent prayer.

God, I don't believe I'm in this position by accident. I can make a difference here, but only if I use Your wisdom to guide me.

"I prefer to promote from within rather than hire an outsider, and we do have qualified senior reporters who can make the jump. We're here today to start evaluating them."

The managing editor shuffled through a folder containing personnel files.

"These are the ones I see as legitimate candidates at this time. Anyone who thinks I missed somebody or if somebody I mention can't cut it, let me know."

He opened the first file. "We have Miranda Sanchez, who's been with us four years now."

He rattled off impressive information from her annual reviews.

"Next we have Raymond Styles, who's been here just over a year, but who has done phenomenal work and has shown editorial potential from the start."

He presented a dazzling array of compliments about Ray's work ethic, his nose for news and his diligence before winding down, to Max's relief. Another shuffle through the folder brought forth the last name.

"And finally, we have Fred Bennett."

<center>~~~</center>

"Man! Told you we should've come on time."

Yolanda reluctantly agreed. Calvary's biweekly Friday bowling nights had grown so much that they now rented the entire facility each time they came.

"You're right, Fred. Well, maybe we can jump on the lane with someone else."

"Fred! Over *HERE*!"

Fred looked up, and cursed under his breath, followed by a quick apology to God. Symone Donovan, the most blatantly single woman in the entire church, waved him over to the lane where she and someone Fred didn't know were practicing.

She's been on me since New Members Class, Fred thought. *I've seen hungry lionesses pay less attention to a herd of zebra.*

"We have room. Join *US*!"

Fred looked helplessly at Yolanda, who shrugged in resignation. "Either we join them or we wait an hour for a lane to open."

They made their way through the crowd, greeting friends as they went. Symone met Fred with a big hug, and to Yolanda's surprise, Symone greeted her the same way instead of acting snarly due to Yolanda and Fred's closeness. Like many in attendance, Symone wore a Calvary UAC Young Adult Fellowship T-shirt and blue jeans. However, Symone's clothing gripped her formidable body like a hungry anaconda. Yolanda wondered if Symone could breathe properly.

"Glad you could *COME*! Fred, Yolanda, this is my twin brother Symon."

Fred turned to shake hands, and blinked in surprise to see a massive bear of a man standing there. He was six-foot four, nearly two hundred and forty pounds and the same honey brown complexion as Symone. He also wore a Calvary UAC Valiant Men T-shirt and blue jeans (looser fitting), and his biceps each looked as big as Symone, who barely came up to his waist.

Fred looked from Symone to Simon and chuckled.

"Just a wild guess, but I'm assuming you're fraternal."

Symone laughed loudly, causing both Symon and Yolanda to turn and look at her strangely.

It wasn't that funny, Yolanda thought. *This could be a long night.*

Symon looked at Yolanda and chuckled, caressing her hand gently as they shook in greeting. "We're fraternal all right. Symone got the looks and I got the height."

Fred smiled. "Sure beats the other way around."

They all laughed this time, at the thought of an Amazonian Symone and a short Symon.

Symone didn't get all the good looks, Yolanda thought. *He looks like The Rock.*

Fred and Yolanda beat Symon and Symone soundly in the first game, causing Symon to suggest a realignment of teams; him and Yolanda against Fred and Symone.

You ain't slick, Fred thought. *You've been drooling over Yolanda since we got here, and now you have an excuse to get your mack on.*

Symone rolled a gutter ball to start the game, and sighed dramatically.

"Fred, help! How do I get the ball to go *STRAIGHT*?"

In the interest of teamwork, Fred ignored Symone's blatant effort to lure him closer and helped her select a lighter ball. He demonstrated how to grip and release it properly. Her next roll took down six pins, which sent her into a spasm of squealing cheers, followed by a big hug for Fred. Yolanda rolled her eyes and grabbed her ball, releasing without much thought to proper form. She rolled a strike, and Symon's eyes widened.

"Wow! You must practice a lot; that's your third strike tonight."

"Yeah, I do." Yolanda smiled. "I bowl a lot, and thanks to Fred, I'm getting better."

Symon laughed. "Anybody who can get Symone to stop rolling gutter balls is definitely a good teacher."

Symone stuck her tongue out at Symon and then rubbed Fred's arm appreciatively as they all laughed. Fred disengaged himself, grabbed his ball and rolled a strike of his own. Symon whistled in surprise.

"Man! I better come with it or you're gonna run us clean off this lane!"

Symon laughed at his own joke, and then grabbed his own ball. After about an hour of posing and flexing designed to highlight the Omega brand on his left bicep, he released the ball with all his strength. It obliterated the pins for yet another strike.

Yolanda smiled in spite of herself. "Uh Symon? I think the rule is that the ball has to touch the floor before it hits the pins."

They all laughed.

"Sorry. Guess I don't know my own strength."

Yeah, right Sir Flex-A-Lot, Fred thought. *Keep showing off.*

In the end, Fred and Symone defeated Symon and Yolanda, much to Symone's delight. Citing tiredness, Fred and Yolanda begged off of a third game and prepared to leave. Symon gave Yolanda a hearty hug and Fred a bone-crushing handshake, while Symone slobbered all over each of them in turn.

"This was a lot of *FUN*. We should get together more *OFTEN*."

Fat chance Symone, Fred thought. *We definitely crossed the "Too Much Donovan" threshold tonight.*

"We'll see. Good night, and thanks for letting us share the lane."

With Yolanda's diplomatic reply hanging between them, Fred and Yolanda made their exit. Three lanes over from the Donovans, Ted Stansbury waved as they passed. His bowling partner and fellow usher Dee Winston didn't look as happy to see them, but said nothing.

"How's it coming?"

Donna looked up from the computer screen. "It was easier when I didn't have time to prepare."

Max laughed, and massaged her shoulders. She sighed with pleasure and leaned back to fully enjoy his ministering hands.

"I guess so. I didn't hear one stammer or stutter at Merry's service, but now you have writer's block. Or is that preacher's block?"

"Funny. You try writing an initial sermon and see how well *you* do, smarty."

Max kept massaging. "I know how *I'd* do. It's not my calling, which means the sermon would be the verbal equivalent of me fighting Lundy Burroughs."

They laughed, remembering last year's Calvary church picnic when Max got into a fistfight with Burroughs, a huge sexual predator with a mean right cross and a strong desire for Donna. There were police officers nearby who could have arrested Lundy without Max's help, but he took matters into his own hands. Because Max was out of line with God's will, he also took a nasty beating.

"Can you use the same Scripture you used at the home going?"

Donna reached back and caressed her husband's hand lightly. "'Fraid not. That's what I've been trying to work from, but apparently it's not what God wants for this sermon. I think I'd rather have gone bowling."

Max laughed. "Let's get back to basics."

He wheeled Donna's chair back away from the computer, knelt in front of her and took her hands. Donna smiled and bowed her head.

"Lord, it's us again."

Max's standard opening for their joint prayers brought a giggle to Donna's lips.

"We come to you tonight thanking and praising Your holy name. Thank you for bringing us together, for allowing us to share our lives. Thank you for Your many blessings.

Lord, thank you for giving me a wife who is obedient to Your call on her life. You've called Donna to preach your Word, and now it's time for her to start. Let her know what You would have her to say. Show her which scriptures to lift up, so that someone who hears Your Word coming through her will want to seek a closer relationship with You."

Max paused, and Donna took up the prayer. "Lord, thank you for sending me such a wonderful, supportive husband. Bless him Lord, because as I start this new journey, he's starting it with me. Please grant me the ability to be submissive that I will never try to step on his authority as head of this household even as he doesn't try to block me from serving You."

They alternated in prayer for ten minutes, reaching the Amen together. They sat together in silence, enjoying their closeness.

"Thank you, Max."

He kissed her lightly on the lips. "You're welcome."

Suddenly, he reached for Donna's Bible.

"Do you have an idea for me?"

Max flipped a few pages. "Listen to this."

"*How fair is thy love, my sister, my spouse! How much better is thy love than wine! And the smell of thine ointments than all spices! Thy lips, O my spouse, drop as the honeycomb: honey and milk are under thy tongue and the smell of thy garments is like the smell of Lebanon.*"

By the end of his reading, Max stood directly in front of his wife, staring into her eyes. Donna frowned, trying to place the scripture.

"That sounds like the Song of Solomon."

"Yup, from Chapter 4."

Donna looked at Max suspiciously. "What kind of sermon can I do with that?"

Max had mischief in his eyes. "It might not work for your sermon, but for what *I* have in mind- - -."

Donna laughed and turned off the computer.

Yolanda yawned suddenly. The sound echoed in the closeness of the car, causing Fred to smile.

"That a hint?"

She blushed, and then chuckled.

"Yeah, that I need to start going to bed earlier!"

"Hey, it's Friday night. You're supposed to stay up late. I think it's the law."

They laughed and got out of Fred's car, cramped from having sat in conversation for nearly an hour after returning from bowling.

Yolanda hesitated as they reached her door, and Fred extended his hand.

"Allow me."

Yolanda smiled and handed over her keys. Fred opened the door for her.

"Wait here."

Fred made a gun with his right thumb and forefinger, and, imitating every television police show he'd ever seen, slipped inside.

Yolanda giggled. *He knows I'm still getting used to living alone. Nice of him to always check the place out for me.*

"Hey! What you doing in here? You betta jet 'fore I call the cops!"

Yolanda stepped inside and flipped on the light. Fred sat on the couch facing her, legs crossed and a playful smile on his face.

"Very funny."

He chuckled and stood to leave. Yolanda gave him a sisterly hug as he approached the door, and Fred tried hard to ignore how well her five foot seven inch frame fit into his arms. At six foot two, he didn't meet many women who did.

"Thanks for taking me to the bowling social tonight, Fred. I really appreciate it."

I didn't want you going alone, Fred thought. *I knew Usher Ted would be there drooling, and now Simple Symon's macking too.*

"No problem. It was nice."

Fred was painfully aware of Yolanda's presence; her perfume was more fragrant, her dark eyes were deeper and something about her drew him in.

I need to get up out of here. She's looking entirely too good and I know she ain't thinking about me like that.

"Yolanda?"

"Yes?"

His heightened awareness of Yolanda intensified, and he knew that if he didn't guard his tongue, he'd say something that both of them might regret.

"I just wanted to thank you too."

She looked puzzled. "For what?"

"For being there. With Merry, and then getting used to being in church and all- -I don't know if I could've gotten through it without your help. I really appreciate it."

Yolanda hugged Fred again.

"You're welcome. And you've been there for me too. I'm used to having somebody close by, and now Donna's married."

"Yeah, same here. Max can't hang with me like he used to, and if he tried to, I'd have to slap him and send him home to his wife."

Their laughter was relaxing, but Fred still felt awkward.

I better go now or else I'll end up making a move on her.

"Any big plans for tomorrow?"

Fred perked up, and hoped she hadn't noticed.

"Not really. Saturdays I do laundry, wash the car, shop if I need to and that's pretty much it. Oh yeah, I have Men's Choir practice at noon. Nothing major though."

Yolanda smiled. "I wanted to visit my parents this weekend, but my car's acting crazy. Can you follow me to the mechanic tomorrow morning? If I drop my car off when they open, they said they'll work on it first."

"No problem. What time?"

She told him, and Fred finally made himself leave. He drove home on automatic pilot, alternately cursing himself for being afraid to tell Yolanda his true feelings and rejoicing because of the chance to spend more time with her tomorrow.

Yolanda slid under the covers and picked up the phone.

I haven't been able to catch Donna all week. It's only a little after eleven; she should be up.

The phone rang four times. Yolanda prepared for the answering machine, but Donna surprised her by answering. "Hello?"

Yolanda was surprised by the sleepy voice on the other end.

"Hola mija, it's 'Landa. Did I wake you?"

Donna tried unsuccessfully to conceal the exhaustion in her voice. "We just got to sleep actually. It's been one of those weeks; church meetings, trying to write this initial sermon; you name it, it happened this week."

Yolanda blushed as she realized what else she probably interrupted.

"I won't hold you then. I just wanted to see how you were doing. Seems like forever since we've talked."

Donna smiled. "It probably *has* been forever. Call me tomorrow afternoon, around two. I should be here then and we can catch up."

"Okay. Good night. Sorry for waking you."

"No problem. 'Night 'Landa."

As Donna hung up, the reason for her exhaustion emerged from the bathroom, still smiling and still naked.

"Who was that?"

Donna chuckled. "Yolanda. You *know* only a single person would call us this late!"

Max laughed and slid back under the covers. "She probably misses you. When you two were roommates, you would have hung out tonight."

Donna nodded her head in assent. "Yeah, we either would have gone to the movies together or watched TV- - -."

Max smiled. "- -or gone to the Diamonds High trolling for men."

Donna playfully popped him upside the head. About a year ago, Yolanda dragged her to that club on the same night when Fred dragged Max. Despite the fact that both of them were way out of their element, that night sealed their budding relationship.

"Hey, whatever works."

Max laughed and shifted position so that Donna could put her head on his chest.

"Fred told me he was taking her to the bowling fellowship tonight. Bet they just got in or she might have called earlier. And I guarantee you *Fred* knows better than to call here this late!"

Donna laughed. "Max, do you think they'll end up together?"

Max stroked Donna's hair with his left hand.

"Fred and Yolanda? Hard to say. I'm pretty sure Fred's down, but I don't know if Yolanda feels the same way."

"'Landa's not sure what she feels about Fred. She enjoys their friendship, but she's confused about where the line is drawn in their relationship, or even if there is one."

Max shook his head. "Darn, you're good! Did your gift tell you all that?"

Donna smiled. It took her awhile to get used to her God-given gift to discern the feelings of others, but now it felt like one of her five senses.

"Pretty much. Last time we talked, I mentioned Fred and then I felt all this ambivalence in her. She's really not sure what she and Fred are; just friends, friends preparing to become more, or what."

"I think they'd be a great couple if they gave it a chance. We can't force them though."

Max thought for a moment. "Donna, how about we have them over tomorrow night? We could play Monopoly or something."

"That's a good idea. We really haven't spent much time at all with them since we got married. Yolanda's supposed to call me tomorrow afternoon; I'll mention it to her then."

Neither of them knew exactly when their conversation stopped, but before an hour had passed, Max and Donna fell asleep in one another's arms.

Gray fog swept across the scene, becoming black as it grew. Max heard a cry for help that quickly stopped. He tried unsuccessfully to clear a path through the smoke.

Max woke up, still trying to hold onto the images he had seen, and slipped out of bed to the bathroom without waking Donna. 5:30 in oversized numbers on the bedside clock greeted his return to bed, but he received no answers about the nature of the foggy dream scene. Max slipped back under the covers and rejoined Donna in slumber.

4

Fred arrived at Yolanda's door promptly at 7:30, and was surprised when Yolanda opened the door wearing her bathrobe and a sheepish expression.

"I overslept. Have a seat, I'll be ready in ten minutes."

Fred swallowed hard and nodded in agreement.

"No problem, take your time."

Yolanda hustled off to shower, leaving Fred alone with his thoughts and hormones. He sat on the couch, placed his back to the hallway so that he wouldn't accidentally see anything and tried not to dwell on the thought that Yolanda was fifteen feet away and naked.

This can't be my life, Fred thought as he heard water running. *It's a Saturday morning. I was out last night with a FINE woman and didn't even THINK about making a move, and now I'm up early so we can run errands.*

The shower stopped. Fred heard the bathroom door open and the light tread of Yolanda's footfalls as she raced into her bedroom.

Yolanda dressed in the first clean sweatpants and sweatshirt she could find.

I can't believe I set my alarm wrong. And of course I overslept when Fred got up early to give me a ride.

Yolanda pulled her hair into what Fred called the world's longest natural ponytail and joined Fred in the living room.

"Hold up. I need to ask you something."

Yolanda stopped in the middle of tying her sneakers. "Huh?"

Fred pointed to her sockless feet, which shone white against the rest of her tan skin.

"Is lotion like Kryptonite to you?" He held a bottle near her. "Nope, you didn't faint. I was wrong."

Yolanda's eyes widened as she struggled not to laugh.

"No you *didn't* go there!"

"You're the one with them ashy feet. Looks like you been kick-boxing the Michelin Man!"

He quickly lotioned them for her, enjoying the intimate contact. Yolanda smacked him lightly upside the head as he laughed and they headed for his car.

Max woke up suddenly, disoriented by his sudden exit from sleep. Donna lay beside him, and while her soft, rhythmic breathing was soothing, he couldn't relax and go back to sleep. The foggy dream scene had repeated itself, and Max wanted to understand why.

Max reached for his glasses and his bedside notebook, which had gone largely unused in the past year. Although he tried his best not to awaken his wife, Donna stirred anyway.

"Max? What are you doing?"

Max finished capturing the details and closed the notebook.

"Writing. I had a dream."

"Okay, if you're one of those folks who takes five hours to buy groceries, let me know now. I'll leave you here and come back tomorrow."

Yolanda laughed. "As I recall, it takes you awhile to finish all your shopping too."

Fred smiled. He and Max met her and Donna nearly a year ago in the same supermarket they entered now (the College Square Pathmark), and the women still teased the men for their blatant lack of subtlety in following Donna and Yolanda around the store. Max and Fred were mortified to learn that their attempt at stealthy surveillance failed miserably, and that Donna and Yolanda had checked Max and Fred out thoroughly without the men noticing.

"Max was the one on a mission, remember? I was just there!"

"Mm-hmm. Max might have been the instigator, but you looked like you were enjoying the hunt yourself!"

"Hey, I just wanted to get close enough to see if all that was really your hair!"

They laughed and started shopping. When Fred realized that it would be at least three hours before Yolanda's car would be ready, he invited her to join him in running errands while she waited. After a McDonald's breakfast, the supermarket was their next stop.

All this running around just to spend more time with her is crazy. I need to just tell her I'm falling for her. No, I'm past falling; I fell months ago!

⌇

Donna listened intently as Max described the dream.

"Have you had it before?"

Max thought briefly. "Not before today, and then I had it twice in three hours."

Donna opened her eyes. "That sounds familiar."

Max smiled as he remembered their first shared dream. He could hardly believe a year had already passed since then.

"Mmm-hmm. And if things go like they did before, you'll be having some variation of that dream before much longer."

"Maybe so."

Neither of them remembered just when they stopped talking and fell back asleep.

⌇

Halfway through their shopping, Fred stopped for shaving products while Yolanda perused the feminine hygiene section. She was exiting that aisle when she felt someone staring. She stopped to check out a sale display of Coke products and stole a sidelong glance. Her reward for stealth surveillance was a glimpse of her observer; a man standing five foot eight, lean and muscular in build with steel gray eyes.

He's Mexican, she thought. *And FINE.*

Yolanda immediately pondered how she looked. She had on one of her, "It's Saturday morning and I really don't care" outfits; gray sweat pants and an oversized University Of Delaware sweatshirt.

Glad it's long enough to cover, because these sweats are a bit tight in the booty. Don't want to thrill the brother too much.

Laughing to herself, she kept shopping, noticing that her admirer followed her while trying to look like he wasn't.

Where have I seen that before?

Raoul left the cookie aisle, turned the corner and saw Heaven. Heaven in this case was a bronze-skinned woman about his same height, hair down her back and the best butt Raoul had seen in months.

The shirt can't hide everything baby, he thought. *And am I glad!*

Not wanting to come off like a stalker, he nonchalantly stopped and pretended to peruse a sales display of Oreos while checking out the future Mrs. Carizales with his peripheral vision. When she moved on to the next aisle, he waited a few seconds and followed, hoping to catch up to her soon, by which time he would surely have a suave line that would put her in his little black book, and hopefully in his bed before long.

I can't wait to tell Donna about this. It's nearly a year to the day of her meeting Max, and now I have a guy chasing me down in the supermarket. If he steps up talking about dreams and visions, I might have to hurt him.

"Find what you needed?"

Yolanda jumped slightly. Fred had come up behind her and she hadn't even noticed.

"Sure did. You?"

"Yup. Shopping's a lot easier when you're not trying to pick somebody up."

Yolanda laughed. "Funny you should mention that."

Raoul rounded the corner and his heart sank. He cursed to himself as Fred approached Yolanda with complete familiarity. Raoul resented their intimacy; they laughed, talked and were clearly very close.

Ay caramba, he thought. *Unless that's her brother, I'm screwed.*

Fortunately for Raoul, he needed to pass through that aisle to get to the rest of the store, and he did so, thankful for the opportunity to act like he hadn't come that way with the intent of picking her up.

Yolanda waited until he turned the corner. She and Fred were heading the opposite way when she tapped Fred on the shoulder.

"Fred, that was your classmate from the You Too Can Pick Up

Women At Pathmark Institute. He must have graduated with you and Max, because he had your moves down pat."

Fred snorted through his nose. "You telling me that Antonio Banderas with braids tried to mack?"

Yolanda laughed. "Why you have to go there?"

"Did he do the "Reach For Something On A High Shelf So I Can Get A Better Look" move? I have it on good authority that one's played."

She giggled again. "No, he just stopped when I did, and checked me out while pretending to decide between Oreos regular or Double Stuff."

"Dag, that cookie aisle's a happening place! Forget clubs, folks need to hang out here. I can see the ad now: One Stop Shopping: get some Nutter Butters and a date all at once!"

They finished their shopping and headed for the nearest checkout lane. Fred spotted Yolanda's admirer before she did.

"There's your man. You need me to act like a boyfriend?"

"No, it should be okay; I think he's given up. Guess he thinks you *are* my boyfriend."

I should be so lucky, Fred thought, but said nothing.

Maybe that wouldn't be such a bad thing, Yolanda thought but said nothing.

Four checkout lanes over, Raoul took what he told himself was a final glance at Yolanda before giving up hope.

Definitely a boyfriend or a husband. They look too comfortable not to be together.

He watched as a small child sidled over to the couple, and spoke shy Spanish to his dream woman. He was pleasantly surprised to hear her answer in kind before the little girl's mother got her. Stealing another glance, Raoul noted that her features appeared to be both Mexican and African-American.

She is incredible. I'm sure her body is even more incredible than what I can see, and she speaks Spanish too! Oh well, she's taken. No sense crying over lost opportunities.

He paid for his groceries and left, resisting the urge to look at his dream woman just once more.

Back in her apartment, Yolanda put her groceries away and settled onto her couch for a nap. Sleep was elusive, as thoughts of her morning with Fred abounded.

After leaving Pathmark, Fred drove her back to the mechanic, made sure her car was ready and left for his second ever Men's Choir rehearsal.

Second day in a row where a decent looking man paid me some attention. I could get used to that.

Yolanda laughed to herself. *I can't wait to tell Donna about old Gray Eyes. What are the odds of being scoped in the same supermarket and even the same aisle two years in a row?*

Wonder if that means this mystery man is the great love of my life? Sure worked for Donna.

Nah, he's probably a bigger jerk than Symon, and that would be saying something! Actually, Symon wouldn't be so bad if he weren't so arrogant. The supermarket guy's probably the same way. Well, I might draw some losers, but Fred's a great guy. At least I have him to hang out with while I'm waiting for my husband.

The phone startled Fred out of his unplanned nap. Looking around, he noticed that the clock said six PM. He answered on the third ring, trying to sound coherent.

"Hello?"

"Hi Fred."

"Yolanda? Is that you? Haven't seen you in a *long* time! How you been?"

"Wise guy." She laughed "Like you didn't just drop me off six hours ago."

"True. To what do I owe the honor of this call?"

"I'm at Max and Donna's, and we need a fourth for Monopoly or whatever game they're going to lose to us today. Want to come over?"

Fred perked up immediately. His intent was to spend a lazy evening at home, but he hadn't hung out with Max in ages. And of course Yolanda would be there too.

"Sure. Need me to bring anything?"

"Just your over-competitive nature; we're gonna need that!"

Fred laughed. "Fine, be right over."

He hung up, yawned, and looked for his sneakers. The thought that board games with his friends had replaced clubbing as a great way to spend a Saturday night made him laugh as he headed out.

Raoul stared at his computer screen, wishing that the report of his last old major case would type itself and spare him the trouble.

I know what I want to say. Found a piece-of-human-sewage-repeat-sex-offender kidnapping eight-year-old Reggie Messenger. Suspect resisted arrest, cheerfully blew his pedophile behind away. Case closed. Unfortunately, my reports might get subpoenaed in court someday and I have to make sure they're worded properly.

He called up his calendar file, and checked to see if he had made any important appointments during the upcoming week. Nothing stood out and he started to exit the calendar file, but a note caught his eye.

Call Yolanda Mason, teacher at Brookshire Middle School, and confirm safety lecture for fifth grade class. A week from Thursday?

Raoul called the school and left a message on the secretary's voice mail confirming that he would come and hung up, entering this commitment into the calendar file before closing it.

Hope she calls soon. I don't like going into classrooms without a basic idea of what they want me to talk about. That gives me time to organize my speech, and maybe grab some props to make it interesting.

His thoughts drifted back to the magnificent creature he'd spotted in the supermarket and how he wished she weren't spoken for.

They were too comfortable together not to be a couple. And, for them to be hanging out dressed like that, they're probably married. Oh well.

Distressed that he was still replaying that incident in his mind, he saved everything, exited his Microsoft Word program and shut off his computer to prepare for Coral's imminent arrival.

DeShawn Carry-Winslow rubbed her throbbing temples and signed off her computer.

I give up. Since Bert has Wade this weekend, I thought I could get some work done, but nobody told me this was Act A Fool Day.

When her accounting firm took off a year ago, DeShawn bought a building to house it. She chose Southbridge, a part of Wilmington that many black and white Delawareans avoided like the plague. DeShawn grew up a block from her office building, raised by hard-working parents to be successful and to remember where she came from. She had no problems setting up shop close to her childhood home until days like this.

Since her son was with his father this weekend, coming to the office had seemed like a good idea when she woke up. Unfortunately, the day didn't go as she saw it in her head. She arrived at her office at ten a.m. and learned that the repairman who was supposed to have fixed her broken air conditioner a week ago still hadn't done it. Undaunted, she'd opened her window and sat down to work. Within minutes, two men chose to have a profane difference of opinion at the top of their lungs directly underneath said window. After spending a good ten minutes assassinating each other's characters, they parted company with a complex handshake and a friendly farewell. "A'ight man!" "Later, yo!"

The day went downhill from there.

After Cursers One and Two left, she returned to her paperwork, only to be distracted by the German Shepherd and Rottweiler from across the street. Apparently Batman and Robin took exception to the fact that the sun was shining and decided to race up and down the street and bark until it stopped. It took DeShawn an hour to realize that she'd read the same set of numbers twenty-seven times, and that the rest of the file registered in her mind as "Arararararararf! Roofroofroofroofroof! Grrrrrrr!"

When hunger and frustration forced her out of the office, the dogs took on their customary roles as Neighborhood Watch. After their customary severe sniffing, she rewarded their diligence by stroking each of their heads. Satisfied, they returned to their busy barking schedule.

The Four Brothers Soul Food restaurant had the doors open, and the smell of chicken and catfish had been tapping her on the shoulder all morning. DeShawn returned to her office with a chicken leg sandwich drenched in hot sauce, homemade peach cobbler and a cold Coke, determined that after she ate, she would finish her paperwork, no matter what.

Deshawn noticed a strange odor as she neared her building, but she couldn't place it. Then she saw a wisp of smoke emanating from her basement window. As she raced to investigate, the odor became more pervasive. She entered her building, and her head ached as she recognized the aroma.

Oh no they're not. If this is what I think this is, I'm gonna hurt somebody.

She put her lunch on the empty receptionist's desk and stormed downstairs to verbally maul whomever she found. Just as she suspected, her soon-to-be-ex custodians were enjoying a Cheech and Chong retrospective moment in the basement that they were supposed to be cleaning.

"Barkley" and "Gator's" eyes widened as their boss stormed in and demanded to know why they were smoking marijuana in *her* building, especially when they were on the clock. Barkley's lame excuse that they were on break didn't sit well. After the profanity and the dogs, two doped-up employees was the last straw.

DeShawn fired them on the spot, and let them know that, because they violated her "smoke free building" policy, their final paychecks would go towards deodorizing the walls and carpets. When Barkley protested, DeShawn reminded them that she could also have them arrested for possession. They stormed out, stopping long enough to steal her lunch on the way out the door.

How they gonna smoke weed in MY building and think I wouldn't mind, she thought as she closed her briefcase. *They were smoking so hard that the whole office will probably get a contact Monday morning. And then the trifling Negroes took my food!*

Shaking her head, she left for the day, wondering if white entrepreneurs ever had days like this.

⌇

"Man, I *told* you we shoulda waited till after work to get into that!"

Roger "Barkley" Jackson glared at his friend. They were sitting on the couch in the house Barkley recently inherited from his father, contemplating unemployment.

"Shut up! How was I supposed to know the heffa was gonna come in on a Saturday?"

"She did today, and now we ain't got no jobs!"

Barkley, nicknamed in his opinion because of his alleged basketball skills but in reality because of the size of his bald head, licked hot sauce off his fingers.

"How she gonna make us her janitors anyway? After we done grew up together, the best job she could give us was sweeping her floors?"

Tim "Gator" Simmons rolled his eyes and ate more peach cobbler, not wanting to hear more of his friend's persecution complex in action.

"Ever since she bought that building, she thinks she all that. Strutting around the neighborhood like she own it, buying all them fancy elephants just because she can. Heffa."

Gator polished off the last of the cobbler. "She ain't being snotty. It's some sorority thing."

Barkley was in no mood to have his moral outrage interrupted. "Whatever. She just think she all that, and I ain't taking it no more."

Barkley explained his brainstorm. Gator listened, wondering if his friend was serious or if the weed hadn't yet worn off.

～

5

"And now we'll be blessed again with the ministry of music from our Men's Choir."

The choir stood up. When they sang the first selection, Max, Donna and Yolanda smiled to see Fred in the first row of tenors. This time, the three of them blinked in astonishment when the director handed Fred a microphone.

Donna nudged Max. "Can he sing?"

"Of course. He used to use his voice to get women."

The three of them muffled their giggling. Fred stared over their heads and focused on the clock.

If I look at them, I am done.

Max was surprised to hear the organist play the opening chords for "Jesus Is Love."

They haven't sung that since Bro. Stanley moved, Max thought. *Fred better work this solo or folks will dog him out for the rest of his life.*

Just then, the director finished the introduction and looked Fred's way. Fred nodded in acknowledgement and sang like he'd been in the choir twenty years instead of two weeks.

"Father/Help your chil-dren- -."

That one phrase in Fred's golden voice was enough for the congregation to erupt.

After the solo, the choir came in with perfect four-part harmony. The congregation shouted approval, and as Fred continued his solo, they jumped to their feet, clapping and singing along with the choir.

Soon, the song reached the point where the choir hummed in harmony as Fred ad-libbed. Fred forgot that he was nervous and that Yolanda sat in the third row. He focused on the song, pouring his heart and soul into each note.

The director started to end the song, but one look at Fred changed his mind. Smiling, he signaled the choir to keep going. Fred kept ad-libbing, demonstrating an amazing vocal range as the choir followed him, grinning at the revelation of a strong new solo voice.

Yolanda was unable to keep her seat at hearing Fred sing with such authority. She brushed aside joyous tears, enthralled by the unexpected revelation of Fred's gift. Beside her, Donna smiled as she felt Yolanda's joy at Fred's singing along with a wave of something more.

Fred snapped out of it all at once, and the director, now grinning ear-to-ear, signaled the choir to end the song. Despite the fact that the song was far longer than the usual, the congregation was on its collective feet, lifting loud praises to God. Pastor Nathan made no move to preach allowing the Holy Ghost to have His way. Turning to face the choir, he gave Fred and the rest of the choir a thumbs-up. Embarrassed, Fred smiled as he sat down, thoroughly exhausted and filled with the Spirit.

Pastor Nathan turned back to the microphone wearing a huge smile. "I guess I can stop threatening to join the choir now. They found a brother who can *sang*!"

The congregation laughed and prepared to hear the preached Word.

After service, Max, Donna and Yolanda couldn't wait to talk to Fred, but they had no choice. Fred couldn't walk two feet without someone else telling him how much his singing had blessed them. He saw Max and the women coming and rolled his eyes. It was clear by the expression on Max's face that Max couldn't wait to tease him. After about the 700th set of congratulations, Fred finally reached his friends, who awaited him with amused expressions on their faces.

Max stared hard at Fred. "Okay Donnie McClurkin, where'd you hide Fred? We need him back."

Fred laughed. "You're the one made me join something, and then when I do, you got jokes."

"I said join the choir, not run it! How you gonna make one rehearsal and have a whole song that quick?"

Fred rolled his eyes. "I sang "Jesus Is Love" when I was a kid, at my grandfather's church in Jersey. And it was two rehearsals, wise guy!"

Yolanda hugged him, and Donna smiled at the distinct not-just-friends pleasure Fred felt.

"You were great!"

Fred smiled, ending the hug reluctantly. Max and Donna both noticed that Fred didn't release Yolanda's hand and Yolanda didn't rush to pull it free.

"Thanks. I always loved that song, but now I actually understand what it means. Back then, I only did it because I'd just learned that the girls in our church liked boys who could sing."

As the teasing kicked into high gear, Symone Donovan blew past Max and physically separated Yolanda from Fred by throwing herself into his arms. Donna nearly laughed out loud at the sudden burst of panic she felt from Fred at Symone's passionate arrival.

"Fred, that was *wonderful*! I didn't know you could sing like *that*! Your solo was such a *blessing*!"

Fred unconsciously winced; at close range, the extra volume Symone customarily put on the end of her sentences was painful.

"Uh, thanks Symone. Thanks a lot."

Fred tried to simultaneously hold a conversation with Symone and figure out how to escape her less-than-holy hug. In reaching up to plant a kiss on Fred's cheek, Symone managed to display her cleavage, press her breasts firmly into Fred's chest and apply a back rub with her free hand at the same time. Her less than modest light blue dress nearly exposed all of her secrets as she stood on tiptoe to congratulate her much taller New Members Class classmate.

Nearby, Max and Donna fought back laughter. Yolanda didn't have that problem. Her mood darkened, and it didn't take the gift of discernment to see that Yolanda's temper was suddenly as short as Symone's dress.

Lord, have mercy, Fred thought. *Please get this woman off me before I relapse.*

Symone finally let Fred go and swayed off into the crowd, leaving a lipstick-stained Fred in her wake. Once she was out of earshot, Max and the others lost the battle with laughter. He clapped Fred on the shoulder and started towards Fred's car. Max was amused by both the mildly distressed look on Fred's face and the stony one on Yolanda's. Donna sensed that neither of her friends faked those feelings.

"You okay Fred?"

Fred affected a glassy-eyed stare and accepted the tissue Donna offered him.

"Jesus keep me near the Cross."

Wiping his cheek clean, he looked up towards Heaven. "And while You're at it, can You get Symone a new top button for her dress? The one she got ain't working."

Max, Donna and even Yolanda had to stop walking so they could laugh.

—

DeShawn looked at her watch for the tenth time in the past hour and fumed. *Why can't his trifling behind bring my son back home on time?*

On cue the phone rang. DeShawn knew before she looked at the Caller ID she'd soon have an answer.

"Hey, 'Shawn. It's Bert."

DeShawn unsuccessfully fought down a growing wave of anger and sarcasm. "And you're on the other end of the phone instead of here returning Wade because- - -?"

"I know we're late, but the game went extra innings, and then we went for pizza and Wade fell asleep on the couch when we came back and I didn't have the heart to wake him."

DeShawn took a deep breath, determined not to go off on her ex-husband yet again. "You *do* realize he has school tomorrow."

"I was thinking since you have to work, I could just bring him back to you tomorrow afternoon, when you get in from the office."

DeShawn's voice turned colder than the Arctic tundra. "Wade's grades are not so good that he can skip school every time you start having "father not in the house-itis."

Bert protested, but DeShawn cut him off. "I will call his school tomorrow morning. If for any reason Wade is not at school on time, I will call the police to have them search for him."

Bert's voice went up an octave. "The police? Why you got to go there?"

"Because technically, my son is missing. According to our custody agreement, he is supposed to be back here no later than nine P.M. on Sunday night when you have him for the weekend. It is now two hours past that. Since I know he's safe, I'm willing to overlook that fact for now, but should he miss school tomorrow for no good reason, I'd have to reconsider."

Bert promised to take Wade to school in the morning, muttered a few choice words under his breath and hung up. DeShawn slammed the phone down, willing herself to be calm.

Thinks he's slick. He's always making excuses to keep Wade longer. He's lucky I don't push for a stricter custody arrangement.

She spun on her heel and stomped off towards her bedroom, knowing that sleep would be elusive tonight.

6

"Princess? That you?"

Donna smiled as she recognized the woman waving to her from across the room from past temp assignments.

"Tina!"

They bridged the gap between them in seconds, and Donna found herself smothered in a huge hug. Tina Winchester's ample bosom reminded Donna of her deceased grandmother.

"I ain't seen you in over a year! Nice to know you're on this job with me. How you been?"

"Blessed. How about you?"

"Same old same old. Ricky's still acting a fool, and I'm getting too old for his mess. Other than that, I can't complain."

Tina's eyes locked in on Donna's left hand, and she smiled. "Hold up. What's this here?"

Donna laughed as Tina grabbed her hand and held it up for inspection. "Don't tell me the princess done found herself a prince!"

Donna laughed harder. "I sure did. Best thing that ever happened to me."

"Who is he? Do I know him?"

Donna thought for a minute. "Remember when we temped at Statebank last year?"

Tina nodded.

"Remember that time I got a flat tire and you broke your nail trying to help me fix it?"

"Yeah."

"Remember the fine man who came by and changed it for me?"

"Yeah."

"That's him."

Tina cracked up. "Girl, that sounds like a *good* story! Come on to lunch and tell it to me!"

They laughed and headed for the elevator together.

Fred was determined to finish his story before Max or one of the other editors had to ask him for it, but his eyes began to burn. As soon as he closed them, an image of Symone came to mind. It seemed like she was in the room with him.

He smelled her perfume and saw the well-defined contours of her body in the outfit she'd worn to church when she attacked him after service. Even as he chuckled at Symone's total lack of subtlety, he wondered how she'd look without that dress on.

As Fred's mind succumbed to the images in his mind, his body responded accordingly. Alarmed, Fred forced his mind out of fantasy.

I don't roll like that anymore. God, You have to help me stop thinking like this. I gave up being a player and I meant it.

Refreshed by not having given in, Fred attacked his story with renewed vigor.

"Randy, the writer who called to do an article on you is here."

Theresa's knock startled Dr. Errell. He looked up from his paperwork and saw his desk calendar, where he'd circled his one appointment for the day.

"Okay Theresa, send her in."

Theresa spoke to someone Randy couldn't see, and then opened the door to let the guest enter.

Randy had always considered Theresa tall at 5'6" but this redhead was easily four inches taller, and sturdier. She wasn't heavy, but she had broad shoulders and it was clear that the Mattel people didn't manufacture a Barbie doll in her proportions.

"Randy, this is Sharon Fulton. Sharon, my cousin, Dr. Randolph Errell."

He snapped out of his stupor and stood to shake hands, gladly noting the absence of a wedding ring. Theresa backed out of the office, grinned at her cousin behind Sharon's back and closed the door.

"Pleased to meet you, Miss Fulton. Have a seat."

Randy indicated one of the plush chairs in front of his desk. Not wanting her to think he was intimidating her, he came around the desk, settling into the second chair.

Sharon retrieved her notepad, pen and mini tape recorder from her purse and tried not to dwell on how delightfully tall the doctor was.

"Well, since you were kind enough not to make me screech questions across your desk, I suppose I won't insist you call me Miss. Sharon is fine. Do you prefer Doctor, Doc, Mighty Healer- - -?"

Randy laughed. "A lot of folks call me Doc, but Randy works for me."

He has a sense of humor. That always helps for a smooth interview.

"Wonderful! Now that we're on a first name basis, you can tell me all the secrets I need to write a Pulitzer Prize caliber story about you."

Randy felt as though he'd never laughed before this woman walked through his door.

If I didn't know better, I would swear this was someone Theresa wanted to set me up with.

Sharon opened her notebook, placed her pen within easy reach and prepared to turn on her tape recorder. "I hope you don't mind me taping. Sometimes I have a hard time reading my own shorthand, and when that happens, it's good to have the tape to fall back on."

Randy chuckled. "No problem. Less chance of me being misquoted that way."

He admired Sharon's professional blue suit, noting that the skirt rested near her shins, even when she sat. Her curly hair framed her face nicely, and freckles competed for every square inch of facial space, particularly on her nose. Her eyes were a catlike shade of green, which Randy found hypnotic. He was suddenly glad that he'd chosen to wear a suit today.

"Okay, all set."

Randy snapped out of his second stupor since Sharon entered his office and swore to himself he would concentrate on this interview rather than the interviewer.

⌒⌒

"Fred, got a minute?"

Fred hit Save. "I do now. What's up?"

Max leaned over the back of Fred's chair and pointed to the screen, as if giving Fred input on his story. He spoke into Fred's ear.

"You didn't hear this from me, but tomorrow is a big day. You'll want to be sure your laundry situation is correct."

Fred forced himself to maintain the illusion that Max was micromanaging the editing process instead of giving him privileged information. He pointed to a section of his story, a paragraph about the heads of a corporation he was writing about.

"Would this sentence be accurate in this context?"

Max smiled. "Yes it would. It will be tomorrow morning too."

Fred blinked. "Mmm hmm. And would this story be front page material?"

"It'll be the first thing people see."

Fred smiled as a wave of comprehension set in.

"Okay. Thanks for the input. I'll make sure to adjust things accordingly."

"No problem."

Max straightened up and headed towards a second reporter whose work actually required Max to look over his shoulder.

The bosses want to see me first thing in the morning, and I'm guessing the open assistant editor spot will be the topic of conversation. I'd better dress for success.

Fred refocused his attention on the story he was writing, trying not to dwell on the golden opportunity awaiting him in the morning.

⁓

"Hey, Donna."

Donna smiled. As always, her husband's voice was a pleasant diversion in the middle of a busy workday.

"Hey yourself. How's your day going?"

"Pretty good. The other editors are beginning to forget that I'm "the new guy" and treat me like I've been with them a lot longer."

"Good! Now I know you want to ask me something, or else you would've just waited until we got home to hear my lovely voice."

Max laughed. "Aren't we supposed to be married longer before you start reading my mind? Oh that's right, you got an edge."

Donna laughed, and quickly composed herself so as not to alert her supervisor that she was on a very personal call.

"Anyway, I called so you could remind me what you wanted me to pick up from the store."

Donna sighed, remembering that she'd already reminded Max when they got up this morning and again on his way out the door. She gave him the short list again and they hung up, whispers of love and promises of affection on their lips.

Sharon turned off her tape recorder.

"Well Randy, I think I have more than enough information to do you justice."

Randy sat back and smiled for what felt like the three millionth time that day.

"Good, I'd hate to think we left any stone unturned. By the way, what publication do you write for? Guess I should have asked that sooner, huh?"

Sharon laughed. "Guess so. If I'd told you up front I work for the National Inquirer, you probably would have thrown me out."

She maintained her poker face for a few seconds, and then smiled. "Gotcha!"

"That you did." Randy cracked up. "I almost believed that one."

Sharon chuckled as she put her things away. "Actually I freelance. I write for a lot of different magazines and newspapers."

"Sounds interesting. Who's this story for?"

"I'm going to see if I can sell this to more than one magazine, but it will appear first in Career Day. It's a publication for high schools. You find someone doing a certain job and write about it through that person's experiences."

Randy raised his eyebrows. "So this story is to teach kids how to become a doctor?"

"Sure is. Instead of just the bare facts, I personalize it so the readers can see what the job is about and how to get into that field."

"Sounds interesting. I'd like to see a copy when it's published."

Sharon smiled. "You will."

She reached into her bag and pulled out a form. "I know it looks long, but CD needs this filled out and signed. That way they have your permission to run the story, and by putting your address here, they know where to send you a copy when it comes out."

Randy quickly scanned the form, which consisted of six double-sided pages. "I've seen shorter medical consent forms."

Sharon laughed. To Randy, the cheerful sound was as soothing as classical music.

"Yeah, it does look complicated, but they need all this for background information, in case I don't give them everything they need when I write it up."

"This could take me a little while. When do you need it?"

"By the end of the week, if you can. Oh, and I'd like to make another appointment."

Randy regarded her curiously. "I hope you're feeling okay."

Sharon laughed again, unable to keep her grin from spreading. "I have to take pictures of you to go with the story. Unfortunately, I don't have my camera with me."

Randy grabbed his calendar from his desk. "My schedule looks clear on Friday. Four days should give me enough time to finish filling out War And Peace here, and to get myself together for the camera."

You look just fine to me, Sharon thought, but kept that comment to herself, along with the fact that her camera was buried beneath her other equipment at the bottom of her purse. Carefully evading it, she pulled out her own calendar.

"Friday works for me too. Eleven a.m. okay?"

"Eleven it is."

With no further excuse to linger, Sharon dropped her calendar back into her bag and slung it onto her shoulder with one hand, and shook Randy's hand with the other.

"Randy, thank you for the interview. What I'd like to do on Friday is to take a few shots of you in here and the rest "action shots," basically you doing your job. If your other doctors or nurses or your receptionist or any of your patients want to be in some pictures that's fine, but they'll have to sign consent forms too."

They held the handshake longer than necessary, but neither of them made any special effort to disengage. Randy escorted her to the front door, past Theresa, who, after saying her own farewell to Sharon, found some reason to linger so she could watch Randy watching Sharon. Oblivious to his cousin's presence, he stayed at the door until Sharon got into her car and drove safely away.

7

"**H**oney, I'm home!"

Donna chuckled as she heard her husband's key in the door. *Okay Max, that might have been funny the first ten times- - -.*

She came out of the bedroom, where she'd been looking for her Bible.

"That was fast. Short lines at the store?"

Max fell silent. *Oh great- I forgot that fast! She's gonna love this.*

"You forgot that fast."

Max shook his head yes, looking sheepish. "Too much on my mind, I guess. I'll do it now, while I'm thinking about it."

He searched his pockets for the list he'd written after talking to Donna and realized that said list was still at work.

Without a word, Donna wrote up a new short list and handed it to him.

Another deposit made at Screw-Up National Bank, Max thought. I'll be a millionaire before thirty at this rate.

"Oh, Max? Can you get me thirty dollars from the ATM? I want to take my coworker Tina to lunch for her birthday tomorrow."

You think I'd say no now? Good timing, Donna.

"Sure. Be right back."

Max kissed her lightly on the lips, grabbed his car keys and headed back out, kicking himself for forgetting yet again

God, can You please help me remember stuff? I'm pretty sure I'll have some major screw-ups during this marriage; I don't want to waste my time on minor ones.

↝

"Umph! That man must be treatin' you good- you ain't stopped smiling since we got here!"

Donna cracked up. Tina had readily agreed to Donna's offer of a birthday lunch, at Bennigan's, only ten minutes from their current assignment.

"He forgets to take the garbage out and won't put the toilet seat down to save his life, but overall, he's wonderful; everything I ever wanted in a husband."

Tina exhaled loudly. "And you young too. What are you, twenty-three? Twenty-four?"

"Twenty-four."

"I'm thirty-five, and I *still* ain't got it right where men are concerned. Or any other way when you think about it."

Tina grew silent for a moment. Donna started to speak, but Tina chimed in unexpectedly. "You ever wonder why I call you Princess?"

"I figured you'd tell me if you wanted to."

Tina smiled as Donna paid their bill and they walked out. "First time I seen you, you reminded me of one of them fairy princess girls in the children's books. You always in a good mood and you talk proper without sounding phony. And stuff goes right for you. You seem like you always got it together, like a princess."

Donna laughed. "I have a whole **lot** of days when I feel more like Cinderella being kicked around by her evil stepsisters. You calling me that reminds me that I need to act right so people can see Jesus in me instead of my attitude."

Tina cocked her head and stared at Donna. "You know, I been meaning to ask you this. How is it that people like you seem like you and Jesus is road dogs while the rest of us can't find Him with a flashlight and a road map?"

Donna and Tina shared a good laugh over her analogy.

Thank You God, Donna thought. *Tina's ready to hear about You.*

Tina listened while Donna told her who Jesus is, how to receive Him and the benefits of salvation.

"Now, I need you to listen real careful to this part. Don't think that getting saved will automatically take all your problems away. Take it from me, it doesn't work that way!"

Tina laughed.

"And, giving your life to Jesus isn't just about wanting Him to fix the stuff you're most concerned with and nothing else. You have to let Him have all parts of your life, and you won't regret doing it. Jesus knows our problems because He's been here and done that. He knows all the stuff we go through."

Tina thought things over. "Okay, that makes sense. But how do I know when I'm saved? I mean, if I ask, what tells me that Jesus heard me and said, "Okay, you're in." And how do I know when He starts changing me?"

Donna smiled. "When you accept Jesus, you just know. I can't describe how it would be for you, but for me, I felt peace like I'd never felt before. As for knowing when He is making changes, you can't try to force that to happen. Once you accept Him, you pray, you read the Bible and you go with the flow and let Him direct your decisions. As time goes on, you'll see changes. You won't want to keep up your old bad habits because of Jesus in your heart."

Tina pondered that for a moment. "I like how peaceful you are, and I want that too."

Donna smiled. "You can have it. It's not my peace; that's Jesus inside of me keeping me from acting a fool."

They laughed as they arrived back at work.

"Princess, thanks for telling me all that. And thanks for the birthday lunch. I'm definitely coming to hear you preach tomorrow night."

Donna smiled. "Okay, I'll see you then."

"Yolanda, I need to tell you something. Let's sit down."

They were in her apartment as usual, relaxing with a pizza and an assortment of rented movies.

"Okay Fred, I'm sitting. Is this where you tell me you have a fatal disease?"

Her tone was joking, but deep down, Yolanda was concerned.

"No, nothing like that, but it is serious, and I just have to come out and say it. I love you."

Startled, Yolanda grasped for something to say. "What, I mean when- -, I mean, how long have you felt this way?"

He took her hand and looked into her eyes. "I haven't been able to get you off my mind since we went to dinner last year to talk about Max and Donna. God knows I've tried, but I can't. And I'm tired of trying."

Fred pulled Yolanda into his arms and kissed her to within an inch of her life.

And she woke up.

Yolanda looked around, disoriented. The dream seemed so real that finding herself home in bed was disappointing. She got up to walk around, and prayerfully clear her head in the process. But, a trip to the bathroom, a glass of water and a complete tour of her apartment later, Yolanda still felt hazy. She returned to bed, but couldn't sleep.

Why am I dreaming about Fred? We've been friends for a year now.

Uh huh. If I keep on telling myself that, maybe I might actually believe it.

8

Unlike most Wednesday evenings at Calvary United African Christian Church, nearly every seat in the sanctuary was full.

"Look at this. If this was just Bible Study, it'd be half empty up in here."

Max smiled at Fred's comment. They, Yolanda, the Carsons, and assorted parents, siblings, uncles, aunts, cousins and play cousins of the Randall clan occupied the first two rows on the left side of the sanctuary.

"You're right. Even the biggest CME members come out for an initial sermon."

Fred chuckled. "True. It's folks here who normally wouldn't come on a weeknight unless their child was being held for ransom."

Sitting on the other side of Fred, Yolanda cracked up. Just then, Pastor Nathan, two members of his ministerial staff and Donna entered from the side door and ascended to the pulpit. She nervously took the seat her pastor indicated and sat, Bible in her lap.

The assistant pastor prayed, and the other minister read a Scripture. Pastor Nathan then stepped to the pulpit, grinning ear to ear. "For those who didn't hear Bible Study is cancelled tonight, I'm sure you figured it out when you couldn't find a parking space."

Laughter rippled through the crowd. Behind the pastor, Donna sat stiffly in the "preacher's chair," wishing the formalities would end so that she could get it over with.

God, thank You for the message You gave me. Now, will You please help me over this nervousness so I can deliver it?

As Pastor Nathan spoke, Max noticed Donna taking deep breaths and squirming in her seat. He stared until he caught her eye, smiled, and then gestured as if summoning her to his side. Donna looked perplexed.

What is he doing? I can't just come off the pulpit and talk to him.

Frustrated, Max tried again. When he caught her eye this time, he first pantomimed shivering, and then pointed first to her and then to himself. He then mouthed "Galatians 6:2" to her.

Donna smiled as the message sunk in. *God, thank you for my husband. You've allowed for this to happen between us before. If it's Your will, let it happen again.*

In reply, Donna's nervousness faded, replaced by bold confidence and a resolve to preach with all her strength. Conversely, Max's breathing quickened, and he broke out in a nervous sweat.

"Man, if I didn't know better, I'd think it was you about to preach!"

Max smiled nervously. "Fred, the way I feel right now, it might as well be!"

Having heard the verse Max mouthed to Donna, Yolanda turned there in her Bible.

"Carry each other's burdens, and in this way you will fulfill the law of Christ."

Reading it brought comprehension to Yolanda's mind, and a smile to her face. She looked at Donna, who had transformed from the poster child for nervous into the essence of calm, while Max made that transformation in reverse.

Wish I could just send my feelings to someone else whenever I feel like it, Yolanda thought. *It must be nice.*

Pastor Nathan completed his introductory remarks. "In the United African Christian tradition, the pastor calls Solemn Assembly so the congregation can discuss matters of great importance. To me, there's nothing more important in the life of our church then nurturing the growth of a new preacher."

He paused for breath, swelling with pride in anticipation of Donna's message.

"Donna Carson came to my office nine months ago and told me that she felt called to preach. Her left arm was in a sling due to a gunshot wound, and she had just come from the home-going service of the woman who shot her. From what I hear, she started to say a few words about the deceased and wound up preaching the eulogy! That alone convinced me that Donna was serious about her call. I've been preaching ten years, and if I got shot, y'all would see Rev. Conrad up here instead of me. I'd be home figuring out how much I'd sue the woman for while whining to my wife for more Aleve."

The congregation chuckled again.

"Donna has demonstrated a high level of commitment to God and the ability to love unconditionally, two traits necessary to preach the Gospel. I have counseled her and her husband, and I'm convinced God has called this young woman to preach His Word.

Because her calling isn't to serve as a pastor or as a local elder, she won't be required to attend seminary. She is simply to preach, as she will do shortly. In accordance with UAC tradition, upon the successful completion of her initial sermon, she will be given the title of Evangelist. Following the singing of "I've A Message From The Lord," the next voice you will hear is that of Sister Donna Carson."

Sister Geraldine Campbell moved to her customary seat at the piano and struck up the requested hymn. As the final verse ended, Pastor Nathan moved away from the pulpit, and stepped aside in the traditional show of deference usually given by a UAC pastor to a visiting preacher. Donna and many of the older members blinked in surprise at Pastor Nathan's show of respect. Protocol called for the preaching candidate to let the pastor return to his seat before approaching the pulpit.

I shouldn't be surprised, Donna thought. *Pastor won't do something just because UACs have done it a certain way since Jesus was a boy. He'll seek God and then do it His way. Lord, let me always be like that too.*

She smiled and stepped to the pulpit, Bible in hand, notes tucked neatly inside.

"Good evening, church."

They returned her greeting.

"I thank God for this opportunity, and thank Him more that my family and my friends are here to share it with me. I won't stay before you long, but I do have a message from Him. Will you join me in prayer?"

"Lord, thank You for allowing me to shoulder the awesome responsibility of preaching Your gospel. My husband, my friends and my family members are all here, but I thank You for being here most of all. And thank you for helping me realize that even if there were only a few people here, I would still preach your Word because that's what you've called me to do. In Jesus' name I pray, Amen."

Donna saw Tina sitting near the back of the church. Their eyes met, and they shared a smile.

I did what you asked me Lord and invited her here. Now she's in your hands. And so am I.

Encouraged, Donna opened her Bible and, without glancing at her notes, let go and let God.

"If you will turn to the gospel according to John, Chapter seven, verse thirty-eight, you'll find these words. *'Whoever believes in me, as the Scripture has said, streams of living water will flow from within him.'* By this he meant the Spirit, whom those who believed in him were later to receive. Up to that time the Spirit had not yet been given, since Jesus had not yet been glorified."

She looked up from her Bible. "My topic this evening is 'Go With The Flow.' "

The congregation murmured approval; pens whirred over paper as congregants made sure they'd have an accurate record of her initial sermon to recall in conversation for days to come. Tina smiled and wrote it down as well.

"Webster's Dictionary defines the word "flow" as follows: "to issue or move in a stream," and also "to derive from a source.""

Fred elbowed Max. "Does Webster get kickbacks from the church or something?"

Max smiled; he and Donna had laughed over her use of that particular preaching technique.

"Flow has many connotations here. First, there's the song from our liturgy, "Praise God From Whom All Blessings Flow." God is the One who releases showers of blessing upon us. He is the source of our joy, and we need to stay within the flow of those blessings by seeking His face instead of trying to do things our own way."

Off to a good start, Yolanda thought. *Keep it up, Donna.*

"Then there's menstrual flow. Men, stay with me now. I'm going somewhere with this; don't get squeamish!"

A chuckle rippled through the church.

"That monthly flow comes from the source of our womanhood. It cleanses us of the unused eggs that our bodies form, and it signals that all is well with our reproductive systems. We might not like it, but it's necessary. In fact, this particular flow is even comforting under some circumstances. For those of us who might have backslidden, there are times when we go into prayerful anticipation around that expected time of the month. And when it happens, we know that the blood makes everything all right!"

Another ripple of amusement passed through the congregation. Tina laughed so loud she startled the people sitting around her.

"Then there is the flow that we as Christians can't live without. When Jesus hung on the Cross, He became sin, so that we could be restored to relationship with God. In the Old Testament, when folks lived under the Law, they made animal sacrifices because blood had to be shed for the remission of our sins. The blood had to come from an unblemished lamb; in other words, a pure, innocent source."

Max closed his eyes, basked in the love he felt for his wife and prayed that she would keep letting God use her.

"Jesus came to fulfill the Law; hence, He had to shed His own precious blood for you and for me. In John 20:32-37, you'll find these words. I'm reading this from the King James.

"Then came the soldiers and brake the legs of the first, and then of the other which was crucified with Him. But when they came to Jesus, and saw that He was dead already, they brake not His legs: But one of the soldiers with a spear pierced His side, and forthwith came there out blood and water. And he that saw it bare record, and his record is true: and he knoweth that he saith true, that ye might believe. For these things were done, that the scripture should be fulfilled, A BONE OF HIM SHALL NOT BE BROKEN. And again, another scripture saith, THEY SHALL LOOK ON HIM WHOM THEY PIERCED."

"That last part is important, now. One of Jesus' last words from the Cross is found in John 19:30, where He simply said, *"It is finished."*

Donna knew that her assigned ten minutes of preaching time was almost over and headed into the home stretch of her sermon. Her voice rang out with power and authority.

"When the soldiers saw blood and water flow out from Jesus' side, they knew it was indeed finished. The price for their souls and for ours was paid! They had to witness that crimson flow and know that Jesus, the Lamb of God, shed it for them. In other words, *the blood made everything all right!"*

To the last man, woman and child, the congregation stood, shouting praises and lifting hands to God. Yolanda was in tears to hear her friend preach under the anointing of the Holy Spirit, and Max praised God in a loud voice.

"He shed His blood for those who killed Him, for the thief hanging next to him, for you, for me, for everyone. They had to know- we need to know- that Jesus paid it all! Hallelujah!"

Donna's face was red with exertion as she brought the Word with power. Behind her, Pastor Nathan stood and shouted encouragement to his newest protégé.

"I can't speak for any of you, but I know where my husband and I stand; directly beneath that life-giving flow! As for me and my house, we will serve the Lord! We choose Jesus, who shed His blood for the cleansing of our sins. We will go with the flow!"

Drained, Donna stepped away from the pulpit amid thunderous applause and loud shouts of praise. She moved to her seat, but Pastor Nathan intercepted her and swooped her into a massive bear hug.

"Don't sit down yet. I want you to give the Invitation."

Knowing that UAC tradition called for the pastor to give the Invitation, Donna started to protest. Pastor Nathan waved her off.

"Go with the flow, now."

She smiled, took the cordless microphone, descended the stairs and went behind the altar rail for the Invitation to Christian Discipleship. Some of the older members blinked in surprise at this major deviation from protocol, but no one openly disapproved.

Donna paused, locking eyes with her husband and her best friends. She smiled at the warmth in their eyes, and an idea dropped into her spirit when she saw Fred. She signaled Pastor Nathan for a second microphone. He gave it to her with an amused look on his face, wondering what she had in mind.

"Any time the Word goes forth, we must give people a chance to respond. The preacher can whoop, holler, turn cartwheels or whatever, but if we don't present the congregation with the chance to know Jesus afterwards, it's all in vain. If you don't know Him for yourself, now is your chance. And if you're still not sure what He's done for you, let me make it plain."

She beckoned Fred forward, showing him the microphone in her other hand. He stiffened in surprise, and slowly got up, comprehension dawning. Max and Yolanda snickered, also guessing what Donna wanted.

" 'The blood that Jesus shed for me/Way back on Calvary/The blood that gives me strength from day to day/Will never lose its power.' I'm not a singer, but that song has great meaning for me, and it should for you too. In the absence of a choir, Brother Fred Bennett will come forward to minister that song for us."

Fred took the microphone from Donna and glared flaming daggers at her for putting him on the spot. As Donna skillfully ignored his gaze, Sister Campbell scrambled back to the piano. Opening the hymnbook, she found the appropriate page. Fred glanced at her and nodded his agreement that he could handle the key she played. He sang softly as Donna continued the Invitation.

"You might be saying, "I'll get saved when I get my act together." Then you will *never* get saved. None of us is perfect; we all strive to know Him and to live for Him instead of for the world. If you feel Him calling you now, then come to the altar now. You'll see Pastor Nathan and me standing here, but you'll give your heart to Jesus Christ.

Fred had shaken off his initial nervousness and had reached the chorus.

"For it reaches/To the high-est moun-tain
And it flows/To the lowest valley, O yes!
The Blood that gives me strength/From day to
day/It will ne-e-ver lose/Its power"

Eyes closed and head thrown back, Fred sang with all the power and authority Donna had just preached under. Women wept openly; men either shouted their approval or tried to act unaffected. As Fred's powerful tenor voice hit notes that even he wasn't sure he could reach, two women came to the altar, weeping and holding onto one another for support as they came forward. A man joined them, and Pastor Nathan asked Donna to pray for the women while he tended to the man.

As Donna finished praying for the first two women, she looked up to see a third woman standing at the altar, tears streaming down her face. Whispering a final word of encouragement to the first two women, Donna bid them to stay at the altar if they wanted to receive Christ in their lives and stood to greet the third woman.

"Princess, that- -that was- -."

Tina couldn't finish her sentence, and Donna couldn't speak either. She simply reached out and Tina pulled her into an even bigger hug then the one they'd shared on the job.

～

"When you talk to Donna, tell her next time I see her, her butt is kicked!"

Yolanda laughed. "Like Max would let you. You're just mad because she called you out."

Fred chuckled as he pulled into Yolanda's parking lot. "Yeah, whatever. I should've known she'd pull something like that. Do you know how nerve-wracking it is to just jump up in front of all them people and sing?"

Yolanda cracked up as she got out of Fred's car and joined him for their traditional trek up her stairs. "No, and considering I can't carry a tune in a bucket, I'll never find out!"

Fred rolled his eyes as she invited him in. "You ain't that bad."

Yolanda unlocked her door and let Fred in, still chuckling. "Yeah, but you won't see Donna handing *me* a microphone anytime soon!"

They talked over glasses of lemonade until the question nagging at Yolanda escaped. "Fred, when you sing like that, what do you feel?"

Fred was surprised by the sudden shift of topic. "It feels like I'm doing the right thing."

Yolanda gave Fred a blank stare.

"What I mean is, this is more than just being good at something. I mean, I'm good at writing and interviewing, and I was good at getting women, but this is different."

Yolanda chuckled as Fred continued.

"When I sing for God, I know I'm doing exactly what He wants me to do. It feels right."

"It must be nice to know what God has for you to do and then be able to do it."

Fred finished his lemonade, glad for an excuse not to have to speak for a moment. *Until just then, I didn't realize it, but I'm there! I'm working God's plan!*

"Yeah, it is. I used to be jealous of Max and Donna because they knew what God had for them and I was still guessing. But, deep down, I knew that I needed to be singing."

Yolanda spoke so quietly that Fred nearly missed her next words.

"I still don't know."

She put her glass on the table next to the couch and paced nervously. "I know that feeling you talked about, but I only remember feeling that way when I helped Donna deal with her gift. I don't think I've ever felt that way about something I did for myself."

Fred's heart twitched. *What do I do? How do I help her?*

Comfort her.

Fred got off the couch and hugged Yolanda before he even realized that he'd felt those words dropped into his spirit. She welcomed his embrace like a hungry man reaches for food.

"It won't be like this forever, 'Landa. God will show you what He has for you soon enough."

He gently rocked Yolanda in his arms, and started humming a familiar tune in her ear. Yolanda smiled as she recognized it.

"What God has for me, it is for me- -"

***

"Man, this ain't no good idea."

Fed up with Gator's rebellion, Barkley grabbed him by the lapels and pulled him up off the couch to eye level. Gator's half-eaten cheese steak went flying, adding a greasy ketchup stain to the already busy leopard design.

"Will you stop whining like a little girl? I told you this gonna work just fine!"

Gator surprised Barkley by putting both his hands in between Barkley's and then forcing the slightly larger man to let go of his collar. He then looked Barkley in the eye.

"That ain't gonna work. You're gonna get us both arrested instead of paid.

To Barkley's surprise, Gator reworked Barkley's idea so that it would have a better chance of success. Shocked, Barkley nodded his approval and they revised their plans accordingly.

***

Fred didn't know how much time had passed since he stopped singing. All he knew was that Yolanda was still in his arms and that she felt the same familiar hunger he felt.

You been waiting for this a long time, player. She's ready- go for yours. Get some of this while you can!

This voice was harsher and more like hearing another person speak. As if urged on by the same hard voice, Yolanda looked up into Fred's eyes. What he saw there was unmistakable, and he felt powerless to do anything but meet her halfway.

The first kiss was brief and tentative. Surprised at herself, Yolanda blinked and then offered her lips again. This kiss was anything but friendly, and they surrendered themselves within it.

"Max, pray with me."

Max paused in the middle of preparing for sleep. "Okay. Any special requests?"

Donna was winding down from preaching, but she suddenly looked tense again.

"I feel something in my spirit, Max. We need to pray for Yolanda. Fred too. I don't know exactly why, but they need prayer, right now."

Stop!

Fred pulled away from Yolanda so fast their lips sounded like a champagne cork releasing from the bottle. He slowly took a step back, praying for his heart rate to calm down and for the rest of his body to come under submission.

What was that? Yolanda took her own one step retreat. *Where did that come from?*

"Yolanda, I, uh, I'm sorry about that. I was out of line. I shouldn't have- - -."

Yolanda took another step back. "Fred, it was my fault. I shouldn't have kissed you. I- -."

They fell silent for a moment. Words failed as they realized what would have happened if they hadn't stopped kissing.

Fred took a deep breath. "Do not be conformed to the pattern of this world, but be transformed by the renewing of your mind. Then you will be able to test and approve what God's will is- his good, pleasing and perfect will."

Yolanda smiled. "Romans 12:2. The scripture Pastor Nathan used last Sunday."

"Yeah. And I'm glad God reminded me of that just now. By the world's standards, what just happened here is fine. But we have a different standard to meet. I'm sorry for trying to take you there. And I need to leave *right* now!"

Yolanda laughed. "I'm sorry too, Fred. We do a lot together, but I don't think Extreme Kissing qualifies as a 'friends hanging out' activity."

Fred cracked up as he backed towards the door. "Got that right! I think we need to talk about this some more, but not face-to-face!"

Yolanda laughed as he apologized yet again and beat a hasty retreat, thoughts of a freezing cold shower uppermost in his mind.

<hr>

"Is everything okay?"

Donna burrowed into Max's arms. "Sure feels like it. Thank you for praying with me."

"That's what I'm here for." Max smiled. "After all we've been through, I know that if God says pray, I say, "For how long?"

Donna laughed. "Well, if Yolanda and Fred were in trouble, I suppose it's over now."

Max reached to turn the light off in anticipation of slumber. When he turned back over, Donna rubbed his back seductively.

"Want to show me what else you're here for?"

<hr>

9

"Fred, can you come in my office for a second?"

Fred looked up to see Max standing beside his desk, smiling.

At least it can't be bad news, Fred thought. "Be right there."

Max wasted no time closing the door to his office and offering Fred a seat.

"What's up, Boss?"

Max rolled his eyes. "I wish you wouldn't call me that. Your Sovereign Majesty is sufficient."

Fred laughed. "Okay, okay. What's going on?"

"I just wanted to know if everything's okay with you and Yolanda."

"Why do you ask?"

Max chuckled. "Don't panic. Last night, Donna said we needed to pray for you and Yolanda. Did you guys almost hit a moose or something on the way home?"

Fred laughed. "We almost hit it all right."

He told Max about their near-sex experience, and the conversation that precipitated it.

"I don't get it, Max. She was upset. All I did was hug her and encourage her. Next thing you know, we're kissing each other half to death!"

Max shook his head and smiled wanly. "I should have seen this coming. Okay Fred, counseling time from one who's been there."

Fred chuckled.

"It isn't a good idea for single men and women to spend intimate time alone. I know you didn't go over there thinking, "I'm gonna get some tonight!" All you did was drive her home and hang out like you always do. However, the devil is real good at using your best intentions."

Fred laughed. "You're telling me? I mean, yeah I think Yolanda's fine, but we're friends. I'm not trying to scare her away from hanging out with me. She's not seeing anybody and I'm not seeing anybody, so why not hang out? It beats sitting home alone."

Max nodded. "True. All I'm saying is, you don't need to spend time alone at her place or yours. The devil can't tempt you if the situation isn't in place. Donna and I somehow made it to marriage without slipping up, but we had to fight every day to resist the temptation. And I definitely had to stop going over her apartment when Yolanda wasn't there."

Fred laughed. "No wonder you guys can't keep your hands off each other now- y'all had a lot saved up!"

Max cracked up. "Tell me about it. And while you're at it, tell me this: when you gonna stop playing and ask Yolanda out?"

Yolanda sat at her desk, wondering was going on. Her students were a half hour gone, but she couldn't finish her work and leave.

This is crazy. Fred and I have been friends for almost a year, and suddenly we're acting like teenagers in heat. I know Fred's used to a lot of sex, but what's my excuse?

Fred called her after he'd gotten home, and they both apologized repeatedly for what had happened. After about fifteen minutes, they hung up without discussing what Yolanda really wanted to discuss: their status.

I have no idea if he's interested or just wants to be my friend. I have to admit I've wondered about us, but I just don't know. Do I want Fred because of who he is or because there's no other men looking at me?

Chuckling, she forced herself to finish grading the last few test papers so that she wouldn't have to take any work home.

Fred hesitated with his hand on the door of the store.

Maybe this isn't such a good idea. She could think of me the way she does Donna, and if that's true, I'm really playing myself.

Naw. Max called me out, and he was right. I do like Yolanda, and I can't keep playing friend when I know I want more.

Resolved, he entered the flower shop before he could lose his nerve. A cheerful blonde college student greeted him.

"Can I help you with something special?"

"Actually you can. What do you have in a friendship bouquet?"

"Misty" smiled knowingly. "Oh, not quite sure where you stand with her? Got just the thing."

She opened a book and showed Fred several arrangements. Fred indicated an assortment of carnations, artfully arranged in a decorative vase.

"These look nice."

"We get a lot of orders for those. Do you want to include a note?"

Fred nodded, and stepped out of line to fill out the message. It took him five minutes and three false starts to come up with the right message.

"That'll be $19.95."

Fred handed Misty his debit card. As Misty rang up the sale, he wondered how Yolanda would react when she got these at her job.

This ought to do it. Yolanda is too curious not to ask me why I sent them, and when she does, I'll go there. God, please let me be doing the right thing!

Raoul picked up his pace from a morning jog to a full run, pushing himself to his limits.

Twenty-seven is way too young to start losing it. My life depends on me keeping fit.

Raoul thought back two days to his latest $10,000 bond case from Tyros Vouras. Lowell Hudson had been arrested for driving while intoxicated, and wasn't expected to do any hard time. However, Hudson failed to appear for his court date and Vouras wanted his money back.

Lowell showed up like clockwork every Wednesday evening at an adult entertainment place called Jack's, and Raoul wasted no time locating it. Lowell was alone, which he greatly appreciated; there was no money in beating up friends unless they were also wanted.

Lowell surrendered without incident, but, as Raoul opened the door of his car, Lowell bolted across the highway. He was ten years older and thirty pounds heavier than Raoul, but he ran like a teenager.

Raoul seriously considered shooting Lowell in the leg, but Lowell finally stumbled, and Raoul got him with a flying tackle. Lowell struggled so hard that Raoul was forced to hogtie him and drag him back to his car.

Raoul stopped to drink from his water bottle. *It shouldn't have been so tough to catch a lard butt like him. I can't let myself lose my edge; that could be fatal someday.*

He found himself across the street from Brookshire Elementary School. Normally he jogged an alternate route that took him behind the school, but today's more demanding regimen had him facing it. As he caught his breath, he noticed cars pulling into the parking lot.

It's 6:45. Must be some teachers starting their day. There's a thankless job- they're underpaid and underappreciated.

As Raoul prepared to resume his run, he saw two teachers getting out of their cars and heading inside. His appreciation for the female form kicked in, and he looked them over automatically. The first one was short, not much taller than five feet. She was black and from what Raoul could see, petite, yet very shapely. Her coworker looked black as well. She was much taller and had an incredible figure.

If she's that fine from thirty feet away, she must be awesome close up!

Yolanda felt someone staring, and turned to see if she were just being paranoid. *Who is that?*

She nudged her coworker with an elbow. "Tonya, check it out. We are not alone."

Tonya cut a sidelong glance and sucked in her breath at the sight of the lean, muscular man jogging past the school. His tank top and running shorts revealed a physique that was no stranger to exercise.

"Is that what you call a six-pack of abs?"

Yolanda smiled. "I think so. I can't see his face, but brother is *cut!*"

They laughed and entered the school. Raoul stared after them for a second, and ran on.

After a particularly hectic morning, lunchtime was a welcome refuge. With time to relax, Yolanda found herself deep in thought.

Her best friend preached a powerful sermon not two nights ago, and all she could think of afterwards was how powerfully Fred sang. And that kiss- -.

This is ridiculous, she thought as she finished her tuna salad. *Ever since that dream, I've had all these thoughts about Fred. And then the way we acted right after Donna preached.*

God, please give me a sign. If it's stupid of me to want a different kind of relationship with Fred, please let me know. For all I know, that just happened because he hasn't had sex in a long time. He might think of me the same way he does Max.

A knock on the door startled her into dropping her fork."

"Sorry to disturb you ma'am. You Yolanda Mason?"

"Yes, I am."

Yolanda gasped in surprise as the deliveryman walked in. Red, white, yellow, and pink carnations peeked out from a decorative vase. She found her voice and thanked him as he left the room as silently as he'd come.

God, is this your way of answering my question?

For lack of a burning bush or a booming voice from Heaven, she searched for a note.

Yolanda,
Hope you're having a good day. Thanks as always for being who you are.
Fred

A wave of pleasure swept over Yolanda, followed by a thought.

This can't be a coincidence. Something is going on here and I can't wait to find out what.

10

Yolanda was still smiling when her students returned from lunch.

"Hey, I see you got my flowers, Miss Mason. I know I'm too young for you, but can I at least get an "A" in English?"

Yolanda laughed. Dark-skinned and chubby, Wade Winslow was the class clown, and worked daily to maintain his reputation.

"Afraid not, Wade. See here on the note? You misspelled "kissing up.""

Chuckling, Wade took his seat and immediately told the boy next to him that his mother was so ugly she looked at an onion and the onion started crying. Yolanda let them trade a few quips before bringing the class to order.

"Okay class, I told you that today we would have a guest come in to continue our Safety Week lessons."

Yolanda opened the door to her classroom and nearly fainted when Raoul walked in. *This man is FINE! And familiar.*

"Class, meet Raoul Carizales. He's a former New York City police officer and he's here to teach us how to avoid dangerous people."

The class applauded as Raoul came in. He hid his surprise at the teacher being so beautiful, and in the back of his mind, he realized that he'd seen her somewhere before.

I'll figure it out later, he thought. Right now I have some kids to teach.

"Buenos tardes, estudiantes. For those of you who don't speak Spanish, let me translate for you. WHASSSAAAP!"

The class broke out laughing at his perfect imitation of the popular beer commercial.

"As Miss Mason told you, my name is Raoul Carizales and yes, I was a New York policeman. Officially I'm a private investigator, but I prefer to be called a Child Recovery Specialist. Anybody know what that means?"

The students shook their heads no.

"That means my specialty is finding kids. Parents hire me to bring home their missing children. Who can tell me some reasons why someone your age might be missing?"

Hands shot up all over the room. Raoul called on Wade, sitting in the front row. "Because they run away?"

"Yes, that's a good answer. Anyone else?"

He called on a white girl in the back next "They get kidnapped."

"Another good answer. Those are the two main reasons why I have a job. A lot of kids either run away from home or are taken. If their parents don't think the police can find them, they hire me.

Yolanda watched him as he effortlessly held the attention of even her most restless students.

"Okay, let me ask you this. How many of you like to use the Internet?"

Every hand in the class went up.

"Have any of you ever met anybody using the Internet?"

Almost all the hands went up again.

"Okay, how many of you know somebody online who wanted to meet you in person?"

Half the hands went up this time.

"And have any of you actually gone to meet these people?"

No hands.

"Good. Why haven't you gone?"

Wade raised his hand again. "Because my mom would kick my butt!"

The other students laughed, and Yolanda laughed with them.

"I've never met your mom, but I like her already! Would any of you go meet someone you met on the Internet if you had the chance?"

A short white girl next to Wade raised her hand. Raoul reached for his bag. "Why would you do it?"

She shrugged. "I could make a new friend."

Raoul pulled something out of the bag and had the girl stand up. He opened a cardboard cutout and placed it over the girl's head. The classroom howled with laughter to see a replica of a milk carton, with a hole cut out for the girl's face. The words "Have You Seen Me?" were written above her face.

"And you could also end up like this for real."

Raoul spun the girl around so that all the students could see her. Laughing, Yolanda went to her desk for her camera and took a picture.

"Young people, *never*, under *any* circumstances should you go meet somebody you met on the Internet. There are a lot of sick people out there who pretend to be your age, but when you meet them, they're much older. Most of these sickos are child molesters, and they use the Internet to find their victims. Ever heard about this before?"

The class nodded yes.

"Kids are abducted and molested and sometimes even killed by people like that every day. If anyone on the Internet asks you to meet them, tell your parents. Your telling on them might be what it takes for the police to find and arrest them."

The class was reluctant for the session to end, even though it was time to go home afterwards.

"Okay class, we have ten minutes left. If anyone has any questions for Mr. Carizales, ask them now. He's agreed to stay longer if he has to for those of you who are walkers, so let the bus riders ask their questions first."

After what seemed like an hour (but was really only twenty minutes), all the children were gone, leaving Yolanda alone with Raoul.

"Mr. Carizales, I want to thank you again for coming. My students learned a lot, and they had a great time as well."

Raoul used his best charm-the-ladies smile. Yolanda tried hard not to get lost in his captivating gray eyes.

"Yeah, the milk carton works every time. Sometimes after they see it, kids give the wrong answer on purpose so I'll put it on them next."

They laughed.

"We've been trying to drum safety into their heads all year, and I think you really got through to them about the Internet in particular."

"Good. Too many kids are approached online, every day. They need to know to be on their guard."

Raoul repacked his bag slowly and deliberately. "This is gonna sound really strange, but I've seen you somewhere before."

Yolanda smiled. "I was thinking the same thing. You look familiar, but I'm having trouble placing where I saw you. I know we didn't speak, or I would have remembered your name."

Raoul smiled as the memory of his first sight of her kicked in. "We definitely didn't speak. You were with a man at the time, and I didn't think he'd appreciate it if I interrupted your grocery shopping to try and learn your name."

Yolanda's eyes widened. "Wait a minute. That was you in the Pathmark?"

He smiled. "Guilty as charged."

Yolanda laughed, and Raoul joined her without knowing why. "I'm sorry for laughing, but if you knew the whole story--."

"Tell me. It sounds interesting."

Yolanda explained how she and Donna met Max and Fred in that same supermarket a year ago. Raoul laughed at the coincidence.

"Sounds like that cookie aisle is a happening spot! And you say your friends are married now?"

"Yup. They've been married almost two months now."

"Still shaking rice out of their shoes."

They laughed some more. Yolanda was strangely unconcerned that she was alone in her classroom with a man she just met.

"Miss Mason, I hope you'll tell me if I'm out of line, but is the man you were shopping with that day your husband? Fiancée? Boyfriend?"

Yolanda blushed, caught off guard by Raoul's directness.

"No, es un amigo. Fred and I hang out often. We both had shopping to do that day."

Raoul mentally sighed with relief. "I'm glad to hear you're not attached, Miss Mason, because if you give me the chance, I'd like to change that."

Yolanda reddened even more. *Wow, he sure doesn't mince words!*

"When I saw you shopping, all I could think of was how badly I wanted to get to know you. Now all I can think of is how I'd like to see you again. May I call you?"

Yolanda hesitated, torn between her attraction to Raoul and her desire for safety.

"Wait, I take that back. The Single Woman Rulebook says you're not allowed to give out your phone number to some guy you just met. Puedo que ser un loco (I might be a crazy man) for all you know. I don't want to have to pull out my milk carton."

Yolanda laughed, feeling comfortable at hearing Raoul use the same

English/Spanish patois that she and her family still spoke.

"The thought did cross my mind, but you seem pretty safe. However, I don't like giving my number out these days."

"Understandable."

Raoul handed her a business card. "I won't pressure you. Think it over, run a credit check on me or whatever it is that you women do that we men will never figure out."

Yolanda laughed, her concerns ebbing away by the minute.

"If you'd like to get together, then by all means, give me a call. If you don't want to see me socially but you want me to talk to your class again, I'll do that too. Or you can burn the card and forget I ever existed."

Yolanda felt like she'd known Raoul for years instead of hours. "Thank you for providing such a wide range of options, Mr. Carizales. I'll certainly keep them all in mind."

Raoul laughed, a rich, hearty sound that relaxed Yolanda even more. "Bueno. Y me llamo Raoul."

"Fair is fair. Me llamo Yolanda."

"Yolanda."

Raoul let her name roll off his tongue, caressing each syllable. His resonant, accented baritone gave Yolanda goose bumps.

"Well Yolanda, me allegro podemos encontrar finalmente. I certainly hope to hear from you soon. Good night."

"Buenos noches."

Raoul walked out slowly and confidently.

I got her. It might take a week, maybe even a month, but she will call me.

Hope it isn't to schedule another lecture.

As soon as Raoul turned the corner, Yolanda flopped into her chair and exhaled mightily.

That man is fine and smooth. Lord have mercy.

Just then, the teacher from next door poked her head in.

"Hey, Yolanda."

"Oh, hi Tonya. How's it going?"

Tonya entered and smiled. "Apparently not as well as it's going over here! Why do I get a fat old desk cop for my safety lecture and you get Antonio Banderas?"

Yolanda laughed. "I just got it like that!"

"I guess so. The kids been gone a half-hour and he just left! Did he ask you out?"

Yolanda's answer was a sly smile as she collected her things, taking care not to crush her flowers. Tonya gave her a high five.

"You go, girl!"

"I think we *both* need to go. Come on, I'll walk you to your car."

A black Saab awaited Yolanda's arrival at the door. The driver blew his horn.

"Hi Fred!"

He waved, and unlocked the passenger side door for her. Tonya looked at Fred, and then back at Yolanda.

"Wait a minute. You got Officer Extremely Friendly asking you out and this guy driving you home? Where do I sign up to have *your* life?"

Yolanda laughed. "My car's back in the shop. Fred's like a brother. We hang out, but it's not a love connection."

"Mmm-hmm. *My* brother doesn't send me complex floral arrangements at work."

"Shut up!"

Still laughing, Tonya got into her car, waved and headed for home. Once she cleared the parking lot safely, Yolanda got into Fred's car.

"How'd everything go today? Your safety guy show up?"

"He sure did."

Yolanda rode home pondering the men in her life and the decision that suddenly loomed.

〜

11

As soon as Fred dropped Yolanda off, she hurried to the phone.

"Hello. You have reached the home of Max and Donna Carson. We are unable to come to the phone, but your call is important to us. Please leave your name, number and a brief message and we will return your call as soon as possible. And remember, we can do all things through Christ, who strengthens us." BEEEP

Cursing under her breath at having gotten the Carsons' overly cheerful voice mail message, Yolanda left a "call me" message for Donna and hung up.

It was an effort for Donna not to scream after the most aggravating day of her life. She awakened that morning with a sore spot where Max had accidentally elbowed her arm while they slept. Then her temp assignment ended two weeks early without warning or explanation.

After Max left for work, Donna discovered he'd forgotten the garbage yet again, which meant Donna either had to endure the stench or wrestle it out to the dumpster herself. She was still sweating from the exertion when the phone started ringing off the hook with telemarketers. In between calls, she noticed that not only had Max missed the clothes hamper with his dirty drawers yet again, but he also had yet to master the art of putting the toilet seat down.

Seeing Yolanda's number on the Caller ID didn't gladden Donna's heart.

She probably needs me to solve a problem, and I can't even solve my own. Tired as I am, I might snap at her.

Yolanda replaced the receiver and sighed.

What am I supposed to do about this? First Fred acts interested and now Raoul.

She went into the kitchen in search of dinner, mind buzzing with the sudden abundance of worthy men in her life.

Fred was a hemorrhoid when we met, but look at him now. Until the other night, he never laid a hand on me except to be friendly, and even after that, his attitude's still the same.

Yolanda found a box of spaghetti in the back of her cupboard. Smiling, she pulled out a can of tomato soup, an onion, a green pepper and any other spices she could find.

Fred might not be a player anymore, but he still appreciates beautiful women. I could see that when what's-her-hoochie pushed up on him after church. I thought he was gonna pass out!

Yolanda laughed and put the soup on to warm, stirring in pieces of onion and green pepper.

Symone or Syductress or whoever got a reaction out of him, but he hugs me all the time and we never had any issues until that night. He doesn't think I'm attractive?

Yolanda thought back to how Raoul enjoyed her with his eyes as he left her classroom. She remembered how he caressed her name with his voice, and how warm it made her feel.

A hissing sound snapped her out of her daze, and she turned down the flame under her pasta and stirred the meatless tomato sauce. With culinary disaster barely averted, she dug into the refrigerator for some sort of green vegetable.

Fred's a great guy but, but Raoul is a fine man.

Yolanda finished her cooking, but her mind was on a certain business card in her purse.

Fred took a deep breath as he locked his car.

This is it. I'm about to cross the threshold of no return.

The hoped-for riding home conversation hadn't happened. Yolanda thanked Fred for the flowers and immediately lapsed into a preoccupied silence. Fred chose to let her think rather than get her to talk.

Back home, he'd tried to concentrate on his after work routine and failed miserably. Yolanda consumed his thoughts so much that he forgot to change his clothes and then scorched the fish he tried to cook for dinner before deciding that enough was enough. To Fred's delight, Yolanda called him and invited him over to talk.

We can kiss what we have goodbye when I tell her how I feel. I just hope it's to trade up for something better.

Yolanda buzzed Fred in and straightened things that were already straight as she sought vainly to be calm.

Our whole friendship could change if he says what I think he's gonna say.

Hearing the expected knock, she opened her door. Fred looked handsome in a light gray suit and a slight smile.

He didn't change after work, Yolanda thought. He looks good.

"Come on in, have a seat."

Fred moved to the couch and sat down, praying that his nervousness wasn't evident.

"You look rather subdued today. What happened? Electric blue suit at the cleaners?"

Fred chuckled. "I had another meeting with the bosses today. The Voice is going weekly soon. That means they're stepping up their timetable for choosing the new assistant editor to fill Max's old job."

Yolanda perked up. "Does your meeting today mean you're being considered?"

"Yup." Fred smiled. "I thought I would be because of how long I've been there, but this meeting confirmed it."

Yolanda couldn't suppress a huge grin. "Praise God! I hope you get it."

"Me too, even though it means reporting directly to Max. I hear he's a real slave driver."

They laughed, and kept talking. Fred asked Yolanda about her day, and she filled him in. He enjoyed their familiarity and at the same time, realized he would be comfortable coming home to this sort of closeness every day.

If I don't say this soon, he thought, I probably won't be able to spit it out.

"Fred, I'm glad you came by. I've been meaning to ask you something."

"Sure. What?"

"Promise you won't laugh?"

Fred's heart warmed. *Maybe she's going to make this easy.*

"I can't make promises, but I'll give it a shot."

Yolanda narrowed her eyes at him. "Funny. Remember Pathmark a few weeks ago?"

Fred looked perplexed. "Yeah. We shopped while we were waiting for them to finish fixing your car."

"Remember that guy who followed me around the store?"

"Of course!" Fred chuckled. "We took Scoping 101 together at Mack University."

Yolanda laughed. "Yeah, that's him. He turned up in my classroom today."

"Wait a minute." Fred laughed. "*He* was your guest lecturer?"

"Yup! Small world, isn't it?"

Fred laughed harder. "Real small."

For no reason he could fathom, Fred felt a chill. "Did your kids like him or did they treat him like a substitute teacher?"

Yolanda laughed. "They wouldn't dare. They know I'd wear 'em out with homework for the rest of the school year."

"Yeah, they know better than to mess with Mean Miss Mason."

"Anyway, they loved him! He held their attention, and they even stayed after to ask questions."

"Good."

Fred felt unsettled as Yolanda described Raoul's visit in vivid detail.

Sounds like he made an impression on her too.

"When all the kids were gone, he and I talked for awhile. I'm pretty sure I'll have him come back sometime."

"Yeah, with all the perverts out there, they need all the advice they can get. It wasn't this bad when we were that age."

"Sure wasn't. He has a passion for protecting children. He's Mexican like we thought; bilingual too. He's twenty-seven; he used to be a New York cop, but now he lives here and he's a P. I., focusing on missing children."

Fred's feeling of unease crescendoed.

"A PI huh? You'd think he'd have done a better job of covert surveillance."

They both laughed nervously. Fred took a deep breath, determined to find out just what was on Yolanda's mind.

"Sounds like you two had a good talk."

Yolanda took a deep breath. "We did. And he asked me out."

Fred forced a blank expression onto his face.

This ain't good. He asked her out on the spot; I've known her a year and can't open my mouth.

"What did you tell him?"

She sighed. "I told him I'm not comfortable giving out my number. He understood; he gave me his card and asked me to call him one way or the other."

Fat Usher Ted or Simple Symon, no problem. This guy? Problem!

"Not giving him your number was a good idea. You gonna call him back?"

Yolanda took a deep breath as she pondered her answer.

Fred doesn't sound too upset that another guy asked me out. Then again, what man ever shows his feelings? I wish I had Donna's gift.

"I'm definitely going to call him to talk to my class again. As far as going out with him, that's something I wanted to ask you about."

Fred perked up. "I thought women always asked their girlfriends to teach Dating For Dummies."

Yolanda chuckled. "Mrs. Carson has a lot on her plate these days. I left a message, but she hasn't gotten back to me yet."

Fred heard an edge in Yolanda's voice.

"You're my friend, and I need an honest opinion. Should I go out with Raoul?"

Fred's heart dropped like an anchor.

She does have me in that "friend" category, and kiss or not, it don't sound like I'm getting out any time soon.

"I don't know him. Makes it hard for me to give any kind of opinion."

Yolanda searched Fred's eyes for an answer. "Well, in general, how does he sound to you?"

How about this, Fred thought. *"He sounds okay, but I want you for myself, so my opinion is that he's a jerk." Yeah, that would go over well. No, she's my friend, and I've got to honor that.*

"You have some things in common. Do you know if he's saved?"

Yolanda frowned. "We didn't cover that particular ground."

Fred forced the next sentence out through clenched teeth. "Make sure you find out, but if you're comfortable, I think you should go out with him."

Yolanda blinked in surprise. In all the scenarios she'd envisioned, Fred endorsing Raoul never came up.

Fred clearly thinks of me as a friend, she thought. That means there's no decision.

"Well, coming from the nicest reformed player I know, I take that as a ringing endorsement."

They laughed and kept talking. Later on, Fred remembered nothing after that laugh but the sensation of loss.

After leaving Yolanda, he drove home on automatic pilot with a phrase ringing through his mind. "If you love someone, let them go. If they return, they're yours forever."

Why do I feel like she's not gonna return?

12

DeShawn thought she couldn't hate her ex any more until they went out for dinner.

She thought back to Saturday, when against her better judgment, she met Bert at Michael's to discuss things, namely Wade. When their initial round of small talk was relaxed and non-threatening, DeShawn allowed herself to believe that this could be drama-free.

I was wrong. He might have sounded like the prince I married when he invited me, but he's still the same frog I divorced.

"You know I'm relocating to Atlanta with my job, and that means I won't get to see Wade as often as I do now. He's becoming a man, and at this stage in his life, he needs his father. I'd like him to come with me.

DeShawn aimed a withering stare at Bert. "He needed manhood lessons from you two years ago. Adultery wasn't a good one to start with."

Bert didn't flinch; this particular verbal arrow didn't pierce as deeply as it once did.

"I can't change the past, but I can help to ensure that Wade has a good future. I think you're a good mother, but I don't believe any woman can teach a boy how to be a man. Wade is ten going on seventeen; he needs male guidance to get him safely to adulthood."

The conversation degenerated into an argument. After a few heated exchanges, DeShawn refrained from slapping him, threw money for her share on the table and stormed out of the restaurant. A phone message awaited her at home.

"DeShawn, you know I'm right. When you get through with your hissy fit, you can send me my son so I can make a man out of him. Oh, one other thing. Relocation is a bear, and I need repayment of the rest of the money I

loaned you. In case you forgot, that was $20,000, and I need the remaining $17,000 by the end of the month. This doesn't have to get ugly 'Shawn, but I'm not giving up. I want my son with me, and I'll do what I have to in order to get him."

Click

DeShawn took a deep breath. *I'm really going to hurt that man if he keeps it up.*

⌒

A week after The Conversation, Fred was in a minor depression. Yolanda called to tell him that she and Raoul had indeed gone out. He took her to Masorti's, a fairly new restaurant in New Jersey that she'd heard of, but never been to.

Sounded like they had a great time, Fred thought as he pulled up at the Wawa. Wonderful.

He found an open gas pump and filled his tank, distracted by thoughts of Yolanda slipping away and him helpless to do anything about it.

She'll probably fall in love with this guy, marry him and spawn a village full of children while I'm sprinting around the church hoping that Symone doesn't drag me down from behind.

Fred finished at the pump and reached for his car door when a familiar voice surprised him out of his semi-trance.

"You look like somebody who could break my heart."

He spun, and his eyes widened with recognition as he recognized the woman at the pump across from him, gassing up a silver PT Cruiser. He'd met her two and a half years ago, on a night when he'd gone alone to a new club in Philadelphia. It took less than fifteen minutes for Lenne (pronounced Lenay) Richards to lock onto him. He'd ordered a Bud Light and she and it reached him at the same time.

"I'll get that."

Fred was surprised to see a woman extending a ten-dollar bill to the bartender. She was nearly a foot shorter then Fred, brown-skinned, freshly braided cinnamon colored hair and soft brown eyes that belied her brassy demeanor. Amused, he let her buy his beer and made room for her. She ordered a glass of wine and turned to face him.

"You look like somebody who could break my heart."

Fred smiled. "I probably will, but there's other parts of you I'd rather deal with first."

Fred snapped back to the present and gave Lenne a big hug.
"Surprise!"

"It's been awhile, hasn't it? And you still remember that line!"

"I can't believe you took it there!"

Fred chuckled. "I can't believe it worked!"

They both burst out laughing at the same time.

"So, how've you been? Haven't seen you in almost a year, "playa." I thought you'd got married or something."

Lenne tried to smile, but only halfway succeeded. "Close. I lived with somebody."

Fred's eyes widened. "You mean some brother tamed you? I guess miracles do happen."

Lenne managed a laugh. "They must. I hear you were about to go domestic too."

Fred managed a smile. "Yeah, I was serious with somebody. It didn't work out though."

"Where are you on your way to?"

"Home actually. I got off work early to go to the doctor, and miracle of miracles, he didn't keep me there forever. I actually had time to run errands like a normal human being."

Lenne laughed. "I thought you looked relaxed. I'm off today too. Called in sick this morning; I just needed time for me. Feel like hanging out?"

Fred smiled. "Thought you'd never ask. Hungry?"

"Sure am. And it sounds like we have a lot to talk about."

She reached up to Fred's neck and fingered the small golden cross Yolanda gave Fred when he first joined Calvary. It looked a lot like the one Lenne wore.

"Maybe more than I thought. Follow me."

Smiling, they got into their cars and headed off to continue their conversation.

"So basically you hooked up with Shawn around the same time I met Merry."

Lenne smiled an empty smile. "Yeah, maybe a week or so apart from what you told me. I was in Philadelphia for my nephew's baptism, and Shawn was there visiting with his father. Turns out that my mom and his dad go to church together, and they'd been trying to hook us up! We dated for a month before we got our apartment. We were getting married next year."

She'd told Fred the rest earlier. Shawn died in a car accident less than a month after they moved in together, and a day after Merry's death. The eerie timing unnerved Fred.

"Yeah, I hear you. Folks like us never expect to have it that good, and then when it happens, we start thinking it might last. But then- - -."

"- - -but then reality happens and we're back to Square One."

They were silent for a few minutes, eager to shake off the sadness that threatened to deflate their buoyant mood.

"You were really going to propose to Merry?"

Fred sighed. "Yup. I'd never felt so close to anyone so fast, not even you, playa."

Lenne chuckled, and then listened as Fred told her how he met Merry and how it ended. Lenne's eyes widened as she remembered reading about Merry in the newspaper.

"Wow, and I thought I had some drama."

Fred chuckled. "Anyway. It's like all my time playing the game set me up to meet Merry, and when I did, I felt like it was time to make that change. If things with her had been more normal, we'd probably be married by now."

"I felt the same way about Shawn. Guess God had other plans for both of us."

Fred sighed. "Guess He did."

Lenne finished her iced tea. "And maybe that plan was for you and me to become an "us.""

Fred managed to not snort lemonade through his nose.

"Fred, I'm serious. We're comfortable together, and that's what I need right now. I want to be with just you."

Fred blinked in surprise. *She's serious!*

He sighed. "Lenne, it's not that simple anymore."

"Why? With us it's not just physical. We're actually friends. We know each other- that's why this can work."

"Lenne, I, uh, I don't roll like I used to."

She smiled. "Neither do I; no more games. I still have needs, but I want it to be just us."

Fred swallowed hard. *Dag, she's really trying to take me there!*

"Lenne, what I mean is, well, I'm not active anymore."

Her eyes widened. "Excuse me?"

"I'm committed to being a Christian, and since I'm single, part of that means abstinence."

Lenne rolled her eyes. "Oh, please. You mean you can't have Jesus and sex too?"

Fred smiled. "We could, but I'd have to marry you first."

Lenne remained stoic. "As long as it's been, I'm about ready to say yes!"

They both roared with laughter.

"Careful now. I've been cold turkey for a long time too. You keep talking like that, I'm booking the first flight to Vegas!"

Lenne finally wiped her eyes and stopped laughing. "You *know* it's tight when we can say the word marriage without throwing up!"

She looked Fred in the eye. "Think we'd work?"

Fred stared back. "You proposing?"

She smiled wanly. "I wouldn't go that far. What I mean is us having a real relationship. We could even get a place together if you want."

We do get along pretty well. And it's not like Yolanda's breaking down my door these days.

He smiled. "Can't move in, but we can discuss the rest. You ready to turn in your "playa's card?""

She smiled back. "Are you ready to take the chance that I might rape you or something if we start dating?"

"Hey "Landa, it's me. Sorry it took me so long to return your call."

"Oh, that's okay. I only called you a week ago. You have your own life now."

Yolanda unsuccessfully tried to edit the attitude from her voice; Donna felt it over the phone.

"What's going on?"

Yolanda told her about kissing Fred and meeting Raoul.

"Donna, this is so confusing! I really like hanging with Fred and all, but Raoul is different He's fine, he's polite--."

Donna rolled her eyes, knowing the answer to her next question and also Yolanda's reaction before asking.

"Is he saved?"

Silence. "We haven't discussed that yet."

"I thought not."

Resentment rumbled up from Yolanda's belly. *Who is she judging?*

"I don't want to sound like our mothers, but that's the first discussion you should have had. You've been out with him what, twice already?"

Donna braced for emotional impact as Yolanda's resentment intensified. It felt as if someone had placed a bomb in Yolanda's spirit and lit the fuse. Yolanda's Spanish accent emerged, something that only happened when she was upset.

"Yes, twice. Friday will be our third date."

"Oh. Okay."

"And what does *that* mean?"

She's not gonna want to hear this, Donna thought, *but I have to say it.*

"It means I don't think Raoul is right for you. I don't know him, but this doesn't sound good."

"What do you mean it doesn't sound good? Raoul has been a perfect gentleman! We went to dinner the first time and the second time we went to the movies. When was the last time I met a man willing to see a romantic comedy?"

"I'm happy for you 'Landa, but I'm still concerned. Everything you've told me is superficial. I haven't heard you mention where he is spiritually, and if you like him as much as it feels like you do, you should know that. Is he worth your losing your friendship with Fred?"

The emotional bomb exploded, and though Donna expected it, the detonation was more than she could handle.

"Oh, *now* you got advice? Where were you when I had to decide to go out with him in the first place? No time for us lowly single folks anymore, I suppose."

Donna prayed for strength even as she felt Yolanda's rage become her own, double itself and return to sender.

"Well ex-*cuse* me for having a life! In case you forgot, I'm married now. Did it ever occur to you that I *might* have more important things to ponder than today's episode of "Where My Man At Theater?""

Yolanda swore at Donna in Spanish. "Oh, is the high and mighty Mrs. Evangelist Carson having a bad day? Well, I'm sorry I inconvenienced you. Now that I've figured out how to handle my unimportant problems on my own, it won't happen again!"

Still cursing in Spanish, Yolanda slammed the phone down, vowing never to talk to that pint-sized heifer again.

Donna winced at the harsh sound of the phone slamming in her ear and at the sledgehammer assault Yolanda's anger had made on her spirit.

That was real good, Donna thought. *Yolanda's upset and needs to vent, so what do I do? Get smart with her.*

She started to call Yolanda back, but hung up. *It won't do any good right now. We'll just snap at each other some more and that will just make it worse.*

Donna knelt beside her bed and prayed for calmness and discernment and the resolution of this current situation, in His time and not hers or Yolanda's.

Max came in to find Donna having apparently prayed herself to sleep. Smiling at having found her that way, he gently shook her awake and greeted her with a hug.

"What's wrong? You look like you sat through today's editorial meeting instead of me."

Donna tried unsuccessfully to smile and told him about the argument with Yolanda. Max whistled through his teeth when Donna repeated what Yolanda said to her in Spanish.

"Trust me, you *don't* want a translation; I haven't heard language like that in a long time."

"I could feel how upset she was when she answered the phone. Apparently she's mad because she and I can't talk like we used to, and it all boiled over."

Max sat on the bed beside his wife.

"She's mad because you told her that her priorities were off. She knows you're right, and hearing you say so set her off. Think about it. You already have what she's looking for; a husband and the "perfect" life that comes with being married."

Donna laughed. "Keep forgetting to take out the garbage and I might give you to her."

"And have Raoul beat me to death?" Max cracked up. "No thanks."

Fred channel-surfed, wishing he could rewind the last week and start over again.

Encourage her to date Raoul. What was I thinking?

For the past two weeks, Yolanda drove herself to church instead of carpooling and sat across the church from the rest of them. After the benediction, Yolanda vanished into the crowd.

I was hoping we could talk, but clearly Raoul made a claim on her post-church time today.

The phone rang, snapping Fred out of his pity party. "Hello?"

"Any ex-players available I could speak to?"

Fred laughed as he recognized Lenne's voice. "Might be one or two lying around. Any one in particular you're looking for?"

"Think I found the right one. Any plans for the rest of your day?"

"Actually no. I was just planning to chill out."

"Ahh, we can do better than that. Let's go see a movie."

"Fred, I have a problem."

Fred had just hung up with Lenne when the phone rang again. He was pleased to hear Randy Errell's voice. Over the past month, their conversations had become a Sunday afternoon tradition.

"A problem?"

"Well, actually not a problem. A situation, something unexpected- - -."

"What's her name?"

Both men laughed. "Was it that obvious?"

"Only a woman can reduce men like us to babbling idiots."

Randy laughed again. "Yeah, you're right. Her name's Sharon. She's a freelance writer who came to do an article on me."

"And you're hooked just like that?"

"From the second she walked in the door."

"Sounds interesting. Tell me more."

"There's something about her. She doesn't hide anything; what you see is what you get."

Fred smiled. "And clearly you liked what you saw and would like to get it!"

"I wouldn't put it that way, but that does sum it up." Randy laughed. "When we did the interview, I felt like I was talking to a friend about my job instead of interviewing."

"Ahh, the old "lull him into feeling comfortable and then write an expose" trick."

Randy laughed. "Actually she did have me believing that she worked for the National Enquirer for a second, but that was just a joke. She has a great sense of humor. And she's tall, almost our height."

Fred thought for a moment. "Okay. Do you think she's interested?"

"Definitely. The interview was Monday, and then she came back Friday to take pictures. It was noon when we got done, so I invited her to stay for lunch with me and Theresa."

"I take it from the smile in your voice that she stayed."

Randy chuckled. "She did. Theresa ordered pizza, and we spent the whole time laughing."

Fred smiled. "Sounds like a winner to me. So, what are you going to do about it?"

"About the time Sharon was ready to leave, Theresa went to check on a patient whom she'd just checked on right before Sharon arrived. This time I wasn't mad at her for matchmaking because I really *was* working up the nerve to ask Sharon out."

Fred chuckled. "Did you?"

"We went to dinner last night."

Fred could hear the smile in Randy's voice.

"All right! How did it go?"

"Great! We agreed to go out again, but she's tied up until next Sunday. She invited me to come to church with her."

Fred perked up. "Church? She's a Christian?"

"Sure is. Since she was seventeen years old she said, and she's really sincere about it."

"If that's true, then this is huge. I suggest you buy a new suit and get to stepping!"

Randy laughed. "So you're saying her inviting me to church means this could be serious."

"Trust me, church is a big deal. This is a step below her taking you to meet her parents."

Randy hesitated. "I don't know if I can be as excited as she is. I mean, I believe in God, but until Theresa started dragging me lately, I haven't gone to church on a regular basis since I was a kid."

"Until last year, I didn't go either. If you really like Sharon, you should go just to find out why she likes it. It's just like if a woman likes opera or something and she wants you to come with her. Go with an open mind; you'll be surprised."

Randy laughed again. "Okay, will do. I was thinking of buying a new suit anyway; now I have a good excuse."

"I'm not trying to blow you off, but I've got to get ready to go." Fred chuckled. "I have a date myself, and I've got just under an hour before I'm supposed to meet her at the movies."

Randy smiled. "Good for you! Have fun, and of course you know I want details."

They laughed and hung up.

13

"**Y**ou know what? That guy over there with the braids looks familiar."

Fred looked where Lenne indicated, and his blood chilled. Raoul and Yolanda entered the theater, looking very much in love.

"I think I went out with him once. If that's him, once was enough!"

Apparently Yolanda doesn't think so, Fred thought, *but held his peace.*

Raoul looked up, and did a double take when Lenne smiled and waved at him.

What a time to run into an ex, he thought. *At least there's no history with this one. For some reason, she didn't want to put out. Her loss.*

"Fred, I need you be a boyfriend. I'll explain later."

Fred almost laughed. "No problem, playa."

She took Fred's hand as they walked leisurely in Raoul and Yolanda's direction.

"Long time no see, Raoul. How've you been?"

Raoul was glad to have Yolanda with him; ex situations were much better handled with suitable company on hand.

"Been doing good, Lenne. You?"

"No complaints."

She leaned into Fred's arm. "Raoul Carizales, Fred Bennett. Fred, this is Raoul Carizales."

Raoul introduced Yolanda, and bit back laughter as he realized that this was Yolanda's shopping partner. The two men shook hands, taking each other's measure with particularly firm grips. Beside Raoul, Yolanda's eyes lost every measure of joy as she recognized Lenne's name from conversations with Fred.

Raoul smiled to himself. *This is too good,* he thought.

"You know, I think I've seen you somewhere before, brother."

You're loving this, aren't you? Fake Antonio Banderas looking- - -.

"Maybe so. I meet a lot of people in my line of work. I'm a senior reporter for City Voice. And I hear you're a PI. Child recovery, right?"

"Ah, my reputation precedes me."

Fred bit back a snide remark. "That it does. Matter of fact, I'd like to talk to you sometime. I think the Voice could do a feature story on you."

They exchanged business cards while Yolanda fumed.

What in the world is Fred doing with that ho?

"We're going in and get our seats now. It was nice seeing you again, Lenne. Fred, good meeting you. Give me a call and we'll set up an interview."

"Okay, you'll hear from me soon."

They shook hands again, and as they let go, Lenne leaned into Fred. The gesture made Yolanda want to slap the resulting smirk off of Fred's lips. It was all Fred could do not to laugh at the look of sheer disgust on Yolanda's face as he steered Lenne towards the snack counter.

Why shouldn't she get an idea of how it feels? Nice to know she's jealous.

⁓

Raoul smiled as he escorted Yolanda to a seat halfway up the aisle and slid in beside her.

Looks like Fred's moving on, Raoul thought. *Maybe Lenne will distract his attention from Yolanda for good. I hope so; it would upset Yolanda if I had to put him in the hospital.*

⁓

On the opposite side of the theater, Lenne smiled as she, Fred and their popcorn sat down.

I just wanted to yank Raoul's chain, she thought. *but he and Fred have issues. I bet it's over Yolanda. Well, that's their problem. He's with me now, and it's staying that way.*

Hoping that Yolanda might be looking their way, Fred draped his arm over Lenne's seat in a proprietary manner. Lenne smiled and leaned into him as the movie started.

⁓

Randy sat back, reviewing the best Sunday he'd had in a long time.

From the moment he walked into Trinity United Christian Church with Sharon (wearing his new tan double-breasted suit), he felt right.

I really enjoyed the service. The people there were glad to see me come for a visit, and that preacher- wow!

Rev. Barnabas A. Shelby didn't fit Randy's stereotype (a big-haired preacher asking for money for his car and woman fund). He preached from his soul, and showed a genuine love and concern for those under his teaching.

Randy reread Rev. Shelby's text for the day, Matthew 19:1-16. When Rev. Shelby read that scripture in service, Randy felt like someone punched him in the stomach

If I didn't know better, I'd swear that reading was aimed at me.

Randy read another scripture Rev. Shelby referenced, and let it marinate in his spirit.

""For the love of money is a root of all kinds of evil. Some people, eager for money, have wandered from the faith and pierced themselves with many griefs." I Timothy 6:10

He said that this one is always misquoted. It's not money that's evil, but the love of money. That makes sense. Obsessing over anything can get you in trouble.

He read the other scripture he'd written down, Luke 12:16-21. This was the first time Randy had ever read the parable of a rich farmer with many crops.

He said that too many folks put their value in money and goods and not on their souls. I've always known you can't take it with you, but have I really believed it?

Randy read on, losing himself in the Word.

⌐

Fred couldn't focus on Pastor Nathan's sermon. Good as it was, his mind kept wandering back to yesterday's phone call.

After all this time, now Lorraine wants me to help her and Bryan clean out Merry's house. God, you're gonna have to get me through this, because I sure don't think I can handle that on my own.

⌐

Twenty minutes later, Fred had said goodbye to Max and Donna when Yolanda tapped him on the shoulder.

"Fred, can you come by this afternoon? We need to talk."

Surprised, Fred agreed. Doing her best to smile, Yolanda grabbed something from under the pew behind them and headed for the Lost and Found.

⤲

"That's the last of it."

Ted Stansbury and fellow usher Dee Winston had spent the last fifteen minutes retrieving discarded worship bulletins. Dee smiled as she trashed the final handful.

"Half the church complains they don't know what's going on. They would if they'd just read these!"

Ted chuckled and held one up that had a surprisingly well-rendered drawing of an angel on the back.

"Got that right. Maybe we should put drawing pads in with the Bibles and hymnals. That way, these parents could keep their bulletins and they'd know when Usher Board meetings are!"

"Bet they still wouldn't come out if they did!"

They shared a laugh. Dee smiled, enjoying their lighthearted banter. She didn't feel so comfortable with many people, and she basked in the feeling while she had it.

Just then, Yolanda entered the sanctuary, holding something in her left hand. Dee didn't miss the rapid diversion of Ted's attention. The pleasant feeling left Dee as quickly as it came; she suddenly felt shorter and plainer.

"Hi Dee. Ted, somebody left a Bible. What do I do with it?"

Ted was in motion almost before the sentence cleared Yolanda's lips, covering the distance to Yolanda's side in record time for a man his size.

"Here, I'll take it. I'll put it in the Lost and Found so whoever left it can go get it later.

Yolanda smiled and handed the book to Ted. "Okay. See you later."

Ted watched Yolanda leave, unaware that nearby, his fellow usher's heart was breaking.

⤲

Yolanda noticed Fred leaning on his Saab when she pulled into her parking lot.

Good, he came right over. God, be with me because I have to say some things he won't like.

They entered in silence. Yolanda settled them on her couch with glasses of iced tea.

"So Yolanda, what's going on?"

"The usual. Keeping busy, trying not to let those kids get the best of me."

"I'm surprised you asked me over. We haven't seen you after church lately; I would have thought you'd be out with Raoul by now."

Fred hadn't meant to sound bitter, and wondered if coming had been a mistake. Yolanda felt the same way and decided to forgo any further pleasantries.

"He's working this afternoon, and I needed time for myself anyway. Fred, can I ask you something?"

"Sure. What?"

"What is your problem?"

He looked surprised. "What are you talking about?"

"Your "date" the other week. Have you lost your mind?"

Fred blinked in astonishment at the anger in her voice, even as he felt some of his own welling up in the pit of his soul. "Excuse me?"

"I thought you were serious about your Christian walk. Why in the world are you going out with every man's best friend?"

Fred gritted his teeth. *I know she's not dissing Lenne. Not with what she's dating.*

"We go way back. Lenne is the only woman I was ever friends with before you and Donna."

Yolanda sucked her teeth, still reeling from her argument with Donna. "Lenne's been friends with a *lot* of men from what I understand."

Fred could hear Yolanda's accent emerging, but this time he didn't care if she was angry. "Yeah, she's been around. So have I."

"But *you've* changed. Hanging out with a hoochie mama is just asking for trouble."

The past month's frustration exploded out of Fred without warning.

"First of all, you don't know a *thing* about Lenne or you never would've cracked your lips with that garbage. Second of all, you might want to check yourself before worrying about who I'm dating. And since we're going there, when was the last time Raoul saw the inside of a church? Has he been yet this decade?"

"This isn't about me!"

Fred smiled knowingly. "I think it is. *You* don't want me, but you don't want anybody else to have me either. God forbid you should lose your designated taxi service/shoulder to cry on."

Yolanda couldn't answer- Fred's barb hit too close to home.

"Let me tell you something, Miss Hypocrite. Lenne has been through stuff that'd make you wanna curl up and die. She's trying to change, but if nobody gives her a chance, she won't make it. I've been where she's been, and instead of turning up my nose at her, I'm there for her as a friend. After all, I *do* have plenty of time on my hands these days."

Yolanda glared at Fred as his second verbal spear pierced her.

"Okay, I'll give you that. Maybe I don't know her like you do. And you don't need to "know" her in the biblical sense, which is just what's gonna happen si no tienes cuidado (if you're not careful)."

Fred's nostrils flared at Yolanda's deadly return fire.

"I could say the same to you. You don't know Raoul any better then you know Lenne, but *I* know a player when I see one. He's acting right now, but God help you if you ever give him any. You ain't nothing to him but another potential notch on his belt. *Si no tienes cuidado.*"

Before Yolanda could stop herself, she jumped up and swung a vicious slap. Fred ducked her backhand and grabbed her wrist with contemptuous ease to prevent a second swing.

"Oh, it's like that. I tell you the truth, you try to beat a brother down. Be like that. I'm out."

Fred tossed her hand away, and before she could swing again, he grabbed his keys, snatching the door open and prepared to slam it shut. He turned back to Yolanda with an afterthought.

"If your car breaks down or you need to go shopping or if you think someone broke in your place, I hope *Raoul* is there when you call. Have a nice life."

He cleared the door just before Yolanda could slam it on his rear end, and descended the stairs with a satisfied smile.

Who needs her anyway? How she gonna tell me who I should date when she's with the player of players?

Fred pulled out of Yolanda's apartment complex, cursing Yolanda under his breath. As he drove, Fred surrendered his spirit to the anger and frustration that had been present since the day Yolanda told him about Raoul.

I almost wish he would play her. That would knock her off her perch. Thinking she all that. Huh. She deserves to be going out with that longhead son of a- -.

- - --S-curl wearing so-and-so, Yolanda thought as she stormed into her apartment. *Try to warn that joker and he acts a fool.*

Yolanda cleaned her apartment, which in this case, amounted to her rearranging the items on her coffee table and slapping at the exposed areas with a dust rag while she fumed. Normally she'd call Donna to get her friend's insights. Right now though, Donna was the only person she'd want to talk to less than Fred.

Fred stomped into his apartment and slammed the door, just running out of creative ways to complain about Yolanda.

Hope Max is there, he thought as he dialed. I could really use some of his Brady Bunch advice right about now.

"Hello?"

Fred smiled in spite of himself; Max sounded exhausted. "Hope I ain't interrupting anything."

"Think I would've answered if you were?"

Fred laughed. "Naw, I woulda got your new answering machine message." He affected a pompous sounding voice. "You have reached the home of Max and Donna Carson. We're making love right now and can't answer the phone. Please leave your name and number, and when we're through making love, we'll get back to you when one or both of us has recovered."

Max roared with laughter. "Anyway. What's on your mind?"

Fred described the call from Lorraine Lucas, the situation with Yolanda and Raoul, and the altercation between him and Yolanda.

"She swung at you?"

"Yup. She tried to slap me, and I told her don't call me and I won't call you."

"That tends to put a strain on a friendship."

"Tell me about it."

"Now I understand why it's been so quiet at church lately. Bad enough Yolanda and Donna had words, but now you don't like her either!"

Fred laughed. "She's mad at Donna too?" Max explained, and Fred whistled through his teeth.

"Man, I feel kinda sorry for Yolanda now. All she's got is Raoul."

Max laughed. "You make his name sound like malaria or something.

So what led to your blowup with Yolanda?"

"Remember Lenne?"

Max thought for a moment. "The female player?"

"That's her. I ran into her right after Yolanda told me about Raoul. We went to the movies last Sunday afternoon and guess what fun couple we ran into?"

Max cracked up. "Must have been fun."

"It wasn't pleasant. Yolanda asked me to come over after church today so we could talk and you see how that came out."

There was silence on the other end for a moment.

How did this happen? I just knew Fred was going to make a move on Yolanda soon, and that she'd be receptive.

Fred broke the silence. "You think we can salvage this?"

"That's up to you and her. At some point, one or both of you is going to have to apologize or else the church carpool will die a slow death.

Fred smiled in spite of himself. "It's on life support now."

They both laughed.

"Hey, I have a spiritual question for you. Is it okay to pray that she starts hating him?"

Max laughed. "'Fraid not. But, cheer up. Yolanda will quickly realize that this guy's all flash and no substance. She'll be back."

"And if she *doesn't* come back?"

Max smiled. "Then you can ask Symone why everywhere she has to go in the sanctuary, the only way to get there is to squeeze past you."

Fred laughed. "Oh, you noticed that too, huh?"

"You kidding me? If she presses any harder when she hugs you, we'll be able to read her bra size on your shirt!"

They both roared, struggling to catch their breath.

"Yeah, she is kinda obvious. I'm staying away from her. The last thing I need is willing booty in my face."

Max laughed. "That's how it works. When I was *trying* to be a player, nothing. Soon as I promised God I'd abstain until marriage, I got three booty calls in two weeks. I never got one my whole life until then!"

Fred told Max about Yolanda's warnings.

"Can you believe she had the *nerve* to call me out when she's dating the King Of Players?"

Max took a deep breath. "I think you have a point. Yolanda wasn't ready to see you with anybody. I think she wanted to test the waters with

Raoul, and still have the security of knowing you'd be there if it didn't work out."

Fred smiled, glad that someone agreed with him. "She can't have it both ways, and that's what I told her. I suppose I could have been a bit more diplomatic."

Max smiled. "Probably so."

He hesitated. "Yolanda had a point too."

"What?"

"She would've hated on any woman she saw you with, but I'm concerned about you and Lenne too."

Fred tensed up. "Why?"

"Because you have a history with her, because she's not into abstinence, and because you're both vulnerable right now."

"Man, all we did was go see a movie. We ain't checking into Motel Six any time soon."

Max laughed. "All I'm saying is, be careful. The best way to resist temptation is to avoid it."

Fred started to answer, but heard a muffled female voice in the background.

"Let me guess. The wife wants you for something?"

Donna stood in the bedroom door, wearing only a smile. "You might say that."

Fred roared with laughter. "Talk about temptation!"

Max didn't hesitate. "I'm married. What's your excuse?"

Fred laughed. "Got me! Okay newlywed, handle your business. I'll talk to you tomorrow. And thanks."

"Anytime."

They hung up. Max turned toward Donna and smiled. "Sorry, but you can't keep coming here. My wife would kill me if she found out."

Donna laughed. "Keep it up wise guy, and I'll go get dressed!"

"Yeah, right!"

Grinning, he lunged at her. She ducked into the bedroom, laughing as he caught up to her and closed the door.

Just like before, a dense black fog engulfed the area. Children laughed and some screamed as they tried to get their bearings. Donna saw an overweight boy near the edge of the fog. The fog covered him briefly, and then dissipated. But, as the fog left, the chubby boy vanished with it. She saw a tan van speeding away from the fog.

Donna woke with a start, jumping so hard that she woke Max up too. He asked her what was wrong, but she shook too hard to answer. He held her, and his closeness enabled her to relax and write down the details of the dream. Max waited patiently for her to finish.

"Was it the same dream?"

She nodded yes. "There was more this time, Max. I saw Yolanda's school this time." She described the rest.

"Max, I think there's going to be a kidnapping!"

Bertram Wade Winslow, Sr. rubbed his temples against the throbbing headache that was forming.

Come on Bert, he thought. *Be a man and do this. It's the only way I'm going to be able to help my son become a man instead of a mama's boy. I can't stall. If I'm gonna do this, it's gonna have to be today.*

14

$\mathbf{Y}$olanda groaned as the phone assaulted her eardrums.

Go away! It's not even five AM yet. I got another forty-five minutes I can sleep; give a sista a break!

She rolled over and checked Caller ID. Surprised that either Carson would call so early, she picked up the phone before remembering she was mad at Donna.

"Quien es?"

"Yolanda? It's Max."

Yolanda relaxed a bit, but it was still early for her to be coherent.

"Mm hmm. Que quieres?"

"Sorry to call you this early, but we thought you needed to hear this."

Max described the dream he and Donna shared. Yolanda snapped fully awake at the word "kidnapping."

"Yeah, that does sound important. Thanks for warning me. I'll make sure to keep a close eye on my kids when they're on recess."

Now wide-awake, Yolanda slid out of bed and dropped to her knees to pray for guidance.

～

"Do you think she believed you?"

Max hugged Donna tightly. "I think so. Whether she's mad at you or not, she's always taken our dreams seriously."

Donna sat up in bed, unconsciously drawing the covers up to her chin like a frightened child.

"Even so, thanks for calling. I don't think she would have been able to receive anything from me after the way we fought."

Max looked solemn. "Hope it helps."

Donna paced the length of the apartment and started back again, praying as she walked. Her promised new temp assignment fell through, but under the circumstances, Donna wasn't upset.

That dream was a warning. I don't know just when, but something's about to break and I need to be available when it does.

Max sat at his desk, trying in vain to edit a story.

I can't shake the feeling that something's going to happen. Glad we warned Yolanda.

"Okay, hit it."

The smoke machine sprang to life and engulfed the playground in black mist. The children laughed at first, but then the cloud thickened to the point where they couldn't see their own feet. Yolanda called to her students to stay where they were. Surprisingly obedient, they froze.

A shadowy figure stepped to the edge of the fog and chose its prey. Before Wade could cry out, a meaty hand clamped across his mouth and another one twisted his arm behind his back.

"Scream and you die. Got me?"

Wade nodded, but struggled as he was forced into a nondescript van. The shadow threw the fog machine in next to him and took off. Behind them, a dark green Toyota Tercel screeched to the curb. Donna jumped out, and nearly cursed to see the van already speeding away. She scribbled down the license plate and went to see if she could help.

After what seemed like an eternity, the fog dissipated. Yolanda counted, hoping all her students would be there and knowing they wouldn't. Her count came up one short.

Maybe somebody decided to sneak off to McDonald's. Maybe it's not what I'm thinking.

Her heart dropped into her shoes as she realized who was missing.

Wade wouldn't run off. Class clown or not, he's one of the more levelheaded kids in my class.

"Miss Mason! Look at this!"

Yolanda turned to see one of the girls holding a shoe.

"Is this Wade's?"

"Yeah. He always wears his Iverson shoes now that he finally got 'em. He showed 'em to me yesterday."

Yolanda's heart sank. *Somebody took him. He loves those shoes- he'd never leave one behind.*

"Somebody took him."

Yolanda nearly jumped to see Donna right beside her. She showed Donna the shoe.

"Yeah, I kinda got that idea myself."

Donna sensed Yolanda's growing agitation, and chose not to respond to her friend's sarcasm. She kept her voice low so as not to alarm Yolanda's students.

"I saw a van, tan, real plain looking. I got part of the license number, but I didn't see the driver."

"I'm glad *you* saw something. I was stumbling around playing Blind Woman's Bluff while somebody took my student!"

Donna winced at the wave of frustration and anger coming from Yolanda. She reached for her cell phone. "Want me to call the police?"

Yolanda took the phone. "I better do it. I'm the one on recess duty. I can't look completely incompetent, after all."

Yolanda called, and then tried to calm her students. Other teachers came out to help, including Yolanda's classroom neighbor Tonya. Leaving the teachers to their young charges, Donna looked around for any other clues. Finding none, she prayed.

God, we need Your help. There's a missing boy, and You warned us he'd be taken. Help us to find him, and to bring him home safely.

Without warning, Donna was beset by overlapping images. She saw Wade in a shoe store, Wade and a man (his father?) selecting a pair of Iverson sneakers and taking them to the cash register, Wade showing them off proudly to his friends. The last image was a shadowy man tying Wade up in a basement or a warehouse. Surprised, Donna bent over, feeling faint.

"You okay?"

Donna nearly jumped as Yolanda approached, returning Donna's phone. Donna put it back in her belt holster.

"Yeah, just felt a little light-headed."

A thought occurred to her, and she pulled her phone back out to call Max.

"Is that all you saw?"

Donna nodded. "Unfortunately. I wish I'd seen more."

Yolanda's eyes narrowed, and she fidgeted in her seat on the couch. "Me too."

Despite the fact that Yolanda still had issues with Donna, she came over to the Carsons' apartment when she was through talking to the police. They'd spent the last two hours going over the dreams, and everything they saw happen.

She's blaming herself, Donna thought, *but there was nothing she could do. I mean, we literally saw it coming and we couldn't stop it.*

Yolanda got up and grabbed her purse.

"I can't just sit here. I'm going to see Wade's mother. This must be killing her right now."

And you too, Donna thought as Yolanda left, but held her peace.

15

DeShawn felt like someone parked a UPS truck on her forehead with the engine running. She could hardly think straight since receiving the news that Wade was missing.

He'd never ditch school, and if he had, I would've found him by now. He would have gone to the arcade or to a friend's house.

Calling Bert was hard, namely because she knew he'd blame her. She'd barely finished telling him that Wade was missing when he lit into her about her allegedly inferior parenting skills. DeShawn hung up on him and refused to answer the phone when he called back to finish venting.

He has his nerve blaming me for something beyond anyone's control. What I ever saw in that jackass I'll never know.

A knock at the door startled her out of her thoughts. She raced across the room to answer, praying that it was Wade, that this was just a misunderstanding.

Wade's teacher looked every bit as upset and concerned as DeShawn felt. Not wanting to be alone, DeShawn invited her inside and offered her a seat on the couch.

"Have you heard anything?"

DeShawn shook her head no.

"The police haven't called yet. Some of the neighbors are out looking, but I haven't heard from them in hours."

DeShawn closed her eyes against the pain of her headache. Yolanda felt a gut-wrenching sadness pulling at her, and knew that if she felt this way, DeShawn must feel worse.

"Miss Mason, who would want to take my son?"

This woman needs a friend, Yolanda thought. *And frankly, right this minute, so do I.*

"You can call me Yolanda if you want to. I don't feel like straining my brain trying to be cool and professional right now."

DeShawn laughed, and agreed to be on a first name basis.

"I don't know. It's clear that whoever did it, used that fog for cover. They may have created the fog just to do this."

"But why Wade?"

Yolanda sighed. "I wish I knew. But I do have an idea. Did Wade tell you about the safety lecture we had recently?"

"Yes, he did. He raved about this private investigator Raoul something."

"Carizales. He is a P.I., but he focuses on finding missing children."

DeShawn's head snapped up. "He does? Does he have any experience with kidnappings?"

Yolanda pulled his business card from her purse. "Why don't we find out?"

Raoul paced like a caged tiger. He couldn't summon the patience to surf the net or watch TV or anything else he normally did between cases.

Maybe I should call Vouras and see if he has any FTAs for me. I don't want to lose my touch just sitting around.

Just then, he heard one of his cell phones ringing. A quick glance at the coffee table revealed that it was the black one he used for business calls only.

All right! Might be getting some action after all.

"Carizales."

"Hello Raoul. This is Yolanda Mason."

Raoul smiled inside and out at the sound of her voice.

"Hola, mija. Como estas?"

Yolanda smiled despite herself. "I wish I were better. Unfortunately, this is a business call. We need your services."

Raoul sat up on the couch. "Who is "we?" "

""We" is me and the mother of one of my students. We have reason to believe that her son was kidnapped. I'm with her now."

"Put her on the phone, por favor."

Yolanda handed the receiver to DeShawn. She gave Raoul directions on how to get to her house and hung up.

"He says he'll take the case! He's coming over to talk to us now."

"Dee, look at me."

Dee Winston lifted her head and looked at her friend and sister in Christ. Sister Annie Nathan was in full "pastor's wife" mode- her voice was warm and affirming.

"I don't ever want to hear you put yourself down like that again. You are God's child, and God doesn't create junk."

The tears flowed. Donna put a reassuring hand on Dee's shoulder, praying silently for her as Sis. Nathan continued her counsel. The three of them had stayed after the women's ministry meeting adjourned so Dee could deal with her pressing issues away from the scrutiny of the entire group.

"I want to believe it, but it's hard sometimes. I lost weight, but I still feel like that chubby girl who didn't have any dates in high school, not even for the prom."

Dee hung her head again, and Sister Nathan put a hand under Dee's chin and lifted it.

"Sista, I've been there. I was nearly six feet tall in the sixth grade. It took me years to stop believing I was a freak and to start seeing myself the way God sees me- and you; beautiful."

Dee sniffled, and Sister Nathan handed her a tissue. Impulsively, she pulled Dee into a hug as she and Donna prayed for her. A few minutes and half a box of tissues later, Dee's tears subsided.

Sister Nathan smiled impishly and let her Jamaican accent out of its box. "Okay now sista, give it up. What brother's got ya all hot an' bothered?"

"Ms. Winslow, I need to ask you some questions. I realize some of them might seem strange, but I need to cover all the bases."

DeShawn took a deep breath. "Whatever it takes, Mr. Carizales. Ask me anything you need to if it will bring Wade home."

Raoul took out a miniature tape recorder and a small notebook. "Tell me when you found out Wade was missing."

"I was at my office in Southbridge when somebody detonated a stink bomb on my front steps! We had to evacuate the building, call the police- it was a mess. That was around noon. When we got back in the building around three PM, there was a message on my phone to call the school. That's when Yolanda told me that Wade was missing."

Yolanda gave Raoul her side of the story. He took notes before turning back to DeShawn.

"I need you to tell me *anyone* you may have angered in the past year, even if it seems insignificant to you."

DeShawn listed two clients who were dissatisfied with her services, a man whose romantic advances she'd rejected repeatedly and her former receptionist, whom DeShawn had to fire for laziness. Their parting wasn't peaceful.

Raoul looked up from his notebook. "Is the former receptionist the only employee you've ever fired?"

"No. I fired my idiot custodians not long ago for smoking weed on the job."

Raoul suppressed a smile. "Names?"

"Roger Jackson and Tim Simmons. They go by their nicknames, Barkley and Gator. Both of them live here in Southbridge."

Raoul finished writing and asked his toughest question.

"What about Wade's father?"

After Dee left, Donna and Sister Nathan exchanged glances.

"Child, I wish I'd known this sooner. Travis and I been trying to hook that man up ever since he came to Calvary!"

Donna laughed. "Max told me that Ted's a charter member of the I Need A Wife club. He's looking hard, and she's working side by side with him every Sunday."

Sister Nathan frowned. "I see the problem. Ted's not thinking about Dee because he's into your friend."

Donna was incredulous. "He likes Yolanda?"

"You haven't noticed? Every time she comes around, his face lights up like a Christmas tree."

Donna looked thoughtful. "That explains why Dee doesn't like Yolanda. If Ted's drooling over Yolanda, why wouldn't Dee be jealous?"

Sister Nathan regarded Donna curiously. "I haven't seen Yolanda much lately. Is she okay?"

"As far as I know. I haven't heard much from her since she started seeing this new guy."

Sister Nathan looked thoughtful. "Are you and Yolanda all right?"

"If you want an answer, I hope you have a spare hour."

"Wade's father and I had a disagreement last weekend. No, it was past disagreeing- we fought!"

The three of them chuckled.

"Bert asked me to dinner so we could talk about Wade. Our custody agreement is clearly spelled out, but Bert always finds excuses to bring my son back late when it's his weekend."

Raoul took notes on a small notepad. A micro-recorder whirred away on the seat beside him.

"This time, Bert asked me to let Wade live with him for an undetermined length of time so that Bert could 'teach him to be a man.' Like he'd know."

Yolanda winced at DeShawn's rage concerning her ex.

I hope I never fall out of love as hard as she did.

"Bert's moving to Atlanta with his job next month, and he wants to take Wade with him. I told him no, and that pissed Bert off."

Raoul's eyebrows raised. "Really?"

"He told me he'd take me to court to get Wade, and he demanded I repay all the money I owe him."

Raoul perked up even more at this statement. "How much?"

"$17,000. He gave me $20,000 to help me start my business while we were married, and when we divorced, part of the settlement agreement was that I repay him. We hashed out a schedule and I have yet to miss a payment. But, since I refused to let him take my son, he demanded that I repay the whole thing by the time he moves to Atlanta. If I had it, I would have paid him long ago to get him off my back!"

Yolanda could see the gears turning in Raoul's head, and wondered if he thought the same thing she did.

Of course he is. He does this for a living. If I'm suspicious that Bert knows more about this then he's telling, I know Raoul is a step ahead of me.

Raoul closed his notebook and turned off his recorder.

"Ms. Winslow, thank you for your cooperation. You've been more than helpful."

Raoul rose and headed for the door. DeShawn had a cold fire in her eyes that could make Satan nervous.

"Please find my son. If you learn something, call me, no matter how late or how early. And if there's anything else you need from me, just ask."

Raoul was impressed by the quiet strength this small woman exuded, as well as by her figure.

If I weren't so into Yolanda- - -.

"Don't worry. I haven't lost a child yet, and I don't intend to start now. I'll find him and whoever took him. You have my word on that."

It was after one a.m. when Sister Nathan dropped Donna off at her apartment after their talk about her strained relationship with Yolanda. She smiled to find Max sitting up in bed reading, clearly waiting for her.

"How did it go?"

Donna sighed heavily as she undressed. "It had the potential to be ugly. I'm glad Sister Nathan was there; she's really good at listening without getting all upset. I'll tell you all about it in a minute, but I need to brush my teeth and all. How'd the intervention go?"

Max filled Donna in as she got ready for bed. He finished his story as she came out of the bathroom and crawled into bed next to him.

"Okay, your turn. What kept you so long?"

Donna told Max about Ted Stansbury's unintentional ignoring of Dee Winston.

"We cheered her up, but it'll take counseling for Dee to get past her inferiority complex. It would help if Ted would open his eyes and see what's right in front of him."

Max chuckled. "I think they'd be a great couple. They're good friends, and they have a lot in common."

Donna laughed. "In the absence of any prophetic dreams, that's a good place to start."

The clock showed 1:45 AM when they prayed together and went to sleep. Max drifted off, dreading having to get up for work far too soon and feeling thankful that Donna didn't have a new temp assignment yet and could sleep in.

"Fred, we need you to take on the Winslow kidnapping story."

Fred's mouth fell open. *Talk about your early morning surprises, he thought.*

"Take it on? You mean like completely?"

Max sat behind his desk, as cool as a penguin sleeping on an ice floe.

"Completely. You're to make sure this story is fully and accurately covered, which means you'll assign reporters to the various aspects of this coverage, from the main piece to the sidebars. And you report directly to me."

"Wow. All I can say is, I appreciate this opportunity and I won't let you down."

Max finally smiled. "You never have before, and I'm sure you won't start now."

Fred left Max's office in a daze. *If anyone but Max assigned this to me, I'd swear he was being a smart aleck.*

He contemplated his new assignment, knowing that his success or failure would help the brass decide who to promote to assistant editor.

I'm glad they're considering me. The pay raise would be great, and I'd finally get to show them what I can do aside from just writing the stories. But this- - -.

A burst of comprehension hit Fred like a punch in the face.

They asked Max to assign it not just to test me, but to test him too. Everybody knows we're tight, and they needed to see if Max feels comfortable ordering me around. And, they also needed to see if I feel comfortable with him doing it.

Fred sighed, dreading his first step in the process without fully understanding why.

Bert Winslow stretched as he got out of his car.

Talk about a long day- - -. You'd think they'd ease up a little since they know I'm getting ready to move.

He retrieved his mail, he balanced it and his briefcase while he withdrew his house keys, totally unaware that he was under surveillance.

Okay loser, Raoul thought, *you're mine. Sooner or later you'll lead me to where you're holding your son.*

He settled in to wait. His black Suzuki Grand Vitara was parked half a block away from Bert's house, obscured in shadows. A hi-tech binoculars/camera combination sat beside him on the seat, and his gun was within easy reach.

This guy's smart enough not to keep the kid here. Sooner or later he'll lead me to him.

As if on cue, the door opened and Bert came back out. Whistling a tune, he got back into his car and drove off. Raoul waited a few seconds and pulled out, keeping a car in between them.

Three minutes later, Bert pulled into the parking lot of a Damon's restaurant and disappeared inside. He came back out five minutes later, carrying a takeout box.

Not a bad idea, Raoul thought. *Hurry up and blow your cover so **I** can get something to eat!*

Bert retraced his path, leading Raoul back to his house. Raoul frowned as he resumed his previous parking spot, deciding to keep surveillance awhile longer.

━━

Barkley pushed Wade down the last two stairs into the basement, causing him to stumble. He looked back and glared at his captor, who glared back, unblinking.

"Okay kid, here's where you're staying until your mom starts paying."

Wade rolled his eyes. "Can't you ever just say something without either trying some lame rhyme or using some movie line? Dag!"

Barkley pushed Wade towards the couch. "Don't push your luck, Beat Box. The plan is to give your fat butt back to your momma alive. Don't make me flip the script."

He tossed a TV remote control onto the couch next to Wade. "There's a bathroom over there. We got cable and Gator's old Nintendo hooked up down here, and since we need you alive, we'll bring you food-when we feel like it. Everything's sealed up, so don't waste your time trying to break out. Alcatraz'd be easier to get out of then this basement."

Laughing at his own lame joke, he turned and left, slamming and locking the door behind him. When he heard the lock click, Wade got up to check the door Barkley just left through, the back door, the window and even the bathroom window. All were sealed tight as a crypt.

My daddy wasn't no good, Barkley thought as he climbed the stairs, *but he left me a decent crib. Guess I should thank his trifling butt.*

"See Gator? Told ya this'd work out. Don't nobody know we did it or where we at."

Gator nodded approvingly. "A'ight, I'll give you that. I still don't know where you stole that fog machine from, but that was tight! And that stink bomb going off at the same time you grabbed him at the school was decent too."

Barkley touched fists with Gator. "Good job. It'll take a month to clean that up. Glad we ain't still working there!"

The two men laughed and planned how they'd spend the ransom.

16

Fred rubbed his eyes and tried again to focus on his task. Determined to get off to a good start, he came to work an hour early to work on his new assignment.

I think I've got the right reporters to handle the sidebars, and Ray should do well on the main piece. Now comes the hard part.

Fred looked at the business card as if it were a wasp that would sting him if he looked away.

He's a major part of this story, Fred thought, *and someone has to talk to him to pull it all together. Unfortunately, I'm best qualified.*

Fred said a quick prayer, dialed the number and as expected, got voice mail.

"You have reached Raoul Carizales, Child Recovery Specialist. I'm not available at this time, but leave a message and I'll get back to you as soon as I can. If this is an emergency, please page me at 212-658-9997."

Fred left a message and hung up, praying for a reasonably fast call back. He wrote down the pager number for future use, but for now, he felt that this didn't constitute an emergency.

God has a sense of humor. That's the only explanation for this.

—

Raoul checked his messages, and laughed. *Looks like Yolanda's buddy finally got around to calling for an interview,* he thought. *Bet it killed him to make the call, all things considered.*

Guess I'll cut him a break and call him back- when I finish this surveillance.

—

Max fumed silently and looked at his watch for the seventy-fifth time in the past few minutes.

Guess we can kiss being on time goodbye. I hate CP time, but it looks like we'll have no choice.

Max heard singing from the shower and almost laughed. *"Your Grace And Mercy" is a good song, but under the circumstances, "Soon And Very Soon" would be better.*

Max discarded the idea of calling out to Donna again, knowing from experience that it would only prolong her shower. He picked up his Bible and paged through the gospels, resisting with all his strength the urge to hurry Donna along.

I need to just commit to being late for the rest of my life. Not to mention never getting a hot shower again.

A passage of Scripture caught Max's eye, and he smiled.

Why not, he thought. *Nothing else works.*

Max stepped to the bathroom door and cleared his throat. "Lazarus! Come out!"

The shower shut off just as Max spoke in his best project-to-the-back-row-without-a-microphone-in-church voice. Water ran in the sink, teeth were hastily brushed and within three minutes, the bathroom door finally opened and Donna emerged, wearing a towel and the meanest scowl this side of Adolph Hitler.

Max tried to look innocent. "We need to leave in the next fifteen minutes if we're going to be only fashionably late."

Donna maintained her glare while fighting the inexplicable urge to laugh and disappeared into their bedroom. Max stepped into the steamy bathroom to shower and brush his own teeth.

That was a 9.5 on the "Annoy Your Wife" scale. I'll have to remember that one.

He smiled again at the faint sounds of laughter coming from behind the closed bedroom door.

Max and Donna arrived at the church just as Mrs. Nathan did; they greeted her and went to the pastor's office together.

Pastor Nathan was finishing a call; when he saw them in the doorway, he motioned to them that he would only be another minute. They sat in the small row of chairs outside his office.

Lord, help us learn what we need to learn, Max prayed silently. *Marriage is a blessing God, but it sure is hard work!*

Beside him, Donna squeezed his hand.

I'm glad Pastor has mandatory monthly post-marital counseling for the first year, but I think both of us would have asked for this if he didn't.

"Okay y'all, come on in."

Mrs. Nathan entered first, followed by the Carsons, who looked like they'd rather walk through a pack of wolves wearing steak sneakers then admit how badly they needed this counseling. Pastor Nathan came around his desk, and he and his wife put chairs in a circle. They say, the pastor prayed and he sat back and smiled at the Carsons.

"Let me guess. Marriage isn't what you thought it would be."

They sheepishly nodded their heads yes, as Mrs. Nathan snickered.

"Know how I knew what you were thinking? Because when Annie and I got married, the first month kicked our butts!"

Julianna Ann-Marie Nathan raised her hand as if in worship, causing all four of them to laugh. Pastor Nathan recovered first.

"You aren't the first couple to think that, and unfortunately you won't be the last. Most of the couples I marry are so happy they found somebody that they haven't thought much about what it means to spend the rest of their lives together."

Max and Donna looked at each other and laughed.

"Pastor, that's true! We spent so much time deciphering prophetic dreams and foiling murder plots that we didn't take enough time to get to know each other before we got married!

Donna chimed in. "We spent hours together every day, and we talked about all kinds of stuff. I honestly thought we were okay!"

Pastor Nathan looked thoughtful. "But obviously you're not, or you wouldn't be so happy to come for counseling."

Max smiled sheepishly. "Yeah."

Mrs. Nathan chimed in, choosing to use her Jamaican accent this time. "Oh, so you t'ought de only part of intimacee ya still needed to learn was in de bedroom!"

There was silence for a second, and all four of them roared with laughter yet again. It took them another few minutes to get themselves together.

Pastor Nathan smiled. "A lot of newlywed couples make that mistake. There's a lot more to intimacy then just the physical. Intimacy means closeness beyond anything you've ever experienced, and you can't get that overnight."

He glanced at his wife, who also smiled and nodded yes to his unspoken question.

"We're going to do one of my favorite activities, Truth Or Consequences. You're going tell each other the truth in love or else face the consequences; namely, spending the rest of your lives feeling like you do now.

Max and Donna chuckled as Mrs. Nathan took over the conversation.

"Donna, I'm going to ask you to share with Max one thing he does that really bugs you and why. Max, when she's through, you speak on the topic. We'll see how many small things we find that could become huge issues if you don't discuss them."

Max and Donna nodded, and settled back into their seats.

"Okay sista, look your man in the eye and tell him something."

Donna smiled. "Herman."

Max looked blank. "Who's Herman?"

"The garbage. We've agreed it's your job to take it out, but it stays in the house so long I've named it."

They cracked up and Max sheepishly agreed not to let Herman get comfortable. Pastor Nathan made eye contact with his wife and nodded that he would moderate for Max.

"Your turn, Brother Max."

Donna cringed. *I know what he'll say first.*

Max looked Donna in her eyes as she had him. She struggled not to giggle at his answer.

"Lazarus."

I knew it!

The pastor and his wife exchanged bemused looks before the pastor continued to moderate.

"Donna had Herman, so I guess you can have Lazarus. Want to explain that one?"

"It's why we were late getting here. Donna, I love you, but I wish you'd take less time in the shower than Lazarus spent in his grave."

Despite their valiant efforts to be professional, the Nathans burst out laughing, and the Carsons joined them.

Fred threw open the door to his apartment; alone or not, home was inviting after a Friday like this.

Raoul's ducked me all week and I have a deadline. It's all a big mind game with him. Bad enough he got Yolanda and I didn't, but now he's rubbing it in by jerking me around in any way he can. Punk.

Fred removed his suit jacket, loosened his tie and slumped onto the couch, luxuriating in the comfort of the plush pillows. He thought back three weeks, remembering the last intimate time he spent with Yolanda before Raoul.

She wanted to bring furniture from her parents' house, and I was the one she asked for help.

They took her white Geo Prizm because his Saab was unsuitable for transporting large objects. Yolanda abused him most of the way to Baltimore for having an impractical car and for driving like a drugged senior citizen. Fred reminded her that he was mean enough to put her out of her own car and make her walk the rest of the way to Baltimore. They spent most of the trip laughing.

Yolanda finished vacuuming her living room and sat down, wondering where Raoul was.

Probably working on some lead connected to the kidnapping I hope he finds Wade soon; DeShawn is frantic.

She sat down to channel surf.

Guess I can't get mad at him for breaking a date while he's on a case. It is more important for him to find Wade then for me to have a dinner date.

Her channel search brought her to Telemundo, and she paused when she heard a lilting Spanish melody.

Sounds like Dad on his guitar.

Yolanda smiled as she recalled her father's latest masterpiece. When she and Fred retrieved her bureau and chairs from Baltimore, she had a long conversation with her mother.

I wondered where Fred got to while Mami and I talked. I should have known Dad had him. He's always writing songs; he's got more unfinished cuts than the guy from In Living Color.

Yolanda was amused when she found her father playing a Spanish melody while Fred made up lyrics.

Raoul returned to his apartment, frustrated. He'd spent the entire week shadowing Bert Winslow to no avail. Today he learned that Bert initiated court proceedings to win full custody of his son the day Wade was kidnapped.

If he took Wade, he wouldn't have gone the legal route.

Raoul crossed Bert Winslow off the list and called DeShawn with her daily progress report. After filling her in, he hung up and looked at the next suspects on his list: Barkley and Gator.

They're not professionals, which means they won't have gone too far from Southbridge. With any kind of luck, I can wrap this up and give Ms. Winslow her son back by Monday.

Fred sighed, remembering the Spanish words that he put to Mr. Mason's music. The translation reflected his feelings for Yolanda.

Closer than a sister, better than a friend;
Nothing could be better than life with you
What we have is special, only God can give
Wonderful companionship that makes me
warm inside.
My love, my friend. Love so special with you.
My love, my special friend; Perfect love so
true, with you.

Fat chance of that happening now, he thought. *She chose Raoul, and from what I saw, she thinks he's got it going on.*

A flash of light caught his eye, and he checked his answering machine for messages.

"Fred, this is Lorraine Lucas. Just wanted to confirm a date with you when we can take care of Merry's house. Give me a call."

17

Raoul sighed as he reviewed what he'd learned so far about Wade's kidnapping.

Time to check the Moron Twins. They're ghetto rats, which means they won't be far from home. It shouldn't be tough to toss Southbridge until I find them.

An idea formed, and Raoul smiled as the pieces came together. He searched his wallet for a certain business card.

DeShawn looked at the ringing phone like it was a scorpion. Yolanda, who had come over to visit right after church, looked over at her.

"Do you want me to answer it?"

DeShawn shook her head no, summoned all her courage and picked up the receiver. "Hello?"

The voice on the other end was an unnatural soprano, indicating that the speaker either had no talent for disguising his voice or had been castrated within the last five minutes.

"Did you lose somebody?"

"What?"

Deshawn activated the record and speakerphone functions so that someone else could verify this bizarre conversation. The voice (which sounded a lot like Eddie Holman singing "Hey There, Lonely Girl") repeated the question, but was interrupted. There was a scuffle for the phone, and "Eddie Holman" was replaced by a grizzly bear with asthma.

"We got Wade with us. You want him back, it'll cost twenty thousand bucks. We'll call again to tell you when and where, but you best have the money when we call."

CLICK

DeShawn sat speechless, still holding the receiver as a dial tone blared from the speaker. Yolanda gently took the phone from DeShawn and hung up.

"My God."

DeShawn looked to be on the verge of tears, and Yolanda felt like joining her at the thought of Wade being held hostage.

"Those were the worst fake voices I've ever heard."

Yolanda's eyes widened, and before she realized it, she was laughing. She tried to stop, but inexplicably, DeShawn joined her.

Barkley slapped Gator upside the head so hard that Gator's teeth rattled.

"Didn't I tell your dumb behind to let me make the call? You sounded like a little girl!"

Gator glared at his friend. "Better then sounding like Barry White with a cold."

Barkley gave Gator his best glacier-melting stare. Gator was less than intimidated.

"Anyway. Now she know how much it's gonna cost to get her fat son back. We call her tomorrow and tell her how she gonna give us the money."

Gator looked confused. "How is she gonna give us the money?"

"I got that. You just make sure Little Bighead don't get out somehow."

The phone rang suddenly, and Fred almost jumped. He caught it on the third ring, noting that his Caller ID read Wireless Caller and a number he didn't recognize.

"Hello?"

"Fred? Raoul Carizales, returning your call."

Fred masked his annoyance behind a practiced friendly demeanor. "Good to hear from you! I've been trying to catch up so we can arrange that interview."

"I'm working this Winslow case now, and that requires almost all of my time."

Fred forced himself to breathe in and out. *I'm not gonna let him duck me.*

"Any open time in your schedule in the next few days? I'm flexible; let me know when you're free."

Raoul smiled. "How about coming with me tomorrow while I check some leads? You can get an up-close look at what I do; might make for a more interesting story than just me talking."

Fred perked up. *There has to be a catch, but I can't pass this up.*

"Works for me. What time?"

"Eight a.m. I'll pick you up at your job."

Raoul hung up without further conversation. Fred chuckled to himself. *This will be interesting. Oh well, at least I finally get the interview.*

He put the letter aside and went to cook dinner.

Yolanda graded a ton of spelling tests. She focused on the quality of her students' work and not on the fact that she graded for one less student this time.

Wade would've aced this test, like all the others. I don't know who has him, but God, please bring him back alive. And please help DeShawn and her ex to share their pain instead of lashing out at one another. They need each other to get through this.

Yolanda kept praying as she finished the last test.

Fred exited the City Voice building to find Raoul waiting in the parking lot. He unlocked the passenger side of the car door and indicated that Fred should get in.

"We've got something to work with. Since her ex-husband is in the clear, the most likely suspects are a pair of geniuses named Barkley and Gator, who live in Southbridge. Ms. Winslow fired them both not long ago and they're definitely the kind to hold a grudge."

"Those their real names?"

Raoul chuckled. "No, but if I ask their friends about Roger and Tim, nobody will know who I'm talking about."

Fred looked Raoul in the eye. "Ask their friends?"

"We do this the old fashioned way. We go to Southbridge and find someone who knows them."

Two and a half hours later, Raoul had what he needed.

"Barkley moved out of his mother's house two months ago. Either nobody we talked to knows where he lives, or they won't tell me."

Fred regarded him curiously. "What's the next step, Sherlock Holmes?"

Raoul smiled enigmatically. "You might have a lot of contacts, but I'm about to introduce you to the best source in the entire state."

They got back in Raoul's black Grand Vitara and rode off.

"How could you let this happen? What kind of mother are you?"

With Bert cleared as a suspect in the kidnapping, DeShawn felt compelled to call him with regular updates. Her surprise at his reaction swiftly became anger; her neck and hips engaged as she returned fire.

"I *know* you didn't just accuse me of bad parenting! *I'm* not the one who ran out on his family! *I'm* not the one who gave such a poor example of manhood that Wade needed a mentor!"

"And *I'm* not the one who spent so much time working her family had to work themselves into her schedule! I almost had to call your secretary and make an appointment to have sex!"

DeShawn slammed the phone down so hard the windows rattled.

That pitiful excuse for a father has the nerve to accuse me of being a bad parent, she thought. *He's lucky he's not standing here in front of me.*

Her eyes wandered around her office and strayed to her elephant collection, resting on a two-foot tall brass one. She entertained fantasies of either cracking Bert over the head with it or shoving it into an inconvenient body cavity as she tried to calm down.

Fred passed Al's Deli on many occasions as he walked up and down Market Street Mall, but never found occasion to go inside until now. To hear Raoul tell it, that was a huge mistake.

"I know the owner from when we lived in New York. His name is Alberto Quiñones, but everybody calls him "Big A.""

We're going to solve a kidnapping by going to a deli, Fred thought. *What's going to happen, we order a sub and the kidnappers happen to be standing in front of us in line?*

Deftly avoiding the milling lunchtime crowds, Raoul pulled his car into a parking spot in front of the Grand Opera House. "There it is."

Fred looked where Raoul was pointing and burst out laughing at the sign in the window.

"AL'S DELI: COME IN AND GET A "BIG A SAMMICH."

Raoul chuckled as well. "I've seen that sign a million times and it still makes me laugh every time. Brings in the customers though."

Inside, Al's Deli was bigger and cleaner then it looked from outside. Customers occupied most of the tables and booths, and both the lines to order and to pay were also full.

At six-foot-five, two hundred eighty pounds, Big A embodied his nickname. He and three employees were hard at work frying up cheese steaks, making sandwiches and selling cold cuts. Big A had a smile on his face that said he was in his world. A sign in the middle of the menu illustrated the "Big A Sammich," a monstrous creation composed of every kind of lunch meat known to man, two cheeses, lettuce, tomato and pickle on a steak roll. Just looking at the picture made Fred's cholesterol level skyrocket.

Big A looked up from the grill and smiled. "Hey, Carizales! Punks keeping you busy?"

Raoul smiled back. "They act up, I bring them in. This is Fred Bennett, a reporter who's trying to keep up with me."

Fred rolled his eyes. Big A's hands were a blur as he put a chicken cheese steak on the grill and added onions. He then took a finished cheese steak off the grill and wrapped it for a customer.

"What you need today?"

"Information. I'm after the kid who got snatched off the playground at Brookshire."

Big A's smile faded. "Yeah, I heard about that. Let me get this line down and then we can talk."

I definitely wouldn't have picked this place out of a hat as an information source, Fred thought. *Shows what I know.*

Just then, the door opened and a dark-skinned couple came in. The man came in smiling and staggering, but one look at Raoul changed his expression. He pushed Fred aside and stormed over to confront the man he'd been looking for all month.

Raoul detected nose-hair-burning breath at an intensely personal range. He turned around to find himself nose to nose with Budweiser's best customer. Raoul was surprised to see Coral with him; her smile indicated that her memories of their liaison were as pleasant as his.

Now I have a jealous boyfriend to deal with, Raoul thought. *From the looks of things, I'm not surprised she cheated on him. Oh well, I can use the workout.*

"You need to leave my woman alone."

"You need to invest in some Tic-Tacs."

The other patrons laughed, sensing an impending confrontation. Fred wondered if he should help if the drunk took a swing at Raoul.

He's supposed to be a hotshot P.I., Fred thought smugly. *That tells me he knows how to fight. I'll stay out his way.*

Raoul maintained his poker face. "Either tell me whatever you know about that boy getting snatched at Brookshire a few days ago or take that iguana breath somewhere else."

Raoul was impressed; in one profane breath, the drunk questioned Raoul's parentage and called him out of his gender and species.

"Impressive vocabulary. I get the feeling that either you're going to tell me something useful or I'm going to mop the floor with you."

"You feeling wrong, Taco Bell. You better step before I make you feel something you don't want to feel."

Raoul smiled. "Sorry, not on the first date."

The onlookers laughed, provoking a murderous rage in the stocky drunk. Moving faster than his staggering gait indicated was possible, Beer Breath whipped out a switchblade and lunged at Raoul, catching him by surprise. He cut a small piece off Raoul's sleeve, but didn't draw blood.

Behind the counter, Big A reached down to where Raoul knew he kept a Colt .45 semiautomatic pistol. Raoul waved him off, with a jaunty "I got this," twinkle in his eye and assumed a martial arts stance.

"Put that knife down before somebody gets hurt, namely you."

The man cursed Raoul's family line to about seven generations and lunged again, blade extended. This time, Raoul sidestepped, letting him run headfirst into a table. The drunk roared with pain as someone's Coke doused him. He jumped up and started to attack with the blade again until he realized he didn't have it.

"Lose something?"

Raoul smiled as he held up the knife he'd taken when the man lunged past, and the onlookers cracked up. Thoroughly humiliated, Beer Breath lunged again, hands extended to choke the smart-behind Hispanic who made him look like an idiot.

"Bad move."

Fred agreed with Big A. Not wanting to extend the humiliation any further, Raoul threw a left-right punch combination so fast it looked like he only hit the man once. As Beer Breath staggered, Raoul karate-kicked him in the chest. He flew across the room, barely missing two teenage girls sitting at a table as he bounced off the wall and fell on his face.

"Okay folks, show's over."

The onlookers applauded, and Big A laughed so hard he had trouble talking to the police.

Raoul walked over to the barely conscious man and, using his foot, he nudged Beer Breath into the puddle of spilled soda and rolled him back and forth.

Fred looked on, amused. "What are you doing?"

Raoul smiled. "I told him I'd mop the floor with him. I always keep my word."

Just then the police came in. Still laughing, Big A pointed them towards Raoul.

"What's going on here?"

Raoul nodded towards the prone form of the drunk. "I'd like to press charges against him."

The officer looked around the room. Raoul's opponent was soaking wet and nearly unconscious.

"*You* want to press charges against *him*? Why?"

"He attacked me."

The cop looked at Raoul incredulously. "*He* attacked *you*?"

Raoul smiled. "He's not very good at it."

The entire crowd cracked up at Raoul's statement, and even the two officers chuckled. Fred, Big A and other onlookers corroborated Raoul's story. Coral caught Raoul's eye, mouthed "Call me" and with a suggestive wink, slipped out the door.

After the police left, Raoul took Big A aside to talk. Fred people-watched some more, and focused on an attractive Hispanic woman. He tried not to stare, but except for the fact that this woman's hair was shorter, he would have sworn she was Yolanda's twin.

After Raoul finished his conversation with Big A, Yolanda's twin accosted him, and they held an intense near-whispered conversation in

Spanish. Fred's eyes widened as he mentally translated bits and pieces.

"- - -later tonight?"

The woman's eyes flared. "*Now* you want to talk. Where were you when I needed you?"

"You don't under- -."

Her eyes flashed with anger.

"*Never* speak to me again, you worthless son of a - -."

Raoul tried to plead his case a bit longer and gave up. The woman continued to assassinate his character as he retreated. Raoul returned to Fred's side as if nothing had happened.

"Let's roll. I got us something to work with."

As they left, Fred noticed the Hispanic woman staring after them, and her focus was on Raoul. Fred looked from her to him, and thought he saw a flash of understanding in her eyes.

He doesn't know I speak Spanish, Fred thought. *He doesn't know he's cold busted, and not just by his other woman there.*

"Big A told me that Barkley works out at this gym we're going to. They'll have his address."

Fred shrugged off his new knowledge for later thought.

"So what makes you think that this gym is just gonna give you the man's address?"

"I know the receptionist." Raoul smiled. "She used to give me a lot more than information."

Fred rolled his eyes. "And of course the memory of your dazzling performance is enough to make her swoon and hand you the address on her way to the floor."

Raoul laughed. "Watch and learn, young Jedi. Watch and learn."

Fred and Raoul reached the gym in ten minutes. As he'd forced himself to do all day, Fred hung back and let Raoul take charge.

Let's see if you can pull this off. It might be a game to you, but Wade's life is in danger.

The receptionist, who bore a strong resemblance to tennis star Serena Williams, had her head buried in a magazine as they entered. It took all of Fred's willpower not to laugh as he saw her nametag with LAPOOKIE in bold letters.

This "La" naming trend has officially gone too far.

Raoul casually approached the front desk, putting on his best lady-killer smile.

"Perdoneme senorita, can I have a moment of your time?"

She looked up from Essence, expecting to have to put some Hispanic wannabe player in his place. Her eyes lit up in recognition.

"Raoul!"

She came around the desk and gave Raoul a hug. Fred smiled, admitting that Raoul hadn't underestimated his ability to charm her.

"Long time no see, Pook. How've you been?"

They caught up on their lives since they stopped dating a year ago, and then Raoul got down to business.

"I wish I wasn't on a case. If I wasn't, we could maybe go get something to eat."

LaPookie smiled, and Fred suppressed another chuckle.

You'd be on the menu if you hung out with him. I might have been a player, but this guy's a pro.

Raoul got more serious. "But, I am on a case, and I could use your help."

He showed her a picture of Barkley and Gator. "We're looking for these two. I hear one or both of them works out here."

LaPookie suddenly looked like she'd rather be anywhere but where she was. She composed herself and pointed at Barkley.

"This guy's a member. He brought the other guy in as his guest once or twice."

"We have reason to believe that one or both of them may be involved in that school kidnapping."

LaPookie's eyes widened. "Really?"

"He's moved from his last known address. If this guy's a member, you have his current address on file.

LaPookie took a deep breath and snapped back into professional mode. "I'm sorry Raoul, but I'm not allowed to give out our members' personal information unless you're a cop with a search warrant.

Raoul didn't blink. "I understand that. Mind if we ask around? Somebody might know where he stays."

LaPookie shrugged. "Go ahead."

They sauntered around the gym, and quickly learned that there was a bad case of selective amnesia going around. Despite the fact that Barkley worked out there four times a week, nobody knew who he was, where he lived or who his friends were besides Gator.

Fred looked at Raoul as they completed their last circuit of the gym. "What now, Columbo?"

Raoul smiled as they neared the locker rooms. "We improvise. And by the way, I'm sorry."

"For what?"

"This."

Raoul stuck his foot between Fred's legs, and when Fred stumbled, Raoul pushed with his right arm and sent Fred flying into the women's locker room. As screams arose, Raoul moved towards the exit. LaPookie went to investigate, leaving her files unattended. Raoul found and copied Barkley's contact information, and, his task completed, returned the way he came.

Fred emerged from the locker room amid shouts and hurled objects. Raoul barely kept from laughing as angry and hastily covered-up women looked out to ensure Fred wasn't coming back in.

"Relax ladies, his foot slipped. It could happen to anyone."

They glared after Fred as he and Raoul left. Fred's face was bright red, but he didn't say a word as they got back in Raoul's car. He handed Fred the address as he put his key in the ignition.

"This where he lives?"

"Yup. Maybe we'll find something there that'll lead us to Wade. We could wrap this up by tomorrow."

Fred glared at him. "Good. Because when this is over, I'm gonna break your legs."

Raoul stepped on the gas and roared off down the block, his laughter ringing out loudly.

⌁

With the commotion ended, LaPookie resumed her place at the front desk.

That's strange. I know this binder wasn't open before.

She glanced down the page, and her blood went cold.

Oh no he didn't!

Glancing around, she snatched up the phone and dialed.

⌁

"Man, move your slow butt! We gotta get outta here *now*!"

Barkley frantically searched for his car keys.

"Bring Baby Huey out through the garage. I'll start the car. We got to be out before the cops come!"

Gator rushed downstairs to get Wade. Barkley decided that there was nothing incriminating lying around and raced out the door. As he jumped in his car and gunned the engine, he saw the garage door open. Wade's hands were tied, but his feet weren't. The boy dug in his heels, determined not to cooperate.

We ain't got time for this, Barkley thought.

He jumped out of the car, leaving it running, and raced over to help Gator.

"Get yo' *fat* butt in the car!"

Barkley punctuated the word 'fat" with a right cross to the jaw. Wade staggered, nearly knocked unconscious. "Stuff him in the back!"

The two of them got Wade into the car. Gator jumped in beside him, Barkley backed out of the driveway at warp speed and zoomed out of his father's neighborhood. As Barkley drove, Gator placed a call on Barkley's cell phone.

18

Raoul pulled up half a block from the address he'd lifted and quickly got out of the car. Fred got out too, and was surprised when Raoul reached into the back seat and donned a webbed vest. He quickly filled the pouches with handcuffs, pepper spray and a bludgeoning baton, and slapped a fresh clip into his gun.

"I'm only gonna explain this once. This could be a dead end, but we might hit the jackpot. I'm assuming they're here, and that means I go in hard. Since you're here, I need you to back me up. You ever handle a gun?"

Fred shook his head no.

"Thought not. This wouldn't be a good time to start."

He grabbed a second baton, took a second canister of pepper spray, shook it and handed both to Fred.

"It's gonna play out just like any cop movie you ever saw. Law enforcement folks call this a dynamic entry. I'm gonna kick the front door in and I need you to watch the back. If *anyone* comes out who isn't me, you hit him or spray him, or both if you have to. Whatever you do, *don't let him escape.* Knock him down and we'll sort it out later."

Fred's heart pounded as he accepted the weapons from Raoul and listened for the rest of the plan.

"When you hear me kick the door in, anybody coming out will be on you in about ten seconds. Stand to one side in case he has a gun, and nail him when he comes out."

Fred nodded and headed for the back of the house. He looked warily for free-range pit bulls, and entered the back yard as quietly as he could.

I can't mess this up. It could mean that boy's life if I do.

He winced at the loud creak of the rusty fence, took up a position beside the back door and waited for Raoul's signal, heart pounding.

DeShawn paced from her bedroom to her bathroom and then to the living room. After unsuccessfully reading Essence for thirty seconds, she returned to pacing.

"DeShawn, sit down. You're making me nervous too."

DeShawn smiled and tried unsuccessfully to oblige Yolanda. She'd been this way ever since Raoul called to say he and Fred were investigating a new lead.

"Raoul is a professional, and he's got Fred with him. If they find Wade, they'll bring him back safe. I know they will."

DeShawn tried to smile. "I wish I had your faith. And I wish there was something more we could do than just sit here!"

Yolanda felt a sudden blast of nervousness. She knew what they could do, but to date, she'd never been alone with someone when it was called for. When things got tight, either Max or Donna always took the lead and did what for them seemed to come naturally.

You're here because you want to help DeShawn. Don't wimp out now.

Yolanda swallowed her fear, moved closer to DeShawn on the couch and took her hands.

"There is. Let's pray."

Raoul nonchalantly approached the house, focusing on the moment when instinct would take over. He approached the door, acting like this was his house and he could pull out a key and enter instead of kicking the door in. He started to knock, and then stopped, listening for signs of life. He smiled to hear voices emanating from inside. Ducking down, he peeked through the window, and through a small gap in the closed curtains, he saw two men moving around.

"Dear God, we come to You in the name of Jesus today with a lot of nervousness on our minds. We, uhm, we want to lift up Wade Winslow to you God, for his safety. Tell him that You're with him so he won't be scared. Father God, touch DeShawn. She's worried about Wade, and so am I. Protect him from any harm, and protect Raoul and Fred too. Let them find Wade and bring him home safely. In Jesus name I pray, Amen."

DeShawn was crying by the time Yolanda finished her heartfelt prayer. Yolanda reached out to her, and DeShawn fell into her friendly embrace like a sick child would with its mother. Yolanda forgot her own fears and held DeShawn while her grief over her missing son spilled out.

Fred felt a wave of calmness overtake him, even as he asked God to remove the nervousness so that he could back Raoul up.

I don't want to hurt anybody, but I'll do what it takes to help Wade. Stay with me, Jesus.

Instead of kicking in the door, Raoul knocked, standing to the side so that no one could see him through the peephole.

"Who is it?"

The voice inside sounded suspicious. Raoul remained out of sight. Just then, the door opened a crack, and Raoul leaned out just enough to be seen. Someone cursed.

"It's a cop!"

The person tried to shut it, but slammed it on his own foot and caused the door to swing wide open. Raoul stepped into the doorway and brought his gun up to where he could use it.

"Freeze! Bond enforcement officer! Nobody moves, nobody gets shot! Get on the floor! Now!"

One of the two men in the room dropped on his stomach and laced his hands behind his head. The second man bolted for the back door. Raoul fired, barely missing. He took a moment to remind the man on the floor just how many bullets his gun held and then gave chase.

Outside, Fred heard Raoul's entrance and his opening remarks, followed by a shot and footsteps running his way.

Help me God, he thought. *I can't let this man get away.*

Fred took a step back. As the back door burst open, Fred swung the baton low, tripping the man down the two steps and flat on his face. As the man spat out dirt, Fred put a knee in his back and placed the pepper spray near his face.

"This stuff's nasty. Don't make me use it."

The man surrendered without a struggle just as Raoul ran out, gun drawn.

"I got him."

Raoul smiled. "So I see. Think you can keep him there a minute? I need to get his partner."

Fred nodded and Raoul raced back through the house. He smiled even wider to see the first man lying exactly where he was when Raoul left him.

This is too easy, he thought as he reached for his handcuffs. Just then, two women appeared at the front door. Their hairdos were high, their jeans were tight, their earrings were large and their expressions, confused. The sight of one of their dates lying handcuffed on the floor made them back out of the doorway and run.

Raoul laughed. *Clearly I interrupted something.*

Raoul dragged the first man over, threw him next to the second and went through their wallets. Raoul was disappointed at missing his targets, but glad to learn who he had instead.

"You're not who I came here for, but you make a good consolation prize."

He threw the first man's wallet on top of him.

"You're James Freeman, also known as "Funky." To the best of my knowledge, you haven't done anything wrong."

Raoul stuffed the second man's wallet back into the man's pocket.

"You're Kenny Simpson, also known as "Stinky" and you're in violation of your bond agreement with Tyros Vouras."

Fred fought the urge to hold his breath, as both men lived up to their nicknames.

"I don't know how we missed bringing you in, but I've got you now. Funky, you're free to go, but Stinky, you're coming with me."

Yolanda sank onto her couch with a sigh. She'd just hung up with DeShawn, promising she would call as soon as she heard from Raoul.

They chased that lead all day. They must know something by now.

Yolanda reached for the phone to call Raoul, and as if on cue, her door buzzer sounded.

"Yes?"

Abrela puerta (open the door). It's me."

Yolanda released the door, and before she knew it, Raoul was in her arms. The look on her face told her all she needed to know.

"We missed those jokers by maybe ten minutes. We got their friends, who had asked to use the house to entertain their dates."

Yolanda closed her eyes, fighting back tears.

"Can you track those guys somehow?"

Raoul didn't have a clue as to how he'd find Barkley and Gator now, but he didn't want Yolanda to know that.

"There's always a way. They left evidence at the house; my contacts with the police will let me know what they find."

"What about Fred? He's good at investigative stuff; maybe he can track down a lead or two."

Raoul rolled his eyes. "At this point, I'll take any leads I can get."

Raoul sat back on Yolanda's couch, massaging his forehead. Yolanda leaned in and took over.

"Que pasa, amante? You're so tense you're about to explode."

Raoul took a deep breath. "I thought I'd have this solved by now. I don't want this to get ugly like the Messenger case."

Yolanda kept massaging. "What happened in the Messenger case?"

Raoul opened his eyes and looked directly at Yolanda.

"I killed a man."

"I hate him like a fat man hates salad. If I had to choose between hanging with him and taking a hard kick in the groin, I'd consider the kick."

Max laughed. Fred was at the office late catching up on work, and, needing a break to clear his head, called Max at home for advice.

"He can't be that bad."

"Oh really?"

Fred recounted his experience at the gym. To his credit, Max tried to suppress his mirth, but gave in and let loose howls of laughter.

"I might think it's funny later, but right now I'm *not* amused."

Max tried to stop laughing. "I'm sorry, but I can see you running outta there with women *throwing toilet paper* at you! That's hysterical!"

"I'm laughing my butt off."

"Ok, so he *is* that bad. Hey, maybe hanging with you will help him spiritually."

Fred scowled. "Only if I beat the devil out of him."

"Fred!"

"I'm serious. Everything would be all right with the world if I could put my foot in his butt."

Max tried to stop laughing, but failed. "Fred, Raoul would whip you like a rented slave, and then he'd *really* laugh at you. Face it, he's multitalented."

"Yeah, he's a jackass of all trades."

Max laughed harder. "I hate to agree, but- - -."

Fred scowled more deeply. "So basically I got to put up with him until we bring the kid back. And *then* I get to beat him down."

Max took a deep breath and finally stopped laughing.

"Then you need to pull up. All you have to do is be yourself and let him do the same. Raoul will do whatever it takes to get what he wants, and Yolanda won't have a man like that in her life."

Fred scowled. "I know, but I still can't *stand* the guy!"

"Hold on a second."

Max grabbed Donna's Bible off the nightstand and flipped through it, looking for a scripture they'd discussed just that morning.

"Here you go Fred. Romans 12:19-20.

"*Dearly beloved, avenge not yourselves, but rather give place unto wrath: for it is written Vengeance is mine; I will repay, saith the Lord. Therefore if thine enemy hunger, feed him; if he thirst, give him drink: for in so doing thou shalt heap coals of fire on his head.*""

Fred thought for a moment. "How about I skip dinner and just throw him in the furnace?"

Max cracked up. "You know you wrong!"

⚊⚊

Yolanda's head snapped up in surprise. "What?"

Raoul hung his head, as if suppressing tears. He stood and paced, unable to sit down and still contain the emotions he felt so strongly.

"I was tracking a child molester. I found him in the house he'd rented, with a boy he'd taken. When I kicked in the door, he was about to- - -."

Raoul let his voice trail off.

"The guy knew I had him cold but I guess he was more afraid of jail than me. We traded punches, but when I started winning, he grabbed a hunting knife, and swore he was gonna cut me from my appendix to my appetite."

Yolanda knew where the story was going, and a chill settled over her heart.

"He wouldn't drop it, Yolanda. I warned him to put it down, and when he kept coming - - -."

Raoul blinked back tears. Yolanda put an arm around his shoulder. He leaned into her like a small child.

"I shot him three times at point-blank range. Yolanda. He was dead before he fell."

"You had no choice. He tried to kill you, and he would've hurt the boy. God understands."

"I have to find Wade before anything happens to him. I don't want to go through that again."

Yolanda held Raoul close, wanting to take his pain away. Raoul clung to her like a baby craving a feeding, wanting only to forget the day's failure and to start fresh tomorrow.

"You sure nobody knows about this place, Gator?"

"I didn't even know about it until last month. I got a letter from my aunt's lawyer telling me she left me some property. She was gonna sell bath and body stuff. Thing is, she died before she could even start the business, so all I got is this big-A empty warehouse."

Barkley laughed. "Man, between us, we inheriting like a mug!"

They touched fists lightly, and Wade took the opportunity to try to run. Gator clamped down firmly on his arm.

"Naw big boy, you ain't going nowhere!"

Gator held him still while Barkley looked for the best place to keep Wade. They settled on a section in the back, near the bathrooms, which, thankfully for Wade, had been completed before construction was halted. Gator tied the boy up as securely as he could while Barkley watched.

"A'ight, good job. Now, we can't let him run around loose because it's too many windows and stuff he could get out of. That means you gotta guard his fat butt."

Gator started to protest, but stopped.

I ain't saying nothing. If LaPookie ain't call to warn him, we probably woulda got caught. He must be hitting that just right!

Laughing, Gator took up his post.

"YAAAOW!"

Raoul hopped backwards, pain searing through his right foot like fire. Yolanda somehow managed to look innocent, apologetic and amused at the same time.

"Are you okay?"

Raoul cursed in Spanish and sat on the couch, massaging his foot. "I will be. What was *that* for?"

Raoul had unexpectedly initiated a passionate kiss, one that indicated he was ready to take more than just comfort from Yolanda's embrace. Yolanda felt her body taking her places her spirit knew were bad for her and did the first thing she thought of to make him stop.

"To keep us from making a big mistake."

Raoul winced. "What mistake?"

Yolanda sighed. "We talked about this before, Raoul. Having sex right now would be the worst thing we could do."

Raoul looked startled. "You don't think we'd be good together?"

Yolanda sighed again. *He really wasn't listening.*

"I'm sure we would be, physically speaking. I'm talking about spiritually and emotionally."

Here we go again, Raoul thought.

"You're not ready for this then?"

"No, I'm not. Physically I could do it, and I'm fairly sure I'd enjoy it. But, I told you before how I feel about premarital sex. Clearly you weren't listening, or else you would have stopped kissing me when I asked you to."

I messed up, Raoul thought. *I heard her mouth say no, but her body said yes.*

"I like you a lot Raoul, but I will not give my body to you or to any other man I'm not married to. That's my commitment to God and no one, not even you, is worth breaking my word to Him. If you can't respect that, we can't be together. Entiendes?" (Understand?)

Raoul sighed. "Entiendo. Ay, caramba."

Yolanda chuckled. "If it makes you feel any better, I feel the same way."

Raoul rose awkwardly from his seat, and headed for the door.

"Time to go then; staying here right now could be painful."

Yolanda chuckled again. "Pienso que vas a vivir. (I think you'll live). Llamame manana?" (Call me tomorrow?)

"Si. I'll call you tomorrow, amante."

With a disarming smile, Raoul was gone, leaving Yolanda alone with her emotions.

That was close. If I hadn't stomped his foot, I'd be naked by now and wondering how it happened!

Raoul entered his apartment, still upset.

We've been seeing each other over a month now, he thought. Why is she still holding out on me? I thought sure telling her about the Messenger case would get me in.

His eyes fell on a slip of paper, nearly concealed by the phone. Smiling, he dialed the number. Coral answered on the second ring.

"Would you care to dance again?"

19

"Wake up."

"Hyuhh!"

Fred jerked awake, startled. He reached for his bedside lamp, wondering who had broken into his apartment and why they were being cordial as opposed to killing him where he slept.

"The early bird catches the worm, and we got a kid to find."

Fred was relieved he hadn't awakened to a dangerous intruder standing over him, but he still wished he owned a gun.

"Raoul, I don't remember telling you where I live."

Raoul smiled. "Dancing" with Coral last night did wonders for his stress levels, and he was back to feeling invincible.

"You didn't."

Fred sat up and saw six A.M. on his clock.

"I assume there's a reason for this visit."

Raoul smiled again. Fred filed the image in his brain under Things That Really Work My Last Nerve.

"Here."

Fred looked up in time to see a wad of bills flying at him. He caught it by reflex.

"What's this?"

Raoul smiled. "Turns out our friend Stinky failed to appear for his court date, and part of what I do for Tyros Vouras is to bring guys like him in. He skipped on $5000.00 bond, and when I bring in an FTA, I get ten percent."

"So why are you sharing the wealth?"

"Stinky is the one you tripped when he ran out the back door. You saved me the trouble of having to chase his butt down, and you're entitled to a cut."

Fred counted out one hundred dollars, which he grudgingly put in his wallet.

"Glad I could help. And I appreciate your taking the time out of your busy schedule to give me this in person."

Raoul smiled, letting Fred's comment roll off his back.

"No problem. Buy Lenne something special. I intend to take Yolanda out for a nice dinner myself."

As if on cue, Raoul's cell phone rang. He turned away to answer it, and Fred laser visioned Raoul's back.

You just had to rub it in, he thought. Son of a - ."

He hung up his call and turned back to Fred. "If you really want to get the full story, get dressed. I'm about to investigate a new set of leads. Once I get going, I won't be so easy to get in touch with."

Fred blinked, trying to get it together.

Creep. Oh well, he could have just cut me out of this altogether.

"Give me a minute. You didn't exactly catch me at my best."

Raoul laughed as Fred went to shower.

～

Fred spent most of the day chasing around with Raoul, and filled in the gaps with cell phone calls to the office to keep the reporting team coordinated on the other aspects of the story. After Raoul let him go, he returned to the office to work, and didn't drag into his apartment until nine P.M.

Once we find Wade I'm gonna kick Raoul's butt so hard his kids will be born with footprints.

He checked his voice mail messages, and was pleased to find one from Randy Errell.

"- - -and then she had the nerve to try and call me out about seeing Lenne. Talk about the pot calling the kettle black!"

Randy laughed and shifted the phone to his other ear. "Yes, it does sound like she's not practicing what she preaches. Just out of curiosity, how bad is this Raoul really?"

Fred told Randy about the gym incident and today's antics. "Any more questions?"

Randy tried not to laugh, and failed miserably. Fred chuckled in spite of himself.

"Okay, you convinced me. He really isn't somebody your friend should date."

"Which is just what I tried to tell Yolanda, but she was too busy trying to handle *my* business to watch out for hers."

"Well Fred, I don't know Yolanda or Raoul or Lenne as well as Max might, but can I offer some advice?"

Fred chuckled to himself at Randy's laid-back demeanor, knowing that Max would have jammed advice down his throat long before now.

"Sure can; that's basically what I called for."

Randy laughed, relieved that Fred was willing to hear him out.

"I think you're right about one thing. It bothered Yolanda to see you with Lenne because she has feelings for you. I wouldn't give up on her yet."

Fred smiled. *I knew I was right!*

"And you should also consider that Yolanda may have been right to warn you about Lenne."

Fred's smile faded as quickly as it came.

He and Max are ganging up on me.

"You told me that you and Lenne were both, what's the word you used? Players."

Fred snickered quietly at Randy's extremely European pronunciation.

"You also told me that she's ready to give up being a player, but not give up sex. Am I right?"

Fred felt uncomfortable with where Randy was going. "Yeah, you're right."

"Yolanda was right to warn you then. The way she said it might have been wrong, but the sentiment behind it is right. You *should* be careful because Lenne might try to get you to do things her way instead of vice versa."

Fred was silent for a moment.

"You might be mad at Yolanda, but don't let that stop you from accepting her warning to stay away from Lenne."

"It's not that simple, Doc. Lenne's boyfriend died in a car crash not too long after Merry was killed. Players don't have many close friends, especially a female player. I have Max, and now you. As far as I know, all Lenne has is me."

Randy considered his next words carefully. "That I understand. Be her friend then. She definitely needs someone to talk to or else she'll hold it in until she explodes. Just don't let things get out of hand."

They talked a few more minutes. Randy sat quietly for nearly half an hour afterwards, replaying the conversation in his mind and hoping he gave his new friend sound advice.

It's not like I'm the expert in knowing when a woman is good for you, Randy thought. Jen- Merry- had me completely fooled; him too for that matter. After something like that, how do you know when you're not making a mistake in the future?

That question stayed with Randy the rest of the night.

Fred woke up in the middle of the night, still pondering his conversation with Randy. Doc might be onto something. Lenne does represent the height of my player days. I might have a flashback or something.

No, that's crazy. We used to use each other, but now's our chance to be real friends. I can't leave her hanging just because I'm scared.

He drifted back to sleep, still pondering the true nature of his relationship with Lenne.

When Gator left the room, Wade released the breath he'd held, and was pleased to see slack appear in the rope. A few minutes of wiggling freed Wade's arms and hands. He prayed that Gator would stay away just a few minutes longer and frantically worked at the ropes binding his feet to the chair.

"Why ain't you guarding Baby Huey?"

Gator glared at his friend. "Chill out, Bark. I hadda take a leak. Tight as you tied him, he ain't going nowhere."

Wade took off the Payless sneakers Gator had loaned him so he could move quietly. He looked around, and arbitrarily chose to go left. He prayed they wouldn't find him before he got away.

Gator resumed guard duty, annoyed. *Ain't like that fat boy gonna bust out of them ropes. He wants him watched all the time, let his big head take a turn.*

He reentered the room, and nearly passed out when he saw empty ropes.

***

Wade crept silently down a hallway, hoping the sliver of light he saw was an exit.

All I gotta do is get to that door. Stupid as them guys are, they won't even know I'm gone until the cops bust in.

He opened the door, and was rewarded by a cool breeze. Wade silently pumped his fist for joy, slipped through the door and quietly closed it behind him. He turned and looked straight into the barrel of a gun.

"Going somewhere, Beat Box?"

Wade's hope deflated. He turned around slowly, and saw Barkley standing just to the side of the door. Barkley smiled and motioned him back inside with the pistol.

20

Barkley marched Wade back into the warehouse, hands atop his head like a prisoner of war.

"Lose something, Gator?"

Gator's heart sank; he stammered out an explanation, only to be cut off by a solid smack upside his head.

"Tie his butt up again. And this time tie his hands to the arms of the chair and his feet to the legs. You can't put no ropes across his belly; fat as he is, he'll always have slack in the rope."

Wade glared at him. "That's why yo' momma so dumb she sold her car for gas money!"

Gator finished tying Wade's legs, and Barkley stepped over and pulled each knot extra tight.

"Shut up punk. I coulda been your daddy, but your pops beat me through the window."

Laughing, he gave Gator a high five and turned to leave the room, turning back towards Gator with an afterthought.

"And if Fat Albert escapes again, it's gonna be two of you tied up next time. You better keep a closer eye on him. "

Barkley stormed out of the room, not hearing Wade mutter under his breath about Barkley's big light-bulb head. Gator snickered.

The creep's cutting me out of the loop again, Fred thought. *That's all right though- I need to show up at work more than twice a week or I can kiss my promotion and my job goodbye.*

After spending half the day at the office, Fred gave Max his remaining itinerary, which included two stops designed to give him more information for his story on Raoul.

Max tried hard to keep a poker face, but he couldn't keep a tinge of pride out of his voice at Fred's hard work.

"You're doing a thorough job researching this. I'm impressed."

Fred forced a smile. "Thanks. These are two of the sources he introduced me to, and since I'm not shadowing him today, I figured I'd get back with them and clear a few things up."

An hour later, Fred closed his notebook.

"Okay "Big A," thanks for talking to me. I learned a lot today."

Big A smiled. "Don't look now, but I think you're about to learn even more."

Fred followed Big A's gaze to an attractive Hispanic woman. She was well built and very familiar.

"Hola Big A, como estas?"

Big A smiled and greeted her in Spanish. "Same old same old. Want your usual?"

She shook her head, responding in kind. "I didn't come to eat, but to see your visitor."

She faced Fred and switched to heavily accented English. Big A conveniently found pressing business in the back room.

"I see you with Raoul. I'm Alicia Torres."

Fred recognized her from the first time Raoul brought him to Big A's. "Fred Bennett."

"It is good meeting you, Fred."

She looked at him curiously before continuing. "Hablas Espanol?"

"Si, lo hablo."

"Bueno. I do better when I speak Spanish."

Alicia looked him in the eye and switched languages. "I know you heard when Raoul and I talked, and you understood us. When you see Raoul, tell him I don't know what game he's playing, but I don't want to keep playing it."

"Frankly, I feel the same way about him.

Alicia rolled her eyes and continued in rapid-fire Spanish. "He told me he was only seeing me, but I've seen him with a woman more than once. He fought someone because of her one day, here in the deli."

Fred suppressed a smile at the memory of his first visit to Big A's place.

Alicia took a deep breath. "I also saw him with a woman who looks like me. Do you know her?"

Fred took a deep breath. "She's seeing him. I told her once that she shouldn't trust Raoul. She didn't believe me, and I'm afraid he'll hurt her."

Alicia looked nervous.

"Tell her not to trust him. Raoul treats you well in the beginning, but once he has your heart, he changes. He isn't a man to fall in love with."

She hesitated. "Raoul wants me back, but after what he did, that will never happen."

Fred nodded, a question in his eyes.

"I heard you tell him that. What did he do?"

"Last month I told him I thought I was pregnant. He swore it wasn't his child."

"And that's not true."

Fred couldn't mistake the fire in Alicia's eyes. "He's the only man I've ever- -."

She let her sentence trail off.

"I later learned I wasn't pregnant, but when I tried to tell Raoul, he didn't answer his phone."

Fred cursed Raoul under his breath.

"He heard from friends that I wasn't pregnant, and *then* he wanted to talk. Do you know what he asked when he saw me here? He wanted to get back in my bed!"

Fred cursed Raoul in absentia again. "I knew he was no good."

Alicia turned to leave, but looked back at Fred.

"If your friend will listen, warn her. Raoul tells women he loves them, but he uses us all."

She turned and walked out, leaving Fred wondering.

I can't just let him play Yolanda. But, she might think I'm trying to break them up because I'm jealous. She didn't want to hear it the first time I tried to warn her. But I didn't have any evidence then.

Just then Big A returned, humming a tune.

"Amazing who you meet in a place like this, eh?"

Fred smiled. "That it is."

～

"Yolanda, I know this might be out of line, but I really care for you."

Yolanda froze. She was leaving church after a Women's Day committee meeting when Ted Stansbury came out of his usher board meeting and blindsided her.

Not Ted! He's too nice to just shoot down.

Oblivious to Yolanda's internal struggle, Ted continued.

"I know I'm not as flamboyant as some fellows, and I'm not sure what's between you and Brother Bennett. All I know is that I enjoy your company and I'd appreciate the opportunity to enjoy it further."

Yolanda smiled in spite of herself; Ted's approach was the most honest and humble she'd ever had.

"Ted, I'm honored. You're my friend, and I enjoy your company. I care for you very much as my brother in Christ, but that's all."

Ted did a masterful job of concealing his disappointment, but Yolanda knew that he was hurt by her gentle rejection.

"There is someone for you Ted, and she may be closer then you think. I just know it isn't me."

Ted excused himself and walked away. Yolanda started to do the same, but felt a searing glare from behind. As she turned, she saw Dee

Winston pick up her purse, pretending she hadn't just scalded Yolanda's spine with heat vision a moment ago.

Looks like I was right. Unless I miss my guess, Ted's wife is closer than either of us thought. Now how do we get Ted to see this?

Yolanda walked away; she entertained thoughts of matchmaking all the way home.

"It has to be something that won't make either of them suspicious."

Sister Nathan nodded her agreement with Donna, unaware that Yolanda's thoughts mirrored theirs.

"I agree. We also need to get them out of this church, so they can relax and enjoy each other's company."

Donna smiled.

"Thing is, neither of them has much of a life outside of church. How can we do that without either of them being suspicious?"

Sister Nathan opened her planner and wrote something down. "Already taken care of."

Fred tried to enjoy a quiet evening at home, but he couldn't relax. Bored with channel surfing, he walked into his bedroom, looking for a book. Since getting saved, his bookshelf became home to the likes of

Frank Peretti, Randy Alcorn and Bill Myers. Fred scanned the shelf, but none of his recent acquisitions appealed to him, not even the three Terrance Johnson novels Max bought Fred in response to his complaint of there being no black male Christian authors.

Fred's Bible somehow fell off his desk and landed at his feet, nearly tripping him.

Must be a hint, he thought. I haven't really read this lately.

He scooped up the Bible and returned to the living room. The TV stayed on as Fred turned to the book of Proverbs. He read through the first six chapters without incident, but the seventh chapter drew him in.

Just then, the TV screen caught his attention.

"The Five Heartbeats! Never saw that in the theater."

He put the Bible aside and lost himself in the movie.

It took Fred a few minutes before he realized the noise in his dream was his intercom buzzer.

"Who is it?"

"Lenne. Can I come up?"

Fred perked up, and simultaneously felt a wave of something not unlike panic.

"Sure."

He released the downstairs door.

Lord, I'm glad to have someone to talk to, but if she's here to mack, send her right back home!

Laughing, he opened the door. Lenne was there, preparing to knock. To Fred's relief, she had on "normal" attire; jeans, her favorite Morgan State T-shirt and sneakers.

"Moving in?"

Lenne laughed as Fred stepped aside to let her come in. She had a small overnight bag, the kind normally used as carry-on luggage on a flight.

"I was going to Philly to spend the weekend with my mom, but she got herself a date tonight!"

Fred chuckled. "Dag, your mom's got it going on more than you do!"

"Aw, hit a sister while she's down! No, when she told me that she was going out with this guy from her church, I told her I'd visit some other time. I didn't want to cramp her style!"

"Well, you sure won't be cramping mine! Come on and sit down awhile."

She put the bag beside the couch and they watched the rest of the movie in silence, enjoying each other's company.

⁓

Yolanda flopped on the couch; her half-eaten TV dinner sat abandoned as she fought tears.

"God," she prayed aloud, "why am I alone on a Friday night for the second weekend in a row when You sent me a good man?"

Immediately, Yolanda sensed a presence in the room. She gasped as she felt, rather than heard, God answer.

BECAUSE YOU COULDN'T APPRECIATE HIM WHEN I SENT HIM TO YOU.

⁓

"I never cried for Shawn."

"Huh?"

Lenne's statement came out of nowhere. "Not one tear."

Fred muted the TV volume and gave Lenne his undivided attention. She sat with her knees drawn up to her chest; in the flickering light of the TV, she looked surprisingly vulnerable.

"We were supposed to go out that night, but he never came home. I figured he had to work late and forgot to call. It had happened before."

She unconsciously moved closer to Fred, and he shifted to accommodate her.

"I got a call from Shawn's dad around ten o'clock that night. He said Shawn was hurt and I needed to get to the hospital. I never drove so fast in my life."

Fred shuddered, remembering how he felt when he learned about Merry. The ride to the hospital was the longest he'd ever experienced, but unlike Lenne, he knew Merry was dead before he left his apartment.

"I begged God not to take Shawn, but when I got there, the look on his father's face said it all. The only thing left for the doctor was to tell me the details. Some drunk driving the wrong way up a one-way street hit Shawn head on. Both of them died instantly. Like that was supposed to comfort me."

Fred pulled her closer, wanting to take the pain away from her, but not knowing how.

"Shawn's mom and older sister died in a car accident two years ago, and then Shawn died the same way. His dad was so torn up he couldn't even function. The only other family Shawn had was a great-aunt and some trifling cousins. I made all the arrangements, called people, the works. The thing is, I did all that and I never thought about how I'd miss Shawn. I figured I'd do that at the funeral. But I never *did*."

Her eyes grew misty as she continued. Fred wanted to do or say something, but he couldn't.

"They funeralized him, buried him, had the family get-together, the works and I never cried. Why can't I cry for him?"

Fred took a deep breath. "Maybe because you haven't let him go yet."

A look of comprehension crossed Lenne's face.

"When I heard Merry was dead and then *how* she died, I was crushed. The toughest thing was accepting the fact that I'd never see her again. I kept thinking I could go to her house and she'd be there. I don't think I really accepted her death until I saw her in the casket."

Lenne nodded, the hint of tears appearing in her eyes.

"Some days I think Shawn's gonna come home and tell me he was playing with me, and that everything will be all right."

"Everything *is* gonna be all right, Lenne. It's just gonna be all right without Shawn."

The floodgates opened and Lenne cried like a baby. As Fred held her close, he remembered doing the same for Merry, and unexpectedly burst into tears himself. Not even trying to compose himself, he and Lenne poured out their sadness together.

It took Yolanda several minutes and a lot of deep breaths to calm down enough to form coherent thoughts.

"I don't get it. I thought I was doing okay with Raoul. I listen to him, I talk to him- - -I *do* appreciate him!"

Yolanda half expected another visitation, but her words met silence. She wondered if she'd imagined it until something on the coffee table caught her eye. She reached down to pick up a photograph half-buried under a stack of *Essence* magazines and forgotten until now.

How did this get here?

She looked at the picture and her mouth went dry. It was of her, Donna, Max- - -and Fred.

"Fred, thanks for being here."

He tried to smile as he offered her a tissue from the box they had nearly depleted.

"I'm glad I could help. It's been awhile since- - -."

Thoughts of Merry crossed his mind, and he choked up in mid-sentence.

"You okay?"

Fred shook his head yes. Lenne realized that he was fighting the urge to cry some more, and let him compose himself in peace.

"When Merry and I first got together, she had nightmares. She'd wake up screaming; I would sit and

Lenne's face turned tender. "Oh Fred, I'm so sorry. I reminded you of her, didn't I?"

"You did, but don't be sorry. I miss her, but hearing you talk about Shawn makes me realize how blessed we both are. We each lost special people, but we still have each other."

"You're right. Unless you've been there, you can't really understand how it feels."

They talked long into the night. Fred wasn't sure when he and Lenne started kissing.

"We can't live in the past, Fred. But, we can make our own future."

Lenne's voice was a sultry breath in his ear. She had his clothes off before he could react, and another kiss silenced his protests for good.

21

Fred showered a long time, praying the scalding spray would wash away his guilt.

We were just talking, and the next thing I know, she'd whipped a condom out of her purse faster than Wyatt Earp drawing a gun. A year of abstinence down the drain.

He immediately asked God's forgiveness as the thought of Lenne in his bed induced momentary excitement. The spray cooled, helping to quench his sudden burst of lust. Normally he got out of the shower when the water turned cold, but not this time.

God, I need Your help. Please forgive me for messing up like this. I wasn't trying to have sex again until I got married, but we got caught up.

The last bit of warmth faded from the spray. Fred jumped as the icy jet of water hit him.

Okay, forget the excuses; I messed up. And God, forgive me because I wanted to mess up! I know I shouldn't have let her come up because I knew she'd make a move.

He turned off the water, but stayed in the shower.

Lord, I have to come out sometime, and when I do, there's a naked woman in my bed who wants me to mess up again. Lord, You know I'm weak! Help me, because I can't resist her without Your help. Amen.

Fred dried off slowly. He wrapped a towel around himself, thinking what a poor defense it would be against Lenne's charms. As he left the bathroom, something caught his eye. Fred was surprised to see a crumpled pair of black sweatpants and a green Howard University T-shirt under his towel rack.

All my sweats and stuff are in the laundry bag. I know they are- I stuffed the last pair in yesterday. How did these get here?

Thankful for the unexpected blessing, he dressed and exited the bathroom quietly. He slipped past a sleeping Lenne and headed for the kitchen, rehearsing what to tell her later.

Lenne woke up revitalized. After months of involuntary abstinence, she felt free. The aroma of bacon frying tantalized her, and she heard activity in the kitchen.

Fred's already up. Glad he's okay. We've both been cold turkey for so long, I could've hurt the brother!

Lenne giggled and headed for the bathroom.

Fred heard the shower running and his heart raced.

She's up, and I know she smells this food, which means she won't linger.

Fred transferred bacon from the pan, added a generous portion of scrambled eggs and toast to each plate and put them on the table. As he finished pouring glasses of orange juice, Lenne came to the table in pink shorts and a white New Orleans T-shirt instead of yesterday's jeans.

"A good time last night and a good meal this morning. I could get used to this."

Fred laughed in spite of himself and pulled out her chair. "As I recall, you always did need a good meal after a good time."

Fred sat down, and blessed the food. Lenne's eyebrows lifted at the eloquence of the prayer.

"I'm impressed. Not only can the brother cook, but he can pray over it like a preacher!"

Fred laughed again, thankful that tragedy hadn't damaged Lenne's sharp wit.

"I'm not just going to church to be going. God's working on me, and I'm growing spiritually."

Lenne ignored that remark and dug into her breakfast with gusto, savoring the food and Fred's company.

"You actually have real bacon up in here? What happened to that nasty turkey stuff you usually eat?"

Fred laughed. "I do have friends who haven't jumped on the health bandwagon."

For some reason, Fred couldn't mention Yolanda by name. She was the only reason he had real bacon on hand.

"You can terrorize turkeys all you want. Pigs still need to run when they see me coming."

They both laughed and kept eating. Months of loneliness were a distant memory.

Fred came to his senses quick enough, and now he's acting just like he did when we'd hook up back in the day. He always treated me like a lady, even though I wasn't his girlfriend.

"How'd you sleep?"

Lenne smiled. *Considerate like always. I should have gotten with him like this long ago.*

"Fred, I slept good. It was that kind of sleep where you become one with the mattress."

He laughed.

"Yeah, I didn't feel you move once we went to sleep. You were knocked *out!*"

Lenne finished her juice, pushed her empty plate aside and sighed contentedly.

"That was the best sleep I've had since Shawn died. I guess you were right- I never let go."

"I'm glad you did. Believe me, I know how that feels."

She smiled. "It was ugly! I couldn't sleep, my appetite was down and when I tried to bring somebody home, I couldn't do it. Thanks again for being there for me. I really appreciate it."

Fred finished his eggs. "You're welcome. That's what friends are for."

Lenne cocked her head. "Friends? I'd think we took a step past that, didn't we?"

Fred prayed silently for guidance.

"We took that step two years ago, as I recall. But, we were so busy ducking commitment that we didn't realize what we had all along."

Lenne smiled. *Sounds like he's not trying to back away after all.*

"So, where does that leave us now?"

Fred took a deep breath, still praying. "That depends on you."

Lenne looked at him. "What do you mean?"

"Lenne, you deserve to be happy again, and I'm glad I helped you get there. It was tough for me to let Merry go. I still miss her, but I can enjoy living now without feeling guilty. Give it some time and you'll get all the way there too."

Lenne frowned slightly. "That sounds like a "but" is coming."

"But, I'm not happy about what happened after we talked last night."

Lenne looked shocked. "You mean you didn't enjoy it?"

Fred shook his head. "Come on now. How many men you know can fake an orgasm?"

Lenne laughed in spite of herself. "You got a point there."

"Lenne, it was great. It was just as incredible as ever between us, and just as wrong."

Lenne was speechless. *Be with me God*, Fred thought, *because I'm about to either enlighten her or lose another friend.*

"When we got back together, I told you that I'm not the same Fred you knew back in the day. I'm saved now, by the grace and mercy of Jesus Christ, and I have to live like it."

Why can't he just let it lie, Lenne thought. *We did it already!*

"Fred, I understand you're trying to change, and we're both going to church now. I just don't understand why sex is wrong for two people in a committed relationship."

Fred sighed, trying to get the words out and knowing he'd make Lenne extremely angry.

"With HIV/AIDS and other diseases going around, you can't be a player any more. But why are you so dead set against it being just us?"

"Because our definitions of "us" aren't the same. Lenne, just because I messed up last night doesn't mean it's okay for us to keep on doing it. I can't just live part of a Christian life and conveniently ignore the parts I don't like."

Lenne's neck went on automatic pilot and her eyes blazed with anger. "I don't believe this. You're trying to kick me to the curb!"

Fred fought to keep from exploding as he drew on everything Pastor Nathan had taught him in counseling sessions about this very issue.

"Lenne, listen to what I'm saying here. Sex isn't a toy. God gave it to us to relate to each other *in marriage*. Over the years, people decided marriage wasn't important anymore, and look what happened. We got abortions, we got diseases and we got people with emotional issues because folks decided to ignore what God says about sex and relationships."

Lenne fought tears as she tuned Fred out in her growing anger. "I was good enough to "play" with for two years, but not good enough for a relationship. Is that what you're telling me?"

Fred swore and slammed his hand on the table, causing Lenne to flinch. "You haven't listened to a word I said! I care about you, Lenne. I want to find out if we *can* make a relationship work. But I won't be out of line with God anymore."

Lenne could feel her anger ebb despite her desire to stay angry until she got her way.

"Wow. You're dead serious."

"I am. I told you before; losing Merry made me want to change my whole life, and Max told me how to do it: accept Jesus. I started going to church again after Merry vanished, and after she died, I saw how fragile life is and how much time I wasted avoiding God."

He reached across the table and took Lenne's hands in his.

"I want your company, but I won't have your body outside of marriage anymore."

Lenne absorbed Fred's last statement for a few minutes. She helped Fred clear the table in silence, and then went to the bedroom for her overnight bag.

"Fred, I've been with a lot of guys; you know that. You're the first one to ever tell me something from the heart and then stick to it. Shawn didn't even do that. He said, "I love you" and meant it, but he never let me see the deepest part of himself. You did that this morning, and I respect that. I just can't do it your way."

She leaned up and kissed Fred on the cheek, and left without another word. Fred watched until her car vanished into the distance.

"I know you going through some things brother, and you gonna go through some more. You on the devil's hit list 'cause you changed sides. He wants you back, 'cause ain't nothing more dangerous than someone like you or me who knows all his secrets!"

Fred felt like the shorter man standing a few feet away rammed a hot spear directly into his heart. He nearly dropped the newspaper he'd walked to Wawa for as he tried to hear more. The shorter man didn't notice Fred as he ministered.

"Don't give up! You seen the world- ain't nothing more out here you don't know about. Hold your ground, stand tall and watch God bust a move in your life!"

The taller man, who wore the battle-scarred look of a long-term drug user, sat on the ground with his head in his hands. Fred walked over and sat next to him.

"Your friend is right. I don't know what you're going through, but it don't matter. I'm going through some stuff myself. All I know is this- no matter what it is, God's got your back. Ain't nothing we go through that He can't see us through."

As if they'd planned it, the two men prayed with a man who after today would no longer answer to the name Crack-head Chuck. Fred's neighbor and fellow intercessor thanked him for helping and drove Chuck to the nearest detox center. Fred watched them drive off and then went inside to make a call.

22

"That's awesome, Fred! You mean you just went over there and helped the brother witness?"

"It was deep, Max. I mean, the things he was saying hit me just as hard as they hit Chuck. When you think about it, I used to get as much booty as he did hits off the pipe!"

Max laughed. "You got a point."

"How did you do it Max? Abstain for all that time I mean."

Max chuckled. "Sin is sin, no matter what form it takes, and the solution is the same: Jesus. Whenever I was tempted to go get a woman, I read my Bible until the feeling passed."

"Did it work?"

Max smiled. "Yeah, but one night I had to read the whole New Testament!"

They both howled with laughter.

"Fred, remember what we talked about before? The best way to resist temptation is to stay away from it."

Fred rolled his eyes. "Point taken."

"You messed up this time, but there's no law says you have to do it again. It's tough, but stay away from Lenne, Symone or anyone else offering loose booty."

Fred sighed.

"Yeah, you're right."

"I know you're lonely, but you spending time with Lenne for company is like an alcoholic going to a bar 'just to watch the game.'"

Fred laughed until he cried. Max tried to ask him why, but Fred kept on until he finally caught his breath.

"It wasn't that funny, Fred."

"I know. I just had a visual of some guy bellied up to the bar with eight beer bottles around him going, "What's the score? Who cares! Gimme another cold one!"

They both laughed this time. Just then, Fred heard a familiar beep.

"Hold on Max, somebody's on my other line."

Fred clicked over, wondering who was calling now.

"Hello?"

"Fred, it's Mom."

Silence for a moment.

"Your father is in the hospital."

⌒

"Sister Annie, you set me up."

The pastor's wife looked as innocent as if this were just another after service chat with one of the congregation.

"What do you mean, Dee?"

Dee's face was granite.

"Save the innocent act for someone who *doesn't* know you. First you ask Ted and me to serve on the Hospitality Committee for the conference next month with you and Donna. Then you suggest that since Mount Pisgah UAC is involved, we have some of their ushers on the committee too, and that we meet at the Golden Corral in Dover to accommodate them."

"Travis and I have lots of breakfast meetings there. The meeting room is easy to reserve, and it's a nice change from meeting in one of the churches."

Dee gave the pastor's wife her best "I ain't buying this" glare. "Uh huh. So explain to me again why Ted and I were the only ones who showed up."

Sister Nathan had trouble suppressing a smile.

"Well Dee, like I told you when I called your cell phone, we got our signals crossed. Apparently the Mount Pisgah ushers thought the meeting was next Saturday."

"Mmm hmm. And apparently both your car *and* Donna's alarm clock thought the same thing. Your car didn't start and her alarm clock didn't go off. Or was it her car and your clock? It's hard to keep your excuses straight."

"What can I say, Dee? It was one of those mornings where none of our plans went right."

Dee maintained her glare. "Yet you managed to reserve the room and make sure that our breakfast was paid for in advance."

Sister Nathan's body shook with the laughter she could no longer contain. Just then Donna approached. Dee reached out and grabbed her arm as she tried to slip past.

"Oh no you don't, Donna. You're in this too. Get over here!"

Amused by Dee's uncustomary assertiveness, Donna adopted Sister Nathan's air of assumed innocence.

"Dee, I don't see the problem here. You've wanted uninterrupted time with Mr. Stansbury for a long time. Why are you angry?"

The barely disguised smirks on their faces made it difficult for Dee to verbally maul them.

"Having breakfast with Ted is not why I'm mad. We've done that here at the church on many occasions. In case you missed it, I'm mad at you two for going to such ridiculous lengths to set us up!"

Sister Nathan feigned concern. "Ridiculous lengths?"

Donna nearly laughed, but she managed to contain it somehow.

"You called a whole fake meeting!"

Sister Nathan did her best to look angelic. "Dee, I already apologized for my mistake, and I even bought you breakfast to make up for it. I just don't see the problem here."

Donna finally decided it was time to stop pretending. "Dee, are you gonna yell at us all morning or do we get details about your date?"

Laughter echoed through the nearly empty sanctuary, as it had for the past few minutes. Pastor Nathan peeked in, rolled his eyes and went back to his office to finish his paperwork.

"You two are impossible!"

Donna wiped her eyes and did her best to stop laughing. "And relentless. Details, woman!"

Dee managed to laugh and blush at the same time.

"Once we figured out nobody else was coming and that breakfast was paid for, we agreed to "go with the flow.""

Donna laughed at Dee's subtle dig at her sermon topic.

"And that entailed- - -?"

Dee smiled. "Breakfast."

Donna studied Dee intently. "Mmm-hmm. Judging from that smile, it was quite satisfying."

"O taste an' see dat de Lord is good."

Donna laughed at Sister Nathan's accented humor, and Dee blushed more deeply then Donna thought a dark-skinned woman could.

"I've known Ted for three years, and he's never looked at me like he did that morning. It's like he was amazed at what he saw."

Donna and Sister Nathan exchanged a knowing smile.

"Ahh yes, the famous "I'm seeing her for the first time" look. I remember when I saw that look on your pastor's face. It was just a matter of time then."

Donna chuckled. "What, you mean it took you more than one date? Max looked like that the first time he saw me."

The two women exchanged a high five. Dee had a wry expression on her face.

"So I take it that you two comediennes see this misguided effort of yours as a success."

Just then Donna felt something, and subtly signaled the other two women to follow her gaze. Each woman in turn noticed Ted performing his normal post-service duties, but this time, his gaze moved from the people he said goodbye to and found Dee wherever she was in the room. Sister Nathan had them move a few feet over, and his head snapped around to follow them.

Sister Nathan smiled again. "Any more questions?"

Yolanda came home from the eleven AM service intending to relax, but she found herself unable to sit still.

I'm pretty sure you're going someplace with this, God, Yolanda thought. *Help me out- what am I missing here?*

She thought back over the troubling events of the past few months.

When exactly did things start going south?

Yolanda didn't want to acknowledge the truth, but it became clear to her when things changed.

I fought with both Donna and Fred after Raoul and I hooked up. Neither of them liked him for me, but I thought they were wrong. Now I have a man in name only and I'm still sitting home alone on weekends because I alienated all my friends to be with him.

Yolanda had her shoes on and was out the door before she realized where she was headed.

Fred reached for the phone for the tenth time in the past hour, and put it down yet again.

I know I have to do this, but I can't deal with Yolanda yet. Guess I have some more praying to do.

And he did.

Max answered the door and greeted Yolanda with a hug. "Good to see you, lady. It's been awhile."

Yolanda smiled nervously. "Too long. Is your wife home?"

"I'll get her for you."

Yolanda self-consciously followed Max inside, standing instead of getting comfortable as she would have in the past. Max vanished into the bedroom, and Donna came out quickly upon being awakened from her nap.

Yolanda took a deep breath. "Buenas noches, amigita. Sorry for coming by without calling."

Donna's smile was infectious, and the warmth behind it was genuine. "Girl, you know you can come here *any*time. Unless we're going to do War Of The Funky Attitudes Part II."

Yolanda smiled and pressed first her left shoulder blade with her index finger and then her right. "I'll disarm my neck muscles if you'll disarm yours."

They laughed together for what felt like the first time in ages, and hugged. Max slipped out of the bedroom and caught Donna's eye.

"I'm gonna head out for a bit. I forgot to grab that milk I told you I'd get earlier, and I also promised Fred I'd try to stop by tonight."

Donna smiled, knowing that Max was giving them space.

"Okay. See you later."

A quick kiss on the lips, and Max was gone. Yolanda smiled at the love between her friends, and Donna was pleased not to feel any jealousy or resentment from Yolanda.

"Sit down, we've got a lot to catch up on."

They settled on the couch, facing each other like they used to for their all-night talk sessions as roommates. Donna felt peace radiating from Yolanda for the first time in weeks.

"I've missed talking to you like this, 'Landa."

"Me too. Listen, I'm, uh, I'm sorry I acted up so bad. I- -guess I haven't really got used to not being able to hang with you like we used to."

Donna's eyes widened in surprise. For Yolanda to put her pride aside and make such an admission was amazing.

"Apology accepted. And while we're at it, I apologize for snapping at you that day. It's just, well, I don't have the same way of seeing things. We used to be on the same page dealing with trifling men or the lack thereof. Now instead of worrying about getting a date, I'm worried about whether or not to kill Max if he doesn't take the garbage out."

Yolanda laughed. "Yeah, guess you do have different priorities than I do. But, can we still talk about men sometimes?"

Donna chuckled. "Sure! Of course my part of the conversation will be a bit one-sided- - -."

Yolanda took a deep breath. "I really need your advice."

"You know I'm here for you."

Fred opened the door and found Max standing there, holding a small bag.

"Aw man, don't tell me she put you out already?"

Chuckling, he stepped aside and let Max in.

"Funny. Actually I put myself out. Yolanda came by, and I figured they needed time to talk."

"Yeah, tell me anything. You just didn't wanna get caught in the middle of a raging cat-fight!"

Max laughed. "Man, you're in rare form tonight. Must be the full moon."

He held up his bowling ball bag, and smiled. "If I know my wife, she and Yolanda will talk for hours, which gives me enough time to avenge my last narrow defeat at your hands."

Fred smiled, eager for anything that could keep his mind off of the ocean of tears he'd shed during his trip home to see his parents.

"You don't want none of this. I'll send you home to your wife crying and then Donna and Yolanda will yell at me for abusing you."

Max laughed. "Man, you talk more trash than two garbage men. Get your stuff and see if your canary behind can cash that check your alligator mouth just wrote."

Fred roared with laughter and grabbed his bowling ball.

Donna and Yolanda enjoyed their first conversation in weeks. Yolanda did most of the talking, with Donna interjecting advice now and then. They talked about Raoul and Fred, about Yolanda's revelation and how to proceed.

" 'Landa, you're not gonna want to hear this, but you know what you have to do, don't you?"

Yolanda sighed. "It won't be easy."

"Eating crow never is. You ought to ask Max how tough it is for him to make me admit when I'm wrong! I know something about pride. But you have to let that go, or else you might lose Fred completely, even as just a friend.

"I don't want that. I miss Fred. Nobody's called me Laquita Maria for weeks now."

Donna laughed. "How about Shenaynay Gonzalez?"

Yolanda laughed too. "Nope. I have to admit, it's nice to have a guy friend I can be myself with. I don't feel like I can do that with Raoul."

"That should tell you something right there."

Donna let the subject drop so Yolanda could let that thought marinate.

"Been a *long* time since you just dropped over without calling or anything."

Max took down eight pins, and then faced Fred, smiling. "It's different once you get married. I can't just jump up and go somewhere whenever I feel like it. It took me awhile to get used to the fact that not only does Donna ask me where I'm going, but that she has the right to know! First time she asked, I almost looked at her like she was crazy and said "None of your business!"

Fred laughed and grabbed his ball, awaiting his next turn. "That what they mean by "the old ball and chain?""

"No, that's what they hit you with when you mess up."

They both roared with laughter. Fred caught his breath, and then rolled a strike.

"Donna must have bad aim. You're still living."

Max chuckled. "True. You really have to work at it, but when you find the right woman, it's worth it."

Fred retrieved his ball from the rack. "That's encouraging. Now all I have to do is find my right woman before I'm too old to chase her around the house."

Max matched Fred's strike.

"Somehow I don't think it'll take you that long. Look at me; I just knew I wasn't gonna meet anybody for at least six months after Jenisse, and next thing I knew, I was engaged and wondering what hit me!"

Fred chuckled and grabbed his ball, preparing for his next turn. "In your case, you had to wonder *who* was gonna hit you next! And none of them was even a jealous boyfriend in your case."

"Fred, all I have to say is this: don't give up on Yolanda just yet. You two have something special, and one fight can't destroy all that unless the two of you let it."

Fred rolled a seven-ten split.

23

Yolanda paced around her apartment.

This won't be easy. Fred acted like a big baby and now I'm the one who has to apologize.

The warm feeling from her marathon conversation with Donna last night rapidly wore off, and she felt nervous about trying to patch up her second friendship in two days.

It's not like I'm not guilty too. We were like two little kids fighting and then going "You're not my friend anymore!"

She giggled as she pictured herself and Fred acting like her students did when it came to their petty squabbles. The laughter eased her tension, and she reached for the phone. It rang just as she picked it up, and the name on the Caller ID warmed her heart.

"Hello?"

"Hi, Yolanda? It's Fred."

Thank you God. This could be easier than I thought.

"I'm glad you called. I was just about to call you in fact. We really need to talk."

Fred smiled nervously. "Yeah, we do. I'd feel better talking in person though. Do you mind?"

Yolanda smiled. "Not a bit. Puedes ver aqui?"

"Sure, I'll be right over."

Wow, two major apologies in two nights, Yolanda thought. *That has to be some kind of record.*

Ten minutes later, Fred was at her door, waiting nervously for her to open up.

I acted like a complete jackass, and now I have to be a man, suck it up and apologize.

Inside, Yolanda was tense as she opened the door.

I have to do the one thing I've never been good at: apologize. I threw away a perfectly good friendship for a man I knew nothing about, and now I have to do what I can to fix things.

Fred was there, visibly nervous, but trying not to show it. "Somebody here order a chit'lin and butterbean pizza?"

Yolanda laughed and let Fred in.

"Raoul and I still have things to work out, but that's not important right now. This isn't about who I'm dating or who you're dating. This is about our friendship. I miss you, Fred. I miss being able to call you and talk about our days. I miss how we could go bowling or see a movie without date tension getting in the way."

Fred swallowed and took a breath. "I miss that too. We can be real with each other and have a good time, even if we're not doing anything special."

Yolanda forced herself to look Fred in the eye. "I'm sorry I acted like a brat, Fred. Will you forgive me?"

He answered by drawing her into a warm, brotherly hug.

"Sure. And listen, I'm sorry too. It was my fault we stopped talking anyway. It was real childish of me to act out like I did."

Yolanda smiled. "So, we haven't talked in awhile. Que pasa en su vida?"

Fred winked. "Nada mucho. Patched things up with my mom, helped her lead my dad back to Christ. Nothing major."

She threw her arms around him. "That's great! When did all this happen?"

"Over the weekend. Lenne and I had got in this big argument Saturday morning. I'll tell you about that later, but not long after that, my mom called to tell me my dad was in the hospital."

Fred started with his parking lot experience, and then told her about the appendicitis attack that not only brought Fred home to visit, but also drew the elder Bennett and his ex-wife back together.

"Mom and I hadn't really talked in about sixteen years, but I knew in my heart enough was enough. We put it all out there, and we both apologized to each other for letting things go for this long. I stayed down there, and Mom and I went to church together before I came back. Man, the church gossipers had a field day!"

Yolanda laughed. "I bet they did!"

"Anyway, we prayed with Dad at the hospital, and he rededicated himself to Christ. And when he gets out, he and Mom are getting remarried!"

"Praise God!"

He looked uncomfortable.

"Now, I have to tell you about Friday."

He took a deep breath and told her how he and Lenne didn't resist temptation. Yolanda listened intently, sad for her friend's fall, but happy that he felt comfortable enough to confess this to her.

"I thought I had it all under control, 'Landa. I figured all I had to do was tell Lenne once that I wasn't gonna sleep with her and she'd leave me alone. Guess you were right about her after all."

Yolanda sighed and closed her eyes, remembering her own recent romantic close call. "I wish I weren't. And believe me, I know how rough that situation is. I've had to tell Raoul about nine times to respect the boundaries I set, and he still tries to push the limits. I almost had to cripple him last time to get him to stop!"

Fred cracked up. "Wish I could've seen that!"

"It's getting so I don't trust myself to be alone with him, because each time, I feel weaker in saying no."

"That's the answer."

Yolanda opened her eyes again. "What is? Crippling Raoul?"

Fred laughed. "I wish. No, the only way for folks like us to resist temptation is to not put ourselves in those situations. Especially when that "situation" is *fine*."

He repeated Max's analogy about the alcoholic to her, and Yolanda smiled.

"Makes sense to me."

"You know what helped me get this?"

Yolanda sat up straight. "What?"

"Proverbs 7. I had read chapters 1-6 and was just starting chapter seven when Lenne came over and, well, you know the rest. After she and I talked the next morning and she left, I picked it back up and read this."

He picked up Yolanda's King James Bible, and read Proverbs 7:21-27.

When he finished, he closed the Bible and took a deep breath. "It'd be easy to blame it all on Lenne, you know. I could be like "It's right here in the Bible! She knew I wasn't trying to roll like that and she just kept after me until I gave in. It's all her fault."

Yolanda looked puzzled. "And it isn't?"

Fred sighed. "I'm not innocent. It takes two to tango, and I was dancing right along with her. If I was really serious about abstinence, I would never let have her come over because she'd made it clear that she wanted to get me in bed again. Plus, that wasn't a real big purse she was carrying; that was an *overnight bag*. Duh!"

Yolanda laughed in spite of herself.

"Not only did I let her come in, but I didn't tell her to leave when I should have. She needed to talk, but once she started macking, I should have put her out. I saw it coming, but I figured I'm saved now, so when she made her move, I'd tell her no, ask her to leave and she would."

Yolanda thought for a moment. "Yeah, I guess I see what you mean."

"I think deep down, I *wanted* it to happen. I let her wear me down bit by bit, and I didn't discourage her. Then when she made her move, I had nothing left to resist her with. She might have played me like a violin, but I handed her the bow and the sheet music."

It looked to Fred as if Yolanda was either praying or on the verge of sleep. After a long silence, she responded.

"Thank you for sharing that with me, Fred. You could have easily let it go and figured I'd never find out. I probably never would have, you know."

Fred exhaled in relief. "I started not to tell you, but I couldn't do that. Friends should be honest with each other. I remember when Pastor preached from Romans 3:23 that time: "For all have sinned, and fallen short of the glory of God." It wouldn't be right trying to make you think I'm perfect when you know good and well I'm not!"

"Oh, I know you're messed up. You didn't have to tell me about Lenne for me to figure that one out!"

Fred chuckled. "Ha ha. Anyway, I told you because I you're my friend, and because I want you to pray for me."

Yolanda looked surprised and pleased at the same time.

"I'm weak when it comes to sex, especially with Lenne. Max and Donna both pray for me, but I'm greedy; I want all I can get!"

She laughed. "We can pray for each other. I'm still all confused about Raoul."

"Works for me."

They sat on Yolanda's couch and poured out their concerns to Him who is able to keep them from falling.

24

Fred relaxed as he sat on the couch in Randy's Richmond, Virginia home.

"So, how's it going with Sharon?"

Randy's smile lit up the room as he pulled an engagement ring from his pocket and showed it to Fred.

"Couldn't be better!"

Fred gave Randy a high five and admired the ring. "When you giving her this? And does it come with sunglasses for the glare?"

Randy laughed. "I hope I'll get the chance when we go out to dinner tomorrow evening. I know we haven't been dating long, but this feels right, more right than anything I've done except accept Jesus. I keep thinking I'm going to wake up and it's just a good dream."

"Better not pinch yourself then."

"Since we're on this topic, how are things with Lenne?"

Fred made a face. "You had to ask."

He told Randy about his breakup with Lenne, and his subsequent reconciliation with Yolanda.

"Sounds to me like things are going just like they should."

Fred rolled his eyes. "It's not like Yolanda and I are dating. Right now it's a blessing that we're even speaking."

Randy laughed. "Uh huh. I'm willing to bet your blessing will be far more than that in the long run. Matter of fact, *when* Yolanda realizes that you're far better for her than that Raoul clown, bring her here. Sharon and I will take you out to dinner. I know the perfect restaurant- Sharon and I went there for our first date."

Fred absently picked up a photo album from the coffee table. "Okay, if that unlikely miracle ever occurs, Yolanda and I will sit on your doorstep waiting for our free meal."

Randy laughed and went to get them a drink as Fred flipped through the album. He turned a page and blinked in astonishment.

"Hey Randy!"

Randy stuck his head out of the kitchen. "The iced tea is just about ready."

"I need you to clear something up for me."

Randy came over, wiping his hands on a towel. "What?"

Fred pointed to a photo of a genteel woman in a blue dress. "Who is this?"

Randy looked puzzled. "That's my great-aunt. I never knew her. She was at the center of a family scandal. Seems she married a black man and the family didn't handle it very well."

Fred felt a wave of dawning comprehension wash over him. "What happened to her?"

"My dad told me Aunt Martha was disinherited and basically run out of the family. They didn't actually *tell* her to leave, but they made her life so miserable that she and her husband had no other choice. I remember my father telling me they moved to Rhode Island, and a year later, they moved to New Jersey with his family. Why do you ask?"

Fred smiled. "My grandmother told me she was born in Richmond, and that she lived in Rhode Island before settling in Jersey. She never talked about her family; my mom always assumed they cut her off for marrying outside her race. Her name was Martha Jenkins. And this is a picture of her."

Randy was speechless.

Fred smiled. "I'm willing to bet the black man your Aunt Martha married was named Jenkins, and that he looked an awful lot like me."

Randy chuckled. "I think our family gatherings just got a whole lot more interesting."

Fred laughed. "Hope we do better than Thomas Jefferson's descendants."

At that moment, the word "family" embedded itself in Fred's spirit and wouldn't leave. He cut his visit with Randy short and got back on I-95 North towards home to figure out how "family" fit into his investigation.

Fred nervously waited for his name to be called, silently thanking God for a possible link to the missing information he needed.

I thought nobody outside of a comic book or a novel could hide his past this well, but there's a picture of Raoul next to the word "mystery" in the dictionary.

Fred marveled at how modern technology had brought him here. An online search on Raoul's name and every conceivable combination of the words "child molestation" unearthed a gem. Most of the results were familiar, but one new name surfaced: C.C. Campos.

It didn't take long for Fred to learn that Mr. Campos' current address was Gander Hill Prison in Wilmington, and then to arrange a visit. Apparently Campos didn't get many visitors, and wanted to talk.

I hope he knows something I can use. I'm sick of running into brick walls trying to figure Raoul out.

"Bennett!"

Fred rose in response to the guard's call. After being thoroughly searched, he made his way to the visitor's area. There was a guard and a glass barrier between him and Campos, but as long as they could talk, Fred didn't care.

Fred sat in the lone chair on his side of the barrier and waited. A long minute later, a guard led a lean middle-aged Hispanic man into the room. The prisoner looked like life planted a foot square in his behind and left it there.

"You've got ten minutes."

Having said his piece, the guard withdrew to a position that gave them some semblance of privacy. The prisoner picked up the phone, and Fred did likewise.

"Ten minutes? I thought visits were half an hour."

The gaunt man smiled. "I've been a bad boy. Guess I'm lucky to get the ten minutes."

Fred nodded in agreement. "C.C. Campos, I presume."

"Yeah. You're Fred Bennett? The reporter who wants to talk to me, of all people?"

"That's me. I was hoping you could help me with a story I'm working on."

Campos sighed dramatically. "I hope so. If for no other reason, so someone would remember I exist without wanting to spit on me."

Fred pulled out a tape recorder and held it up where Campos and the guard could both see it. He nodded his agreement to be taped, and the guard made no move to take it. Fred connected it to the phone with a small wire, so the recording would be clear.

"I'm working on a child kidnapping case with an investigator named Raoul Carizales. Some of the things he told me don't match up, and I'm trying to connect the dots. My research indicates you might know something about him."

Campos made a visible effort to compose himself before answering. "Yes, I know him from when he was a child. What do you want to know?"

"I know he was a New York cop, but he left to become a private investigator. I know he's very successful; he's never failed to find a missing child, and no criminal he's gone after has gotten away. Or gone uninjured."

Campos sighed again. "Raoul is very driven. Once he takes a case, failure is not an option."

Fred nodded.

"I understand that you have firsthand knowledge of Raoul's effectiveness."

Campos closed his eyes briefly, and opened them again, clearly fighting back tears. "Yes. I'm in for selling heroin and cocaine. I was one of the first to go down under that rule where you can't deal within five hundred yards of a school zone. Raoul was on the case because a parent of one of my regular customers put a hit on me, so to speak. They wouldn't have me killed, but they hired Raoul to catch me in the act of selling."

Fred pulled out a printout of a story he pulled off of the Internet.

"This says that you and Raoul got into a knock-down drag-em-out fight before he subdued you and made the arrest."

Campos chuckled. "That's partially true. Raoul knocked me down, and when the cops came, they had to drag him off me!"

"So, you didn't resist arrest?"

"I did at first. I knew selling to school kids meant hard prison time. Like I said, I know Raoul well, and I figured I could take him. I figured wrong. To put it bluntly, Raoul beat the stupidity out of me. I've lost fights before, but I've never in my life taken such a beating as I took from Raoul that day."

Fred suppressed a smile. Campos had a slight lisp, which was more likely due to the two missing teeth on the right side of his mouth than his Hispanic accent.

"How badly did he beat you?"

Campos smiled wearily and opened his mouth. "I still had all my teeth before that day. He also broke my right arm and my nose, after I surrendered."

Fred noticed Campos' slightly crooked nose and nodded.

That figures, he thought. *This is starting to make a whole lot of sense.*

"I deserved it though. If he'd killed me, maybe that would have squared things between us."

Fred looked up from scribbling in his notebook.

"Next time you see Raoul, give him a message for me. Tell him this: "Forgive me. I did wrong by you. Please forgive me."

Fred finished writing. He felt a surge of awe wash over him, as if he were on the edge of some major revelation.

"He'll remember you? Do I need to give your full name or will C.C. Campos be enough?"

Campos closed his eyes again. He was quiet for so long Fred thought he'd fallen asleep.

"He will never forget me, or what I did to him. Neither will God."

Just then, the guard signaled that the ten minutes were over.

"Thanks for talking to me C.C.; I appreciate your help."

Campos started to hang up, but hesitated. "Raoul will recognize my name, but he never called me C.C. My full name is Carlos Carizales Campos. Raoul me nombra Tio."

He hung up and the guard led him away. Fred sat for a moment before gathering his things to leave. A second guard ushered him out and returned those items he wasn't allowed to carry in for his meeting. Fred drove home, Campos' last statement nagging at him.

"Raoul me nombra Tio."

That means, "Raoul calls me Uncle."

"DeShawn, it's me. Can I come up?"

Normally DeShawn would have left her ex-husband outside all night, but the stress of Wade being missing lowered her defenses. She buzzed him in and met him at the door. He touched her hand lightly, and DeShawn unexpectedly burst into tears. Even more unexpected was Bert's comforting hand on her shoulder. She looked up through her tears, and was shocked to see tears in Bert's eyes as well.

"They'll find him 'Shawn. Have faith."

Still sobbing, she collapsed into his arms, and they wept together.

Fred was elbow deep in research when his phone rang.

"Fred Bennett."

"Mr. Bennett? My name is Carrie Messenger. I live in Durham, North Carolina. Are you the Fred Bennett who recently logged onto savinggrace.com and left an inquiry?"

Fred perked up. He'd been to that web site, devoted to the counseling and recovery of victims of child molestation and their families, in hopes of finding useful information.

"Yes, that was me. I'm doing a story on Raoul Carizales, a child recovery specialist. I was hoping someone might know more about him then I've learned so far."

There was silence on the line.

"My husband and I know him well. He rescued our son from a molester five years ago."

She doesn't sound overly happy about it.

"Mrs. Messenger, would you allow me to interview you and your husband?"

"Can you come here to Durham? We'll pay your airfare."

Fred was caught off guard. "Well, I- -yes, sure! When would you be available?"

He jotted down the Messenger's contact information and promised to call her back when he made travel arrangements. He literally ran to Max's office to get approval, and almost danced for joy when Max approved the trip.

This will be tight, but I can catch a flight later today and get there by evening. I could be back tomorrow if I do this right.

Fred rented a car at the airport and drove to the nearest hotel. After checking in, he changed clothes and immediately set off to find the Messengers.

Mrs. Messenger wants to talk, and she wants to talk now. Hope her husband is in agreement.

The directions Mrs. Messenger gave him on the phone were perfect, and he found their house easily. He took a deep breath, got out, and headed for the front door.

The Messengers were a charming Caucasian couple. They answered the door together, which to Fred was a good sign. After exchanging pleasantries, they invited him into the family room. He was surprised to see two more people there; an African-American woman around thirty years old and a young blond boy, maybe twelve or thirteen.

"Mr. Bennett, this is our son Reggie. He's the one your friend Carizales rescued."

Fred shook hands, and the boy smiled shyly.

"And this is Dr. April Corbett. We asked Dr. Corbett to be here as well. She's Reggie's counselor."

Whoa, Fred thought as he shook her hand. *This is getting deep.*

They all sat down in the plush den.

"I've got to tell you Mrs. Messenger, I'm dying of curiosity here. I would have gladly interviewed you by phone or e-mail. You didn't have to bring me here."

Ralph Messenger cleared his throat. "We prayed about this, and we felt led to have you come so we could all talk about this in person. We can tell you what you need to know about Raoul Carizales. The man is dangerous."

"He is. And I need to tell somebody why."

Fred was surprised to hear the high, clear voice. He'd assumed that the parents and the counselor would do the talking, not the boy.

Ralph put a reassuring hand on Reggie's shoulder. "My son asked us to bring you here. He's been through a lot the past few years, but he's feeling better and he wants to talk."

Fred moved closer to Reggie and looked him in the eye, smiling warmly.

"That's good, because I want to listen."

Fred got their permission to tape their conversation. Reggie shifted in his seat, clearly nervous, but determined to have his say. Dr. Corbett put a reassuring hand on the boy's shoulder.

"Reggie, it's okay to be nervous. Just take your time, think about what you want to say to Mr. Bennett and say it when you're ready. Nobody's going to rush you."

Got that right, Fred thought. *I'll stay here all week if I have to.*

"When I was eight, I was real little and I got picked on and beat up and stuff. That really sucked."

Fred chuckled. *That kid could be telling my story.*

"We got this new guy at the Boys and Girls Club, Mr. Zee, who would come and talk to us, and he stopped some guys from kicking my butt one time. He encouraged me to stand up for myself when guys picked on me. He was real cool at first, but then he started trying to get me to do stuff."

Fred knew the answer before he even asked the question.

"What kind of stuff?"

Reggie fidgeted some more and looked at Dr. Corbett, who nodded that it was okay for him to answer.

"He wanted me to watch porno movies, and then he kept asking me to get naked with him. I thought that was weird; I told him no and I stopped hanging with him after that."

He paused and took a deep breath.

"A week after that, I was at the club and he told me Mom called to say she was running late and that she wanted him to drive me home. I figured it was true; she did that once, before the porno thing. But when I got in his car, he took me to some old house I never seen before and dragged me in. I tried to get away, but he was stronger than me."

His sentence trailed off, and a distant look crossed his face. Dr. Corbett knelt next to him and spoke quietly in his ear. After a minute or so, he snapped out of it.

"He was trying to take my clothes off and then I heard this loud sound. I looked around and Mr. Ca-razy was standing there, looking mean."

Fred couldn't suppress a chuckle. "Mr. Ca-razy?"

Reggie shrugged. "I can't pronounce his whole name."

Fred smiled. "Ca-razy fits him well enough."

The other adults chuckled nervously as Reggie continued.

"Anyway, Mr. Carazy busted in there like Batman and beat Mr. Zee down. Mr. Zee tried to hit him, but he couldn't fight. Mr. Carazy kept on hitting Mr. Zee even after he said, "Stop, I give up.""

Reggie shuddered, and this time his parents sat on either side of him and put reassuring hands on his shoulders.

"M-mr. Carazy looked at him and said something in Spanish. After that, he pulled his gun out and- -and- -."

Reggie didn't need to finish. The adults in the room, even Dr.

Corbett, were shocked to silence, even though she and the Messengers knew what had happened.

Dr. Corbett was the first to break the silence. "Reggie, can you remember what Mr. Carazy said in Spanish before he pulled out his gun?"

Reggie thought for a moment. "Yeah. He said "No mas."

The clock on Fred's laptop said 3:45 AM, but Fred was determined to keep working. He'd spent four hours with Dr. Corbett and the Messenger family and his mind told him he should be tired. However, he was bursting with energy, which helped him with the task he'd assigned himself upon returning to his hotel.

C.C. Campos made the papers when Raoul kicked his butt. Wonder if their first run-in did too?

Just then, his search for Campos stories struck gold. Aside from the one about Campos' drug arrest, a new one popped up. He clicked on the link, which led him to a back issue of the Wilmington News Journal.

Guess this one didn't make the Voice. Well, the Journal is the biggest paper in New Castle County. If anyone was going to do a story about this, they would.

He read, and a dagger of ice pierced his heart.

Why does it always have to be family who sticks the blade in your back?

Images of Fred's conversation with C.C. Campos flew through his head, intersecting with this new revelation.

Reggie said that Raoul said, "no mas."

"No more."

It was nearly four in the morning, but DeShawn couldn't shut her mind down to get the rest she so desperately needed.

I can't take much more of this. My son has been missing for almost a month.

"God, why haven't you brought him home?"

DeShawn didn't expect an answer to her heartfelt cry, nor did she get one.

I haven't been a regular at church since not long before the divorce.

Why would God listen to me now?

But why wouldn't he?

A scripture floated into her mind, one Yolanda shared with her earlier during her nightly visit.

"We know that all things work together for good to them that love God, to them who are the called according to His purpose."

Yolanda said that it was from Romans 8:28. She said she memorized that verse to help her when she feels like God isn't working in her life.

How does Wade getting kidnapped work for the good?

DeShawn pondered that question until she fell asleep.

I don't believe this, Fred thought. *This has to be the answer.*

Fred had been up all night, and his return flight was scheduled to leave at 8 AM, three hours away. He needed to catch the airport shuttle soon, but a story caught his eye as he was about to log off his computer.

He'd run a search for any family members for either Barkley or Gator, and found a story about Victoria Jackson Clayton, who died of breast cancer before she could expand her rapidly growing bath and body products business. With no husband or children to claim her inheritance, she left the warehouse in Middletown, DE that she was converting for her business to her nephew, Timothy Simmons.

Paydirt.

25

"DeShawn, I'm sorry."

DeShawn's head snapped up. "I must have been asleep and dreaming for a moment. Did you just say you were sorry?"

Bert took a deep breath. "Yeah, I did. And it's way past time too. We've been snapping at each other for two years now, and it's my fault."

DeShawn was speechless. "I never should've cheated on you. I should have told you what was bothering me."

"I wouldn't have listened."

DeShawn's words surprised both of them.

"I was too caught up in starting my business, and then when we argued, it was important that I was right and you were wrong. Nothing else mattered. And W-Wade paid for it."

Their conversation lasted the rest of the night.

"You need me."

Raoul looked at Fred like he just spit on Raoul's floor.

"Excuse me? I need you?"

Until recently, Raoul's powerful presence was enough to beat Fred into submission. However, Fred was working on two hours sleep and full of the knowledge he'd obtained in Durham. Having the upper hand emboldened him, and he glared menacingly at Raoul.

"You need a backup, and I'm all you got unless you feel like calling the cops for help."

Raoul's eyes narrowed. *The day I need the cops to help me take care of two ghetto small timers, he thought, is the day I quit.*

"Think you can handle trouble if it comes your way?"

Fred smiled. "You told me yourself that Barkley probably won't give Gator a gun. We know he's the flunky, which means he's pulling guard duty. The important thing is to keep Wade safe. I'll do that while you take the one with the gun. Unless you think he's too tough for you."

Fred's jibe hit its mark. Raoul stared at him for a long moment.

"What's the address?"

⌐━━

"What do you have to do to get back in good with Jesus?"

Yolanda looked up expectantly. DeShawn had barely gotten in Yolanda's door before asking the question.

"What do you mean?"

DeShawn took a deep breath. "I got saved in college; went to church every Sunday, started tithing, the works. I kept it up until maybe a year after I started working, and then I drifted. My first job out of college was in DC, and I had a good church home there. But, when I came back here, I never found a new one. I drifted further and further away from God, and now I think He's punishing me."

Yolanda took DeShawn's hand. "DeShawn, no! God doesn't work like that! He's not so cruel that He would have your son kidnapped out of revenge for ignoring Him."

"Then why did it happen?"

Yolanda prayed silently for guidance. "I don't know. Being a Christian doesn't mean you have all the answers. You can tell that by the way I screwed up my own life recently."

DeShawn laughed half-heartedly; Yolanda had shared her recent struggles with Fred and their subsequent reconciliation.

"God didn't cause this situation to happen, but He is working within it to reach out to you. He wants you back."

DeShawn blinked back tears. "I don't know how to go back, or even if He wants me after everything I've done."

Yolanda smiled and pulled out the small New Testament she kept in her purse and read DeShawn the account of the Prodigal Son from Luke 15:11-31.

"DeShawn, God's waited patiently for you all these years. He knew the day would come when you would be ready to return."

DeShawn didn't even try to hold back the tears.

"Will you pray with me?"

This time Yolanda didn't hesitate.

"I think I found where they're keeping Wade."

Max blinked in surprise. "Are you sure?"

"Pretty sure. I'm with Raoul now; we're about to go get him."

Max took a deep breath. "Fred, you should call the police about this."

Fred's answer was both firm and quick. "No."

Max sighed in annoyance. "Fred, this isn't a game. Wade's been missing for a month now. If you know where he is, you need to tell the police. Playing hero could get all three of you killed."

"Did you call the police for the bombing in Virginia?"

Max recoiled as if struck. "What?"

"Don't ask me how, but I just know that Raoul has to handle this- - and I have to be there too."

Understanding washed over Max. Fred shifted his cell phone to his other ear as Max regrouped.

"Fine. Do what you have to, but don't let your pride- or Raoul's- interfere with Wade's safety."

Just then, Raoul came out of the deli, looking at written directions from Big A.

"We're about to roll. Pray for us."

Fred hung up just as Raoul climbed behind the wheel, put the key in the ignition and tossed the directions to Fred.

"You're playing navigator. Make sure I don't get lost."

As Max ended the call, a vision hit him hard and fast. He saw two men indistinctly, Wade tied to a chair and a gun lying on a table. The vision shifted, and he saw a warehouse from a distance. The word MIDDLETOWN loomed as the image of the warehouse came into sharper focus. He saw Donna and Yolanda standing next to him as the vision retreated.

They need backup, Max thought. He quickly let someone know that he'd be out chasing a story and ran out the door before anyone else could question his whereabouts.

"You're going where?"

Max sighed. *Should have known Donna wouldn't take this well.*

"Fred called. He and Raoul are investigating a lead that might lead them to Wade. I saw a vision. I don't have time to explain it all, but they need backup."

Donna took a deep breath. "And you're not sending the police?"

"Donna, you know I'm not crazy. I didn't see any police, and I know I need to be there. We'll call the police when we have to, but for now, I've got to be obedient."

"What about us? At least let Yolanda and me come with you. You know we can help."

Max shook his head no, as if Donna could see that over the phone.

"I'll call you again soon, but now I've got to drive like you if I'm going to get there in time to help."

Max hung up before Donna could protest and stepped on the gas, praying he wouldn't get pulled over and that God would honor his desire to keep Donna safe and forgive him for deceiving her.

Donna fumed as she dialed her cell phone.

I'm the one pushed his butt out from in front of a bullet last year, and now he's getting protective on me. And trying to lie when he knows I can feel it every time!

She hadn't had a chance to tell Max that she'd seen Middletown, a warehouse and all of them in a clear vision of her own.

Well Mr. Overprotective, you're in for a surprise.

Yolanda was outside when Donna pulled up in front of her apartment building. Without a word, she jumped into the car and Donna took off.

"Do I even need to ask how you knew I'd be home instead of at work?"

Donna smiled. "You know how this works. Apparently Max and I saw the same vision at the same time, and you were in it. I don't even know why I dialed you at home instead of calling your cell, but I did."

Yolanda laughed. "I called off sick today. DeShawn came over, and you wouldn't believe how tough it was to make her stay put. I told her you guys needed information from me to check a lead. I promised to call her as soon as we know anything."

As they drove, the women promised one another that they wouldn't to do anything rash, but let Raoul and Fred, and Max handle things. They agreed to hang back unless otherwise instructed, and then only by God and not by their desire to help free Wade.

"They're here."

Fred didn't question what tipped Raoul off, but nodded his agreement.

"What's the plan?"

"Let you know in a minute."

Raoul slipped off around the side of the building to reconnoiter. Staying low, he saw everything he needed to form a plan.

"The kid's in a room near the back with Gator. Think you can get the kid while I get Barkley?"

Fred nodded. "No problem."

Raoul slipped into his webbed weapons vest and handed Fred a bludgeoning baton.

"Gator doesn't have a gun, but I'm sure Barkley does, and he'll use it. This is just like before; you do whatever you have to and get Wade out alive."

Fred nodded grimly as he accepted the weapon. "Got it."

With Yolanda gone, DeShawn's plan was to go to her office and do some much-needed work, but she couldn't clear her mind. Even after the insightful conversation she'd had with Bert the night before, she was still concerned.

I hope they find Wade this time. After that first false alarm, I can't take another.

Yolanda sounded optimistic when she shared the news that Fred and Raoul were investigating a new lead, and DeShawn hoped this time it would pan out.

God, I know I haven't been the most faithful Christian. I don't deserve your help, but I'm asking for it anyhow. Please God, let them find my son.

And God, while You're at it, can you tell me how not to step away from You ever again?

All thoughts of work abandoned, DeShawn remained closed in her office and renewed her relationship with God.

26

Raoul moved quickly through the warehouse. Having slipped in through a broken window, he drew his gun and searched for Barkley.

Fred better handle his part. I don't have time to baby-sit him and save Wade at the same time.

He cursed himself yet again for having to depend on an amateur. Gator and Barkley weren't the brightest bulbs in the chandelier, but even a moron could pull a trigger.

Gator's unarmed. Fred might be a punk, but I know he can handle that loser.

Raoul kept searching, hoping Fred would handle his business and enable Raoul to handle his in turn.

Max pulled off the road, trying to keep a safe distance from the warehouse. *I have to be careful. One wrong move and I could get Wade--or Fred or Raoul for that matter- hurt.*

With a prayer on his lips, he moved stealthily towards the warehouse.

"Relax kid, you won't be here that long. Your moms said she'd pay up, and when she does, you goin' home."

Wade started to say something about Gator's mother for about the three hundredth time since the kidnapping, but stopped. Before Gator could turn to see what his captive was looking at, he felt a tap on the shoulder. He whirled, cursing under his breath.

"Bark, get out my face!"

"Surprise."

Before the shocked look could fully register on Gator's face, Fred put all his anger and frustration into a swing of the baton. Gator flew backwards, hit the wall hard and fell flat on his face, unconscious. Fred stood over him for a second. When he realized Gator was out cold, Fred quickly untied Wade.

"That was cool! You knocked him out! Can we tie him up now?"

Fred smiled. "Why not?"

Fred tied Gator's hands together and then tied those ropes to the ones on Gator's feet. He gagged Gator with his own do-rag so that he couldn't alert Barkley. Wade watched, fascinated.

"I saw you before. You gave Miss Mason a ride home when her car broke down."

"Yeah, I did. You were at school that late?"

"I had after school band. Are you her boyfriend or are you just trying to get in there?"

Fred stifled a laugh. "I'm a friend who's just trying to get in there."

"What's your name?"

"Fred Bennett."

"You send her those flowers?"

Fred chuckled. "You don't miss much."

"Nope. Hey, get me outta here and I'll put in a good word for you."

He laughed out loud this time. "I'll take any help I can get! Come on, let's get you outta here."

⌇

Donna and Yolanda pulled over behind Max's car, causing Donna to smile.

"I think we're in the right place."

Yolanda chuckled and pointed. "And that must be the warehouse you and Max saw. Shall we?"

As Max had before them, they quietly went into action.

⌇

Raoul mentally counted three and stepped into the doorway, gun aimed and ready.

"Freeze, vato! Move and I'll kill you!"

With surprising speed, Barkley grabbed his gun from the table and hit the floor. Raoul fired, barely missing his target, and stepped back to avoid any return fire. Barkley shot back to make Raoul duck, jumped up and dove headfirst out the nearest window without opening it first. Raoul missed with a second shot, cursed and then knocked shattered glass out of the way before following him through the window.

Barkley hit the ground and rolled, springing to his feet just like he'd seen in the movie Beverly Hills Cop. Proud of himself for executing the move so well, he leaped to his feet.

I gotta lose him before he busts a cap in my butt. I need a car!

Looking left and right, he saw how he would get away.

Fred set a brisk pace for himself and Wade.

"Our car's over here. Stay quiet and I'll get you away. Raoul can handle one kidnapper by himself; we need to get you home."

The sound of Raoul hitting the ground spurred Barkley into action. He covered the ten feet between himself and Fred in a flash. Before Raoul could aim and fire, Barkley shoved Fred aside and put Wade in a headlock, with his gun to Wade's temple. He turned back defiantly to face Raoul.

"Hold it right there, Pedro. You take another step and I'll bust a cap in this little Negro!"

Raoul held his ground, anger flaring white-hot through him. He reluctantly lowered his gun.

"That's a good start, but you better drop it. Now!"

Raoul complied, cursing Fred under his breath. *Last time I work with an amateur.*

"Good boy. Now stay right where you are. Me and Baby Huey are taking a trip. You try to stop me, I'll kill him and you too. Got me?

And that goes for you too, S-Curl. Keep your yellow behind out my way and nobody won't get hurt."

Kneeling where he fell, Fred nodded in assent. Barkley backed away, pulling Wade with him. Raoul watched intently, waiting for an opening. Off to the side, Fred did the same.

No way you walk outta here, Raoul thought. *You make one mistake and your butt is mine.*

Raoul eyed his gun, hoping for a chance to grab it and use it, but knowing that the odds of that were slim.

Max watched helplessly from a distance.

God, show me what I can do. We can't let it end like this.

Max wasn't surprised to feel a presence behind him, nor was he shocked when he saw Donna, with Yolanda right behind her.

"Don't worry, Max," she whispered. "Let it play out."

Behind him, Yolanda prayed silently, hoping for a miracle.

"Okay Slim Slow, reach over and open it."

As Wade reached slowly across Barkley's body, Fred kicked out with his left foot, tripping Barkley face first into the car door. As Barkley recoiled in pain, Wade twisted free, planted his left foot and kicked Barkley in the crotch with the right. "I told you; I *hate* fat jokes!"

"Wade, move!"

Showing surprising grace, Wade dove away from Barkley, who dropped the gun and doubled over in pain. Before he could straighten up, Raoul crossed the space between them and literally beat Fred to the punch.

"Come on, he might need help!"

Max, Donna and Yolanda sprinted full speed across the clearing. Donna felt the rage emanating from Raoul, and feared that Yolanda was about to learn Raoul's true nature.

Raoul bounced Barkley off of the car a few times and proceeded to beat him like Barkley gave his mom the finger. Barkley tried to fight back, but Wade's kick took the fight out of him. After missing with one feeble punch, he cursed.

"A'ight, a'ight, I give up! Quit hitting me!"

Raoul either didn't hear him or didn't care; he continued his lightning-fast barrage of punches, oblivious to everything.

Enough of this, Fred thought. *He's gonna kill that guy.*

Fred grabbed Raoul's arm as he prepared to throw yet another devastating right cross.

"The man said "uncle." Chill out already!"

Eyes blazing, Raoul whirled, yanked his wrist from Fred's grasp and sent Fred sprawling with a hard left to the jaw. He then drew his gun and put it under Barkley's nose.

"You think you're tough, vato? Well threaten me, then! Come on, try to shoot me!"

Max, Donna and Yolanda stopped short, horrified. Barkley's nose looked broken, both eyes were puffy and he was barely conscious. Raoul's eyes were feral, and at that moment, totally devoid of compassion.

Donna immediately took a deep breath and prayed for calmness. She shut out the world and prayed for peace to rule Raoul's spirit, to replace the rage he'd surrendered to. Yolanda took a different approach.

"Raoul! What are you doing? You're gonna kill him! *Stop it!*"

Raoul was stunned to hear Yolanda screaming at the top of her lungs. *Where did she come from*, he thought? *How did she get here? How am I going to explain this? She hates violence!*

He lowered the gun from Barkley's chin and relaxed his grip. Barkley flopped back against the car, still woozy. For the first time, Raoul became aware of his surroundings. He saw Fred get up, rubbing his jaw and glaring at him. Wade stood with his mouth hanging open, and Yolanda's friends Max and Donna were behind Yolanda, praying.

"Yolanda, I- -I'm- -."

Yolanda found her voice. "Raoul, what's wrong with you? You were gonna *kill* him!"

He felt everything he valued in life slipping away. Determined to hang on at all costs, he forced himself to look Yolanda in the eye.

"I'm sorry you had to see that, Yolanda. He'd threatened to kill the boy and well, I just lost it. I got caught up in the moment."

"And what about those other times?"

Raoul had almost forgotten Fred was still there, but now Fred walked towards him with a determined look on his face.

Now he's gonna hit me, Raoul thought, *and if I defend myself, I'll look worse in front of Yolanda. Well, a fat lip is a small price to pay for keeping her.*

To Raoul's surprise, Fred didn't make an aggressive move. Instead, he leaned past Raoul, pulled a folder out of the passenger seat of the car and opened it. Raoul's heart turned cold as he caught a glimpse of the newspaper clippings inside.

"Why don't you tell us what happened in New Jersey, Raoul?"

Raoul's voice caught in his throat.

"Oh never mind, let me. That's where you caught the drug dealer- your own uncle by the way- pushing coke and heroin to fifth graders. You claimed he tried to kill you and you had to fight like crazy to subdue him. Funny how he and the witnesses I talked to didn't remember it that way. They said he gave up after you hit him a few times, yet you kept hitting him."

He produced a copy of a medical report.

"Broken arm, broken nose, cracked ribs; you did a thorough job."

Yolanda's eyes widened. Raoul stammered out an explanation, but Fred cut him off with another article.

"Hmm, glad you caught *this* guy. South Carolina rapist who'd attacked two teenage girls returned to his second victim. She had a knife this time, and she cut him pretty good. He was about to overpower her when you got there. The girl said you saved her life, but you scared the crap out of her. The guy gave up, and you not only kept hitting him, you broke both his legs."

These revelations stunned Max, Donna and Yolanda. Donna sensed that it was true; Raoul's violent streak didn't start this day.

"This is the one though. That couple from New York hired you to find where the sicko who molested their eight-year-old son ran off to. You found the pervert in North Carolina with another eight-year-old. Thank God you got there in time to stop him before he molested that boy too."

Raoul finally found his voice. "I stopped that scum from ever molesting another child."

Fred's voice was cold as steel. "By killing him in cold blood."

Behind them, Yolanda burst into tears. She believed Raoul when he said he killed a man in self-defense, but now her faith in him wavered.

Fred was on the verge of tears himself. "I've been to Durham. I talked to the boy, I talked to his parents and I talked to his counselor as well."

Raoul's jaw dropped at the last part.

"Oh that's right, you wouldn't know. Reggie Messenger is in therapy. He was already traumatized at almost getting raped, and then you pushed him over the edge by killing the rapist in front of him. He was catatonic for a month after it happened."

Raoul hung his head in shame. He hadn't thought about the boy beyond rescuing him; all he wanted was to ensure that no other child would have to endure the pain, the shame and the mental anguish that he himself once endured.

"It's been five years. Reggie's just now healing from what happened. You saved him physically, but what you did to him emotionally was almost as bad as what."

Fred's accusation hit like a gut punch. He stepped closer so that only Raoul would see the final article and hear his next statement.

"This isn't going to make up for what your uncle did. You *know* what that boy was feeling. You could have helped him through it instead of making it worse. You can't get revenge on your uncle this way, and if you don't deal with this, it's going to eat you alive."

Fred shared the message from C.C. Campos, and Raoul recoiled as if Fred hit him.

Fred raised his voice again so that Max, Donna and Yolanda could hear. "Look at Wade. He's scared to death. Being kidnapped and then having a gun to his head was scary, but seeing what you did to that knucklehead was just as bad. You're supposed to help children, not hurt them even more."

Yolanda was stunned. *Did I ever know him?*

Raoul looked past Fred. The stunned look on Yolanda's face cut him to the core of his soul.

"Amante- - -"

The fierce look Yolanda gave Raoul halted him in his tracks.

"Stay away from me! And don't call me that, because I'm not your "baby" and never will be!"

"You don't mean that, amante. I love you. And I thought you loved me."

"Love you? I don't even *know* you! You lied to me from jump and now you have the nerve to say you love me? Leave me alone!"

"Amante- - -"

Yolanda turned and walked away. Raoul started to follow, but Fred grabbed his lapels and pulled him close.

"Haven't you hurt her enough? Leave her alone."

Raoul hung his head once again.

Fred couldn't resist talking trash. "I don't know karate, but I *do* know ka-*razy*. Hit me again and I'll demonstrate."

Not waiting for an answer, he shoved Raoul away, and caught up with Yolanda.

"It's all right, 'Landa. I'm here. Just let it out."

Yolanda trembled violently, and tears formed in her eyes. Fred's touch was all it took to free them. Ignoring everyone else, he simply held her until her tears were spent.

Off to one side, Barkley finally stirred. He started to get up, but Raoul glared menacingly at him, and he sat back down quickly.

"I wasn't going nowhere; don't hit me no more, man!"

Raoul made Barkley stand against a nearby tree and handcuffed his hands behind it.

"Where's your partner?"

Just then Gator staggered to the door. He'd worked his feet loose; hands still tied and his mouth still gagged, he took in the scene all at once. He heard police sirens coming, Barkley looked like he'd gone eight rounds with Mike Tyson, and the Spanish PI looked like he really wanted to hurt somebody.

Raoul raised his gun. "I really hope you resist arrest."

Gator immediately fell down and mumbled something that, if his mouth weren't gagged, might have been, "Don't shoot! I give up!"

He also wet his pants.

Max had called 911 on his cell phone when he saw the kidnappers through the window, and they arrived in record time. Barkley and Gator were arrested. Yolanda called DeShawn, who broke every traffic law in existence getting there from her office. Once the police let her through to see her son, she wouldn't stop hugging him. By now, Wade's shock had faded, and he enjoyed the adventure.

"Aw Mom, I wasn't in no danger. Those guys are too stupid to hurt me!"

He stuck his tongue out at Barkley and Gator as the police took them away. Somehow, both men managed to give Wade the finger while handcuffed, and somehow, the policeman escorting Barkley to the squad car managed to not prevent him from tripping "over his own feet" and falling on his face. By an amazing coincidence, Gator tripped right on top of him.

Wade laughed and pointed at them. "That's why your moms is so stupid she jumped out the window and fell *up!*"

Everybody cracked up, including the police. Max looked at Fred and smiled.

"Sure he's not your secret son, Fred?"

Fred laughed. "Hey, great minds think alike."

The police questioned the witnesses and gathered information for their reports. Others collected evidence from inside the house, making sure they had enough to put those two away for a long time.

Wade extricated himself from his mother's grasp and sidled over to his teacher.

"Miss Mason, is Mr. Bennett your boyfriend?"

Yolanda smiled. "No."

"He *should* be. He helped rescue me from these guys and he didn't beat up Mr. Carizales even though he hit Mr. Bennett for no reason."

Max and Donna turned away, unsuccessfully suppressing smiles at Wade's astute analysis of the situation. Yolanda glared at them with her peripheral vision as Wade extolled Fred's virtues. Fred stood within hearing range, looking both smug and humble at the same time.

27

Four Months Later

"Fred, somebody's at the door."

Puzzled, Fred got up from the dinner table, where he, Yolanda, Max and Donna were relaxing together.

"Strange, I wasn't expecting anyone else."

He opened the door and nearly fainted. Lenne Richards stood in the door wearing a big smile and a loose fitting maternity blouse.

"Uh uh."

"They really did that to you?"

Around the table, Max, Donna, Randy Errell, and Sharon Fulton displayed expressions of disbelief. Fred smiled wryly, while Yolanda dissolved into a fit of laughter.

"Yeah Doc, they did. My ex-girlfriend and Giggles there thought it would be funny to scare me with a fake pregnant belly."

Yolanda cracked up. "Come on Fred, you have to admit, it was funny."

"Funny. Huh! I almost peed myself!"

The three couples laughed. Randy kept his promise and invited not just him and Yolanda, but Max and Donna as well to dinner at Manna, a new restaurant in Richmond. After telling the kidnapping story, Yolanda explained the joke she and Lenne pulled on Fred.

"Lenne came to me to apologize for coming after Fred at a time when she knew he was interested in me, and in being so sexually aggressive with him. She told me she not only rededicated herself to Christ, but she's in counseling for sexual addiction to boot. She told me she wanted to apologize to Fred too, but she wanted to talk to me first. We kept talking and one thing led to another."

Max cracked up. "I have to admit, that was the first time I've ever seen a light-skinned brother turn pale!"

Fred scowled at him. "Ah-ha-ha. I'm busting a gut laughing. Darn near changed my mind about old girl here after that one."

They all laughed again, except for Yolanda, who turned bright red. After learning Raoul's true colors, she and Fred resumed spending time together. Before long, their friendship transitioned seamlessly into a romance.

Max looked sideways at Fred. "Negro, you know doggone well you weren't kicking Yolanda to the curb after all you went through to get her."

Fred laughed. "Got that right- I was starting to think I'd have to hit Yolanda over the head to get her to see I was in love with her!"

Yolanda blushed again. "I think I knew it all along; I just didn't want to accept it."

Fred put his hand on top of hers supportively. She smiled and kissed him lightly on the cheek.

"I was being stubborn. I wanted to make my own choices, and me getting together with Fred after Max and Donna hooked up sounded too much like the plot of a romance novel."

They all laughed again; it felt like they'd been laughing non-stop since they arrived.

Randy looked at Fred and smiled. "How about you, Fred? Did you think it felt like a bad novel?"

"Heck, no! I was trying to *write* that novel!"

The four couples laughed until tears flowed.

Randy smiled. "Yolanda, you two had to get together. Nobody else could put up with him."

Fred laughed. "See that? Family's always the first ones to turn on you."

Max looked confused. "Family?"

Fred chuckled. "Oh that's right, we haven't told anybody yet. You want to do the honors, Doc?"

"And steal your spotlight? Far be it from me."

"*Any*way. Turns out Doc and I are related."

The others looked shocked. Sharon found her voice first. "Related how?"

"One of my grandmothers was white, which accounts for my bronze good looks."

Yolanda snorted through her nose. Fred stuck his tongue out at her and continued, amid gales of laughter from the rest of the table.

"That grandmother happened to be Doc's great-aunt! That makes us cousins like seventy-five times removed."

Randy laughed. "Not quite that distant, but you get the idea."

Sharon scrutinized Randy's face, and then gave Fred the once-over.

"You two do look alike now that I think about it. I think it's the eyes."

Yolanda stared. "You're right. Hmmm. Maybe we should give Randy an S-curl; that might bring out the resemblance a little more."

Everybody laughed, even Fred.

"All right now Laquita, don't get comfortable. Tyra Banks ain't married; don't make me trade you in!"

They laughed again. Donna could feel the love radiating between Fred and Yolanda, and between Randy and Sharon. The engagement ring on Sharon's left finger bore testament to the strength of their relationship.

"Fred, how did it go with Lorraine and Bryan?"

Donna phrased her question as cautiously as she could, unsure of which way Fred's feelings would sway. Fred smiled confidently, easing Donna's fears.

"I don't know how, but we cleared out Merry's house in two days flat. We even went to church on Sunday and still didn't miss a beat when we got back in there."

Randy smiled tentatively. "We cleared out the house and cleared the air as well. It was cleansing in every way."

Donna enjoyed the contentment emanating from both Fred and Randy.

They really were able to let go, she thought. *I hope Lorraine and Bryan feel this free now too. Maybe one day they'll be able to tell us the whole story, but for now, I can tell they made peace with the whole situation.*

Max started to comment, but Fred and Randy looked conspiratorial. Their poker faces were good, but Donna felt a sense of anticipation coming from them.

They're up to something, but for the life of me, I can't figure out what.

Fred cleared his throat. "Be right back folks; gotta make that move."

"Me too."

Randy and Fred got up from the table, but instead of heading for the Men's Room, they spun in opposite directions. Randy hunched over a small object, but nobody really noticed because of Fred. Yolanda gasped in surprise as Fred knelt beside her chair and pulled a jewelry box from his pocket. He nodded to Randy, who activated a portable CD player. Yolanda's eyes widened as she heard a familiar Spanish melody and familiar words, sung in Spanish.

Closer than a sister, better than a friend; Nothing could be better than life with you.

What we have is special, only God can give. Wonderful companionship that makes me warm inside. My love, my friend. Love so special with you. My love, my special friend; Perfect love so true, with you.

As the tape continued, Fred looked Yolanda in the eye.

"Pride stopped me from telling you how I feel about you once, but I won't let it happen again. Yolanda Thomasina Matilda Mason, te amo. Puedes casar conmigo?

He looked at the rest of them. In case y'all who don't speak Spanish didn't figure it out, I said, "I love you. Will you marry me?"

Yolanda was speechless, and Fred smiled.

"Say something before knees start cracking up in here."

Everyone at the table chuckled, breaking the ice. Yolanda, smiled, looked at Fred and gave her answer. "No!"

Everyone at the table looked stunned. Yolanda smiled.

"Just kidding!"

The table erupted in hugs and smiles, and people at the surrounding tables applauded. Hugs and high fives were exchanged all around, but Sharon broke it off abruptly when she got to Yolanda.

"Yolanda, I do have one question for you."

Yolanda looked puzzled. "What, Sharon?"

"Matilda?"

The whole table broke out laughing again. Max and Donna chuckled politely, but they weren't laughing as hard as the others. Fred wiped his eyes and looked at Max.

"What's the matter, Max? Surprised that the Carsons aren't the center of attention for once?"

Max chuckled; he and Donna suddenly looked as conspiratorial as Fred and Randy had moments before.

"Far from it. It's just amazing that you had this planned for tonight of all nights. We have an announcement too.

Max held Donna's hand, and the two of them gazed lovingly into each other's eyes. Donna turned to the others and smiled.

"I'm pregnant."

EPILOGUE

"How do you feel?"

Donna smiled at the question Yolanda had asked her an average of ten times a day since finding out her best friend was expecting a baby.

"Pregnant."

Yolanda glared at her friend, ignoring the chuckles from Max, Fred, Randy and Sharon. The three couples got together at least once a month, alternating between Randy and Sharon coming to Delaware and the others going to Richmond. This was Delaware month, and the three couples sat at a table in the Fellowship Hall of Calvary United African Christian Church waiting for their turn in the food line. It was Family And Friends Day, and to everyone's surprise, Pastor Nathan chose Donna to preach. This was her first opportunity to preach for a Sunday worship service, and she rose to the occasion with what people now recognized as her trademark fiery fervor.

"Funny. You know what I mean- I ain't trying to have you fall out on me again."

Donna rolled her eyes. "Sheesh! Get dizzy one time and you get profiled. It's not like I hit the ground or anything. Even Max doesn't hover over me like you do since that happened."

Fred smiled. "I bet he would if he ever saw you two shop. You ain't fall out because of hormones or anything- you realized how much y'all spent that day and it almost made you hit the floor!"

Fred ducked playful slaps from both Donna and Yolanda, to the amusement of the other two men. Max started to say something smart to his friend, but two people came in, clearly looking for seats and diverted his attention. He recognized them and waved them over, indicating the last two seats at their table.

"Is this a Couples Only table or something?"

Fred laughed at the man's question. "If it is, you two definitely qualify. Sit on down and join us."

Ted Stansbury and Dee Winston joined them, Dee blushing slightly at Fred's dig. Ever since Sister Nathan and Donna conspired to get them together, Ted saw her in an entirely new light. Once they got through the initial awkwardness of transitioning their long friendship into something more, their romance took off. After four months of dating, Ted proposed and Dee couldn't say yes fast enough. Their six months away wedding couldn't come fast enough for either of them.

Their turn finally came for the buffet line, and the four couples stepped up. By unspoken agreement, the men let the women go ahead of them, and laughed to see that the women made no argument.

On their return to the table, Max raised his plastic cup and invited the others to join him.

Fred chuckled. "Uh, Max? Isn't it kinda ghetto to toast with red church punch?"

"Just go with the bit, Fred."

The others chuckled and raised their cups too.

"I'd like to propose this toast to lasting friendship and new life."

He rubbed Donna's slightly swollen belly, causing the others to chuckle before they lightly tapped their cups together. Fred and his fiancée smiled, enjoying the appropriateness of that toast to their own situation before lifting their own cups.

"To lasting friendship and new life!"

AFTERWORD:
WRITING MORE VISIONS

Like the first edition of this work, this has been a long time coming.

The first edition of To Whom Much Is Given was released in October of 2000, the culmination of a ten-year journey. This book represents five more years' travel, but the direction was different. The first time, I learned how to turn my idea for a romantic short story into a novel. This time I learned how to market a novel. I've been blessed to travel from one end of this country to the other, and in the process, I've met some of the best and the brightest of my fellow authors. And the whole time, I kept writing. Don't worry folks- next book coming soon!

My biggest complaint about To Whom Much Is Given is that I couldn't do more with Fred and Yolanda. I liked them, but I couldn't give them space at the expense of Max, Donna and Merry. My consolation was that I knew they'd be the stars of All Things.

I couldn't tie up every loose end from To Whom Much Is Given here though; if I had, this book would be roughly the size of Roots! I had to decide what to deal with here and what would have to be cut in the name of keeping the book to a reasonable size. Besides giving Fred and Yolanda their spotlight, I also couldn't just let Max and Donna vanish into the ether. And then there was Merry.

Merry Lucas' role in To Whom Much Is Given generated more interest, more questions and more impassioned commentary then Max, Donna, Fred and Yolanda put together! A few readers understood why it had to end the way it did, and even applauded me for having the courage to take it there. But that left me facing a dilemma. How could I have more of Merry in a future book when she died in the first one?

It didn't take me long to realize that while Merry died, her legacy remained. Her actions had far-reaching impact on a lot of the characters in this work, and it wouldn't have been realistic not to show these folks dealing with her legacy. I alluded here to her family wanting to go and settle her affairs, but I didn't have room to pursue that here. That tells me I need to write another book.

For those of you who have yet to read To Whom Much Is Given, I suggest you pick up a copy and get more details on those aspects of Merry's past (and Max, Donna, Fred, Yolanda and Randy's as well). And for those of you who are like me and enjoy sequels, I'm not through with these characters yet. There will be a third book in this series before too long.

Maurice Gray can be contacted at writevision2000@yahoo.com

DISCUSSION QUESTIONS

1) Do you believe it's possible for men and women to be "just friends" without one or both parties having a romantic interest? What problems did Fred and Yolanda encounter as their friendship grew?

2) Yolanda felt torn between Fred and Raoul- why was her decision so difficult? What factors complicated her decision?

3) How did Max and Donna's newlywed status affect their friendships with Fred and Yolanda?

4) How did Raoul's past affect the way he did his job?

5) How could the falling-out between Donna and Yolanda have been avoided?

6) Fred and Raoul got along like cats and dogs. How important was it that Fred not give in to his desire to resolve his issues with Raoul physically?

7) Premarital sex is a major issue, even in the body of Christ. Is Lenne's attitude towards sex and relationships common among churchgoers? Knowing her as he did, should Fred have renewed their friendship?

8) Bitterness and resentment played a major role in the situations between DeShawn and her ex-husband, and DeShawn and Barkley and Gator. How could those situations have been defused before they became so volatile?

9) In what ways did Yolanda and Fred handle their differences correctly? Where did they go wrong?

10) What was the biggest factor keeping Dr. Randy Errell from seeking a relationship with Christ?

11) Fred was at his best when spending time talking with either Max or with Randy. How important is it for saved men to interact with other saved men?

TO WHOM MUCH IS GIVEN

Two gifted individuals learning to trust God.
One woman on a mission of pure evil.
God loves them all.

BLESSED ASSURANCE

This anthology features six diverse authors bringing the Bible to life in a unique way. Each author took an account from the Bible and brought it to life in a modern context.

Maurice M. Gray, Jr. (parable of the Good Samaritan)- Traveling Mercies

Patricia Haley (Abraham and Sarah)- Baby Blues
Terrance Johnson- (Jepthah)- Sword Of The Lord

Victoria Christopher Murray (Hannah)- The Best Of Everything

Jacquelin Thomas (Tamar, daughter of David)- A Sprig Of Hope

S. James Guitard (Samson And Delilah)- Lust And Lies
There are no copies of this book currently in stock at Write The Vision. You may purchase this book at www.amazon.com or www.bn.com

THE SOUL OF A MAN

Short story: Long Term by Maurice Gray

After a season of sowing his wild oats, Nate Carter is a changed man. He's turned his life over to God, but that doesn't exempt him from the consequences of his past. Nate is challenged when a former conquest comes to work for him and wants to pick up where they left off. The man he is now struggles with the man he was. Who will win? God knows.

HOME AGAIN

"Home Again is a compelling journey into the relationships that matter most: family, friends and self. Each story is founded on natural love, but will require the Father's love to heal the brokenness. Travel with husbands and wives, brothers, sisters, friends and families as they maneuver through life's hurts and betrayals while leaning on a power greater than themselves."

Wanda' Campbell's "friends" include Dr. Linda F. Beed, Pastor Bernard Boulton, Tavares Carney, Shenette Jones, Tyora Moody, Dijorn Moss, Trinea Moss and Maurice M. Gray, Jr.. You can learn more at www.writethevision.biz or at www.micah68books.com. Home Again is also available at a bookstore near you.

Family Matters by Maurice M. Gray, Jr.
Erik Dawson and his mother Charlotte "CC" Dawson are barely on speaking terms after an argument, but when tragedy strikes, both of them must do some soul-searching to get to the root of their estrangement.

SOLDIERS OF THE CROSS

In this groundbreaking anthology, three ministers take three nontraditional ways to convert sinners into believers.

In "Lukewarm Saint" by K. L. Belvin, an educator battles two loves only to find he can't serve two masters and must choose between the Lord or lust. Next in "Called Outside The Lines" by Maurice M. Gray, Jr., a pastor who can ball on the court at an NBA level must decide whether taking a high office truly is his calling or just a temptation to elevate himself for personal gain. Finally in "Follow the Leader" by Isaiah David Paul, a minister who used to lead a life of crime must help two new converts stay on the path of righteousness before all three of them stray by the wayside.

There are many ways to the cross, and these Soldiers of the Cross are leading the way

BUSINESS UNUSUAL/HER GIFTS

By Dr. Linda Beed

Business Unusual
Bernadette Lewis' journey towards fulfilling her purpose faces several obstacles that she must overcome. Determined to have what she believes is rightfully hers, Bernadette sets off on a path of destruction. Shrapnel from the explosive decisions she entertains has the potential to block, detour and/or destroy not only her purpose but also that of future generations.

Her Gifts
Treva Scott has dealt with the demons of her past and is ready to move ahead with plans that will transition her from employee to business owner. If everything goes as she hopes, she'll soon receive the gift she's prayed for.

Brian Chin can't envision his future without Treva in it. Believing her to be his soul-mate, he has dedicated himself to praying for her and loving her the way she deserves in order to help her overcome the insecurities of her past. Looking toward the future, he feels that there's nothing that can take them backwards—or is there?

When current circumstances become painfully reminiscent of the past, Treva is forced to answer her own hard question—Can I live without him?

Business Unusual and Her Gifts are available wherever books are sold. For more information, go to www.lindabeed.com.

Jeremiah McAllister lost his entire family before he turned eighteen, but was blessed with another one. As the oldest of more than a dozen young adults mentored by CC and Thurman Dawson, Jeremiah takes his role as leader within their chosen family seriously. To his siblings, he is confidante, emergency contact, babysitter and family ATM. However, some among them push his largesse to its limits.

Jenisse Anderson is perhaps the worst offender. Despite Jeremiah's consistently being there for her, she will neither reciprocate nor discuss his feelings for her, or even deal with the issues of her past.

Erik Dawson (CC and Thurman's only biological child) is currently estranged from his parents, and uses Jeremiah as a go-between for indirect communication. Jeremiah's repeated pleas for Erik to reconcile with his parents fall on deaf ears. Between Jenisse and Erik and the constant demands of the others, Jeremiah is pulled in too many different directions all at once.

As he reaches his breaking point, Jeremiah finds himself at a crossroads in his life. How can he break out of an emotional prison he didn't even realize he was in until recently? Can he face his own history in order to embrace a better future?